I0831280

White Creek

A Fable

Bart Yates

Culicidae Press, LLC
PO Box 5069
Madison, WI 53705-5069
USA
culicidaepress.com
editor@culicidaepress.com

First Hardcover Edition

ISBN: 978-1-68315-007-7

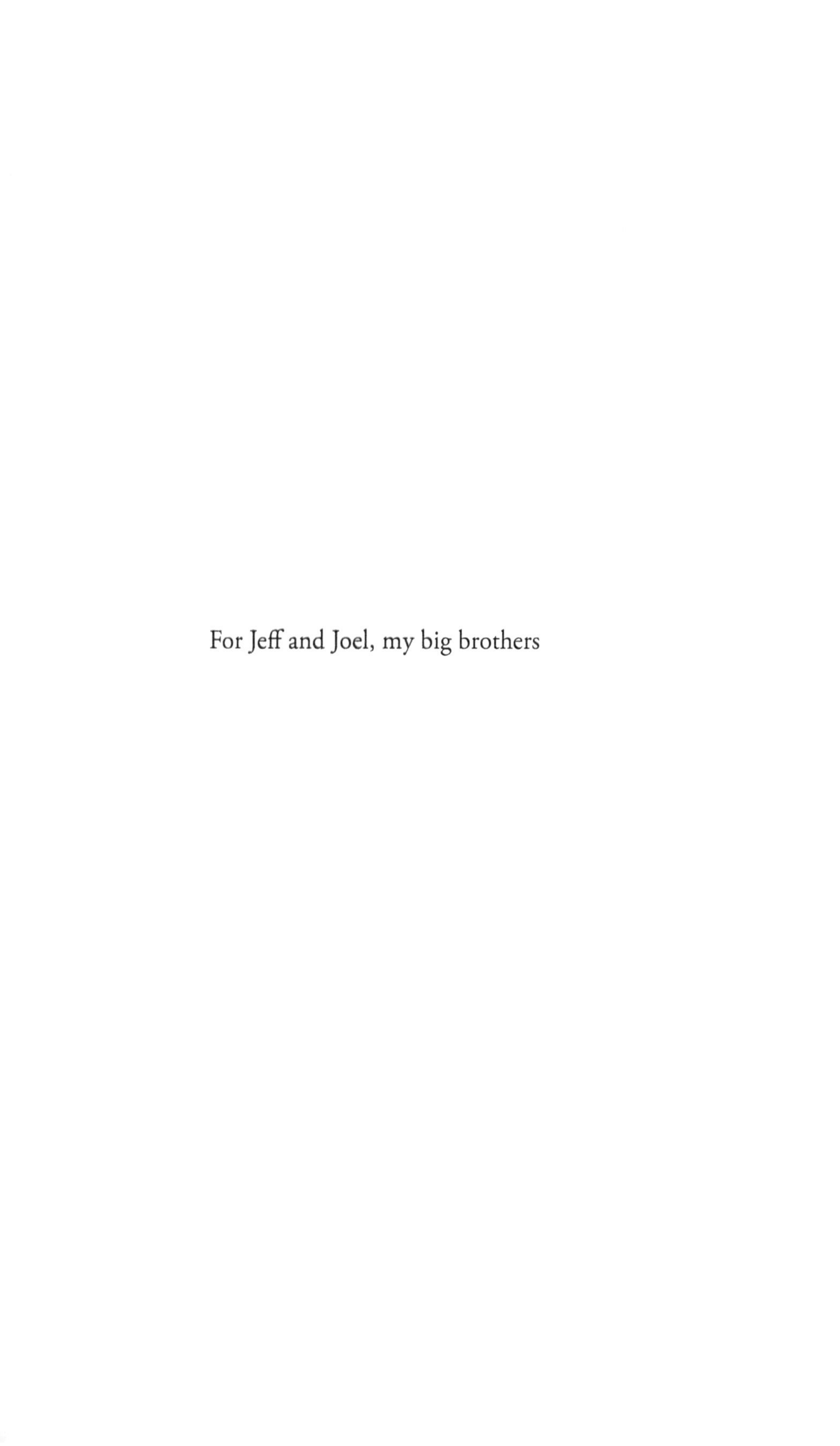

For Jeff and Joel, my big brothers

Table of Contents

Chapter One

The wind scared her. Raging across the plains, manhandling her small blue Camry all over the road like a schoolyard bully terrorizing a kindergartner. Flinging vast sheets and columns of snow at her windshield, time and again, making it impossible to see more than a few feet in front of her headlights on the desolate stretch of highway between Chugwater and Wheatland in southeastern Wyoming. The relentless, banshee howl of the gale was bad enough, but she also kept thinking she saw monstrous shapes in the falling snow—shapes birthed by the wind, vanishing as soon as she became aware of them.

"This is all *your* fault, you greedy little turd!" Sandy Satchell snapped at her cat, Wilbur, who was blinking sluggishly at her from his blanket on the passenger seat, not bothering to raise his head. The vet in Chugwater had knocked out the yellow tabby before stitching the deep cuts around his mouth; the anesthetic was wearing off but he was still mostly asleep. The angry, sewed-up red gashes throughout his whiskers looked like baseball seams. He'd gone rooting through a garbage can that afternoon and sliced open his face on an empty tuna can.

"I can't see a blessed *thing* out here!" Sandy said, white-knuckling her steering wheel.

Sandy lived in Wheatland, but the only vet she trusted lived in Chugwater, twenty-five miles away. The snow had not yet begun to fall when she'd left the vet's, but ten minutes later the sky was nothing *but* snow, obliterating the road and all the usual landmarks Sandy relied on to get home.

On a clear day, the old state highway between Chugwater and Wheatland—Sandy never took Interstate 25 if she could help it—was starkly beautiful. Sandstone cliffs towered above the road every few miles, and random, alien-looking rock formations dotted the prairie here and there like massive headstones, but mostly there was just the vast, treeless emptiness of the Wyoming plains, flat and immense, stretching farther than the eye could see and topped by an endless sky. Little of this remote, lonely part of the world had altered for centuries, and Sandy ordinarily loved it, loved how free and peaceful all that empty space made her feel.

But today was *not* a clear day, and all she felt at the moment was anxious and claustrophobic, penned in on all sides by the blinding snow. All it would take was a bad patch of ice on the highway in front of them, and they'd be in serious trouble; in this corner of the world unlucky travelers died in storms like this one nearly every winter, running off the road and getting stranded. Cell phone reception was nonexistent and nobody lived out this way save for a few isolated ranchers; days could go by without seeing another soul.

"If we freeze to death out here, you little fathead," she muttered at Wilbur, "the first thing I'll do when we get to Heaven is make a nice warm scarf out of you."

Wilbur—a neurotic nuisance of a cat when not anesthetized, prone to yowling fits and unprovoked bouts of clawing and biting—yawned and closed his eyes again.

Sandy glanced at her speedometer. She was creeping along at twenty miles an hour and was worried some lunatic might come speeding up and ram her from behind. The only part of the road she could see was a bit of the shoulder and she wasn't about to risk losing sight of it. If she could just stay on the highway for a few more minutes she thought they'd be okay; there was an intersection somewhere not far ahead that was impossible to miss, blizzard or not, because it was on top of the only hill around for miles. From that hilltop to Wheatland was a straight shot—a five-minute drive at most—and she could surely make it home safely with Wilbur from there.

A gust of wind slammed into her car and she squealed as she felt her rear tires slide onto the shoulder; she fought with the steering wheel and managed to regain the highway. "Oh, Christ!" she gasped, heart pounding. She risked a quick peek at Wilbur to make sure he was unhurt and was relieved to find him still curled up on the passenger seat, oblivious to their near-accident. She returned her attention to her driving with a shaky smile, more than a little envious of the tranquilizer still coursing through his system.

"Oh, shit shit *SHIT!"* she wailed, stomping on the brakes.

In the split second she'd looked away from the road, a small, lonely figure in a bright red coat had materialized in her path, trudging toward her down the middle of the highway. The car went into a skid and fishtailed off the road, missing the walker by only a foot or so, and Sandy cried Wilbur's name as they slid sideways toward an ominously deep ditch.

*

The driver's door screeched as it opened above them, and a blast of frigid air blew into the car, along with a substantial amount of snow. Sandy winced as the icy wind stung her skin and she stared up into the pale, frightened face of a young boy. Her car was tipped on its side at the bottom of an eight-foot incline, and the boy was perched on the frame of the door, leaning in with one hand holding the door open and the other braced against the roof for balance, looking like somebody preparing to clamber through a submarine hatch. Sandy's perspective was somewhat skewed, however, as she was more or less currently upside-down in the cab of the car, her torso wrapped in the painful embrace of her seatbelt as she struggled to free herself. The car, mercifully, had landed almost gently on its passenger side, the impact so minimal its airbags hadn't deployed.

"Ma'am?" The boy was yelling above the wind. "Are you all right? Ma'am!"

"I don't know." Sandy became aware the car's engine had stalled and she reached out in a daze to turn off the key in the ignition, then renewed her assault on the buckle of her seatbelt. "Where's Wilbur?" she cried.

"Who's Wilbur?"

"My cat! I don't know where he is! Wilbur! Where are you?" She heard a tentative mew from somewhere below her suspended head, and a moment later Wilbur's nose emerged in the tight space between the passenger seat and the door. The cat looked addled and weak but unharmed. Sandy reached out a hand to him and he hissed reflexively before rubbing his whiskers against her fingers, his breath warm and moist.

"Oh, thank God," she breathed. "Mommy will get you out of there in just a minute!"

The latch on her seatbelt released at last and Sandy shrieked as she slid out of the driver's seat and dropped toward Wilbur. She landed on her shoulders and thrashed around, bottom-side up, until she finally managed to right herself. She glared up at the boy, daring him to laugh.

"Why are you walking down the middle of the road, you little idiot?" she demanded. "I almost ran over you!"

He was wearing a fur hunting cap with earflaps, and his red, knee-length coat was threadbare and too short in the arms, leaving his bony wrists bare under his mittens. He looked about thirteen, with vivid red hair poking out from under the hunting cap and an army of freckles on his cheeks. His nose was running and his eyes were huge as he gaped down at her; he looked ready to cry. "I'm sorry! I couldn't see where I was going!"

"You shouldn't be out here at all! Don't you know you could freeze to death on a day like this?"

"I'm sorry!" he said again, fighting the wind for control of the door. "I don't know where I'm supposed to be. I think I'm lost."

Sandy opened her mouth then closed it, sidetracked. The boy had to be from a nearby ranch; he couldn't possibly have walked all the way from either Wheatland or Chugwater. "How can you be lost?" she asked. "Where do you live?"

He blinked. "I don't know." He stared into the storm, as if just then noticing the wind and the snow, assailing him from all sides. The bewilderment on his face was plain. "I don't know what I'm doing here."

Sandy's consternation deepened as another arctic gust raised goosebumps on her exposed skin; the temperature had plummeted since she'd left the vet's office. She remembered her earlier terror of being stranded and she shivered, feeling like crying herself. She'd rushed from the house earlier that afternoon without taking time to stock the car with emergency supplies—Wilbur had been bleeding badly and she'd panicked—and now she could strangle herself for being such a fool. Her car offered nominal protection from the elements, but with two wheels in the air it would soon become unbearably cold, its heater useless.

The boy's house *had* to be nearby. She had no idea why he couldn't remember how to get home—maybe he'd fallen and injured his head, or maybe he was just the kind of child who couldn't locate his own belly button in the shower—but he wasn't dressed warmly enough to have been outside for long. Leaving her car in these near whiteout conditions was no doubt risky, but surely they could find his home if they were careful and stuck to the road.

Great plan, she reflected sourly. *I wonder how many people have died out here, thinking the exact same thing?*

"You were walking south when I first saw you," she said, trying to stay calm, "and this is the only road around for miles. Do you remember how long you've been walking?" She coaxed Wilbur from his hiding place then looked back up at the boy. He was still peering into the falling snow, turning his head one way and then the other, and Sandy rose slowly to her feet, clutching Wilbur. She bumped her head on the steering wheel and had to go through several contortions to stand; the topsy-turviness of the car had transformed the bucket seats into bizarre wall ornaments.

"Maybe half an hour or so?" the boy said doubtfully as Sandy's head emerged from the open driver's door. "I don't know for sure." He looked down and seemed startled to find her face so close to his; his lips were turning blue from the cold. Being subjected to the full force of the wind almost took Sandy's breath away, and she quickly stooped again to search for Wilbur's blanket and the pair of gloves she'd thrown in the backseat when leaving the vet's office. She found the blanket by her feet and wrapped him in it—the cat was still stoned enough, thankfully, to allow himself to be ensnared—then resumed her hunt for the gloves.

"We can't stay out in this weather for very long," she called over her shoulder. "We'll be popsicles by the time the snowplows come." She found her gloves and tugged them on, her teeth chattering as she stood again. "Here, take Wilbur."

She thrust the bundled cat at the boy and he almost lost his balance juggling both the door and Wilbur. Sandy bent again to locate her purse, then clawed her way out of the car, panting and grunting, finally ending up sitting on the frame of the door, next to the boy. The wind was brutal and she almost changed her mind at once. From where they were perched her eyes were nearly level with the road—she could see the boy's footprints where he'd stepped down from the road onto the side of her car—but the footprints were already nearly filled with snow and the highway was ridged with drifts, its asphalt surface only visible in patches where the wind had blown it clean. She dragged her legs out of the car to allow the boy to close the door, but he kept holding it open and she realized he was using it, though with little success, as a windbreak.

"God, it's cold," she gasped. In desperation she unzipped her purse and seized her cell phone, praying for it to work, but she already knew it wouldn't. She punched 911 into the keypad and bleakly watched the screen tell her that her network was unavailable. "Dang it," she breathed. "Dang it, dang it, dang it."

She searched the boy's worried, freckled face, knowing he wanted her to tell him what to do. It was impossible not to feel protective of him; he looked so small and vulnerable sitting there with one arm fighting to hold the door open and the other wrapped around Wilbur.

"What's your name, kid?" she asked, dropping the useless phone back in her purse.

He wiped his nose on the shoulder of his coat. "Lucas."

"Hi, Lucas. I'm Sandy." She leaned close so she wouldn't have to shout above the wind. "We have to find your house. Do you remember anything at all? Can you tell me what town you're from, or where you go to school?"

"Wheatland," he said at once, looking relieved to finally know the answer to one of her questions. "I go to school in Wheatland."

"Okay, great, that's a start." She pointed north. "Wheatland's that way, okay? But you were walking toward Chugwater"—she pointed south—"that way. Can you remember if you were on your way home, or walking away from it?"

He bit his lip, squinting into the wind, and shook his head in frustration. "I can't remember anything!" he blurted. "What's *wrong* with me?"

"I don't know, Lucas. I wish I did." Sandy slowly rose to her feet, grateful the car was stable, wedged tightly in the ditch. "Okay, I vote we head toward Wheatland, since it's closer. If we don't find your house soon, though, we'll have to come back here and make the best of things."

Lucas nodded but said nothing, and Sandy wondered if he knew how hard it would be to locate the car once they'd abandoned it. She reached out and took Wilbur; his pointed yellow ears were the only thing she could see of him in the blanket folds. She stepped awkwardly over the gap between the car and the road, eyeing Lucas's footprints on the shoulder. She slipped a little and dug her sneakers into the steep slope, gasping in fright. When she was safely on the shoulder she beckoned to Lucas. The boy struggled to his feet, still holding the door, but as he stepped back the wind whipped up and tore it from his hands. He flung himself to the side and Sandy cried out as the door slammed shut with a deafening bang, barely missing him. Lucas windmilled his arms in a panic to recover his balance but tripped over his own heels, tumbling off the car with a yelp.

"Lucas!" Sandy screamed. "Lucas!" There was no answer and she got as close to the edge of the ditch as she dared. The snowfall was so heavy all she could make out at first was the boy's red coat. He was apparently flat on his back in the bottom of the ditch, near the rear bumper. "Lucas! Are you okay?"

"Yeah, I think so." The patch of red fabric stirred. "There's a bunch of ice down here and I fell on it pretty hard." There was a short pause and all of a sudden he lurched to his feet and began yanking at the back of his coat and pants. "God *dang* it!"

"What's wrong?"

"There's water under the ice! I'm *soaking* wet!"

She gawked at him as he flung snow around like a lunatic, trying to climb out of the ditch. "How can there still be water in the ditch when it's this cold?" Sandy demanded, appalled by this latest misfortune. "Everything should be frozen solid."

Lucas was too preoccupied to answer; his mittened hands had unearthed weeds under the snow and he was using them to pull himself up. As he neared the top of the ditch Sandy held out her free hand, clutching Wilbur to her breast with her other arm. Lucas's fingers groped for hers and she dragged him on the shoulder of the road, both of them red-faced and breathing hard.

"Thanks," he panted. "I thought I was gonna slide back in."

Sandy used her teeth to tug off one of her gloves and laid her hand on his back. The boy's red wool coat was indeed thoroughly wet, and she could already feel the fabric stiffening in the frigid wind.

"Oh, Lordy," she whispered.

She couldn't believe how quickly the day had turned from good to terrible. When the vet had stitched up Wilbur she'd actually been in a cheerful mood, looking forward to getting back to her nice warm condo in Wheatland and roasting a chicken for supper. She'd planned to slip into her pajamas and watch a movie; she'd intended to have some hot cocoa and a big bowl of popcorn.

The universe, however, seemed to have a different plan in mind.

She rose to her feet unsteadily and reached down to help Lucas get up, holding his arm once they were both standing. "We have to leave right now, Lucas, and walk as fast as we can!" she said, trying to hide her fear. "We'll be fine, but we have to hurry and find your house, okay?"

"Okay," he answered, shivering. He squinted into the wind and snow and bit his lip, looking young and scared. "It's really cold."

"Yeah, it is." Sandy faced north, toward Wheatland. "Let's go."

*

Hap Cobb, eighty-two years old and battling arthritis, a sinus infection, and a painfully unwelcome flare-up of nostalgia, put down his book and pondered his reflection in the large mirror above the dining room table. "I may have to diddle myself later on tonight," he said, scratching morosely at the thick white stubble under his chin.

Aaron Littlefield didn't bother to glance up from the book he was reading at the other end of the long table. "Yeah? Why's that?"

"Because I look so damn good I can't stand it." Hap turned his head and gazed out the window at the falling snow. "That's why."

Aaron reached for his wine glass without taking his eyes from the book. "Yeah, you're a real sexy man, Hap."

"Damn right."

The snow was coming down so fast Hap couldn't even see Aaron's old Ford pickup in the driveway, parked less than fifteen feet away. The wind was tearing at the walls of the ranch house, too, and Hap was grateful for both the fire in the wood stove behind him, warming his back, and the gas generator behind the house, keeping the lights on even though the whole county had lost power almost an hour ago. He hated winter, hated being cold, but if anybody was ready for a major storm like this it was Hap Cobb.

"Just like a goddamn boy scout," he muttered. "Hap Cobb, decrepit boy scout and champion self-diddler, at your service. The scout with gout. That's me."

"You're talking to yourself again, old man," Aaron said. "What are you going on about?"

"It don't matter." Hap cleared his throat. "I was usin' too many big words for you to keep up, anyhow." He paused again, wondering why the past was haunting him so much that particular afternoon. He usually got a lot of enjoyment out of bantering with Aaron, but at the moment he was only doing so out of habit. Still, though, the younger man would suspect something was wrong if Hap didn't keep riding him, and the last thing Hap wanted was to have a heart-to-heart about....well, about anything, now that he thought about it. "Oh, yeah, that reminds me, son," he said. "I finally figured out why folks laugh at you when you go to town."

"No one laughs at me in town, Hap."

"Sure they do, behind your back. Anyhow, they're just havin' a good chuckle 'cause they ain't never seen a man drag his knuckles in the dirt when he walks. Looks kinda funny."

Aaron snorted, lifting his gaze from his reading. "You're not going to let me just sit here in peace, are you? You're going to torment me until the snow stops and I can go outside to get away from you."

Hap grinned in spite of his dark mood. "Is shamblin' about like a gorilla a family trait? I never met your folks so all I can do is speculate 'bout what your mama mighta gotten up to when the circus came to town."

Aaron rubbed his head and laughed. "You're a miserable old son of a bitch, you know that?"

"I surely do, son. I surely do."

The White Creek Ranch had been in Hap's family for over a hundred and fifty years. Benjamin Cobb and his wife Sarah—Hap's great-grandparents—moved to Wyoming from Pennsylvania in 1866, trying to get as far away as possible from the aftermath of the Civil War. Benjamin, a corporal in the Union army, had lost his father, two brothers, one uncle and four cousins in the war and he couldn't bear to stay in the east with so many ghosts. Benjamin and Sarah were both young, healthy and conspicuously fertile, so much so that they produced seven children in eleven years: an impressive feat spurred on by Benjamin's oft-stated desire to rebuild the Cobb family.

Sarah was a good sport about this frenzy of fornication for almost as long as it lasted, but when she nearly died giving birth to number seven, family lore had it that she never again allowed

Benjamin's feisty semen anywhere near her equally scrappy eggs, though the aging couple reputedly shared the same bed for the rest of their long and happy lives. All seven of the Cobb children grew to adulthood and raised their own families close by, but none of them turned out to be nearly as fecund as their parents, and after three generations the Cobb line had either died out or drifted away. By the time Hap met Aaron, in fact, he was the only living descendant of Benjamin and Sarah in the entire state of Wyoming.

He was also a widower with a broken heart—and a broken ankle—and worn down with work, and sick to death of living by himself in a huge, sprawling ranch house with seven useless bedrooms, two equally unnecessary bathrooms and a massive kitchen where every scrape of his chair on the wooden floor echoed like a scream in a canyon. He had a handful of workers who came and went with the seasons and helped out with the cattle, but all these men commuted from Chugwater or Wheatland and Hap never took a shine to any of them, at least not enough to offer up a permanent room in his home. He may have been lonely but he was also picky about who he kept company with. Humans were not even close to being Hap's favorite animal, and truth be told, most of the ranch hands he hired were piss-poor representatives of the species—drunks and drifters, largely, or ignorant farm boys about as much fun to talk to as a cow pie.

And then Aaron Littlefield showed up on Hap's doorstep, looking for work.

The first time they met, Aaron had a full head of curly blond hair and was as scrawny as a bantamweight, with a thin, pale face that hadn't yet seen the need for a razor. He was also smart as hell, quiet, and completely unfazed by Hap Cobb's sharp tongue, and Hap, acting on an odd impulse he'd never regretted, had offered him both a job and a room almost on the spot. Now Aaron was bald, stout as a bull, and sprouted a five o'clock shadow by midmorning, but that was as far as the transformation went. His personality hadn't altered a bit through the years; he was still smart as hell, quiet, and the most ridiculously good-natured man Hap had ever encountered.

Out of sheer orneriness, Hap had been trying to rile Aaron's temper for almost three solid decades—Hap prided himself on having the God-given ability to provoke just about anyone he chose into a homicidal rage, up to and including the baby Jesus—but the most he'd ever gotten from Aaron Littlefield was a mild sigh of aggravation. And ninety-nine times out of a hundred what he got instead of that marginally aggravated sigh was a slow, sweet smile—serene, angelic, and utterly endearing—that told Hap he'd failed yet again to get a rise out of the man.

Hap pretended to hate that smile, but in truth it was one of the few remaining things in his life he never tired of seeing.

"Looks like we might not get to town for awhile," Aaron said, stretching his beefy arms above his head and peering out the window. "Thank God we got the pantry stocked up last week."

"Thank *me,* you mean," Hap grunted. "If it was up to you, the only thing we'd have in the pantry would be a banana or two and maybe a can of goddamn corn. We'd be gnawin' on each other's vital parts in three days just to keep from starvin' to death."

"That so? I seem to recall driving to the store last Friday all by myself and bringing home a truck full of food, in case we got hit with a blizzard like this before spring. You haven't left the house in six months, remember?"

"Yeah, and you forgot half of what we needed 'cause you're as useless as my poor old pecker." Hap suddenly narrowed his eyes. "And you can stop *that* right this minute."

"Stop what?"

"Grinnin' like a simpleton, that's what. I'm havin' a crap-ass day and the least you could do is not be so damn *cheerful*."

Aaron raised an eyebrow, and Hap scowled. Whenever the younger man caught wind of one of Hap's periodic black moods he became like a rat terrier chasing down vermin, and Hap had accidentally just given him the juicy scent of prey.

"Oh, Jesus H. Christ," he groaned. "Me and my goddamn mouth."

"You having another bad spell, Hap? Want to talk about it?"

"No, thank you, and keep your big fat nose where it belongs for once in your life, would you?" Hap snapped.

Loud, frantic knocking at the front door interrupted them before Aaron could respond.

*

Lucas had fallen to his knees in the snow twice in the past few minutes, and the second time he fell Sandy had barely managed to get him on his feet again. The boy was shuffling down the highway like an old man; he'd stopped speaking and was shivering violently, and Sandy knew the next time he fell would also be the last. She walked with one arm around his shoulders, supporting his weight as much as she could, and with her other arm she cradled Wilbur against her chest. Wrapped in a blanket and held snugly against her wool coat, the cat was doing far better than the boy, but was still not happy at all, yowling and squirming in the prison of his blanket as the last vestiges of the anesthetic in his system wore off. Sandy's arm ached from holding him but she didn't dare put him down; the snow was well above her ankles and made walking difficult, and if he ran away she'd never catch him.

"It's all right, baby," she crooned in answer to one of Wilbur's angry yowls. "Mommy will find us someplace nice and warm soon." She didn't believe a word she was saying, but she hoped her voice would quiet the cat—and maybe also reassure the frozen, stumbling boy beside her, at least until her own strength finally ran out and they all perished in the snow.

Sandy was exhausted and could feel her resolve waning. In the forty minutes or so since they'd left the car, the temperature had dropped even more and her toes and fingers had gone frighteningly numb, so much so that she was beginning to understand why people who died in blizzards sometimes simply chose to lay down and sleep rather than soldier on. She couldn't see farther than five feet and the only reason she knew they were still on the highway was she could make out—barely—the long, unbroken line of a barbwire fence to her right. For all she knew they might have been farther from the nearest residence now than they'd been when they first set out on this idiotic search for help.

This wasn't at all how she'd wanted to die.

She was only thirty-four. She'd always assumed she'd have a long and fruitful life, with plenty of time for everything she wanted to do. Where on earth had she ever gotten such a fatuous notion? Why had she believed she'd somehow be immune from the ill-fortune of an untimely—and highly unpleasant—death? Good people died every day in horrible ways; why had she never really considered it possible she might be one of them?

Stop that this instant, she told herself sternly. *Just keep moving, and don't even think about giving up.*

Lucas said something she didn't catch and she bent her head. The boy's red coat was encrusted with ice and snow, as was his hunting cap; she glanced down at herself and saw she was similarly shrouded.

"What did you say, Lucas?" she asked, just as her right shoulder collided with something solid, dumping a pile of snow on Wilbur's head in the folds of the blanket. Wilbur hissed in fury as Sandy stared numbly at what she'd run into: a large tin mailbox on the side of the road. She gasped aloud and squinted into the falling snow, praying for further evidence of habitation.

The boy said something else and she leaned into him, her eyes still scouring the surrounding landscape. "I can't hear you, kid," she said, putting her ear close to his lips. "Say again."

His breath was warm on the side of her cheek. "I said, 'Look out for that mailbox.'"

The ghost of humor in his voice surprised Sandy and she gazed into the boy's pinched, bluish face, relieved to discover he had more life left in him than she'd feared. "Very funny, smartypants," she said, smiling for the first time in what felt like years. "Look, if there's a mailbox there must be a house close by, right? Can you see any sign of a driveway?"

Lucas peered into the snow and she felt him go still for a moment before he held up a hand and pointed to their left. "Is that it?"

"Is *what* it? I can't see a blessed thing."

"There's a break in the fence," he said. The chance of warmth and shelter was acting as a powerful rejuvenator; he was standing straighter and seemed to have recovered some energy. "I bet that's it!"

She blinked into the merciless wind. "I can't see what you're talking about. Are you sure?"

"Yeah, come on!"

She let him lead her and after a few steps she saw why he was excited; there was indeed a gap in the snow fence. When they drew even with the fence they both cried out in jubilation as they stumbled over the hard iron bars of a cattle guard—a Wyoming rancher's equivalent of a doormat; to the right of the cattle guard was a small sign Sandy brushed off to read: *White Creek Ranch*. They staggered forward, hurrying as much as they could before Sandy's common sense resurfaced.

"Wait, Lucas!" She gripped the boy's shoulder tightly and forced him to a standstill. There was gravel beneath the snow on the other side of the cattle guard, but if they were indeed on a driveway now, she still couldn't see it. There was also no house in sight, and she reminded herself that driveways in this part of the world were sometimes mini-highways themselves, stretching for miles from the main road to the ranch at the other end.

"Feel the gravel under our feet?" she asked. Lucas nodded, blinking snow from his eyelashes, but she could tell he was impatient to keep going. "I think that's the driveway, but we have to go slow and make sure, okay? If we lose our way out here we're in big, big trouble."

The boy nodded again, unhappily, as her words sunk in. "What happens if the gravel doesn't go all the way to the house?" he asked, voicing Sandy's own fears. "What if some of the driveway is just dirt?"

Then we're hosed, kiddo, Sandy thought, looking away. "I don't know," she said. "I guess we'll just have to hope for the best."

She kept her arm on his shoulders and readjusted her grip on Wilbur. She smelled ammonia and realized Wilbur had just relieved himself in the blanket. She wrinkled her nose, knowing the urine would soon turn to ice and the cat would be even more miserable.

"Stay with me, okay?" she said to Lucas, taking a cautious step forward.

*

"Who in hell's knockin' on our door in a damn blizzard?" Hap demanded, calling after Aaron as the younger man hurried down the hall to the foyer of the house. "What kind of a deficient *idjit* goes outside on a godforsaken day like this?"

Aaron didn't bother answering, aware that Hap's questions, as always, were largely rhetorical. God knew how much the old man loved to hear himself talk, even when somebody was in trouble and needed help, like whoever was pounding on their door at the moment no doubt did. He reached the door and opened it, grimacing as a blast of cold wind and snow blew in. Standing before him on the porch step were a plump young woman and a teenage boy covered in snow and ice; they both looked half-dead.

"Oh, thank God!" the woman cried. "We've been walking forever! Please, *please* let us come inside!"

"Who the hell is it, Aaron?" Hap bellowed from the dining room. "Don't let 'em track any goddamn snow in the house!"

"Lord have mercy," Aaron said, stepping aside. "Come in and get warm, the pair of you."

The woman shoved the boy ahead of her. "I think Lucas needs a doctor." She closed the door behind her and shut out the cold, then leaned wearily against the wall, looking as if she might weep with relief. "He got his clothes wet, and I'm worried he could have frostbite. Can you please help him?"

The boy stumbled in exhaustion and Aaron reached out to steady him. "Good God, son, you're frozen solid," he said. "Come in by the fire and let's find you some warm clothes." The unmistakable sound of a yowling cat caused Aaron to flinch as he glanced at the woman; only now did he see she was holding a blanket in front of her chest, and that a pair of pointy ears—pressed flat in wrath—were visible above the folds of the foul-smelling blanket.

"Uh oh," he said, sighing. "Hap sort of has a thing about cats."

"WHAT WAS THAT GODAWFUL *NOISE* I JUST HEARD?" Hap roared. "THAT SURE AS *SHIT* BETTER NOT BE WHAT I THINK IT WAS!"

"Everything's fine, Hap," Aaron called out, rolling his eyes for the benefit of the woman. "Make yourself useful, would you, and get some blankets? We've got company, and they're in a bad way." The yellow tabby yowled again in displeasure and the woman spoke softly, trying to calm it. That she was more concerned for her cat and the boy than for herself made Aaron's heart go out to her. "Don't worry," he murmured. "Hap's an acquired taste, but he doesn't mean any harm."

The boy's legs suddenly gave out on him but Aaron caught him before he fell, alarmed by his blue, strained face. Aaron lifted him with a grunt and carried him quickly to the dining room, ordering the woman to follow along.

"Better hurry with those blankets, Hap," he said, setting Lucas down by the wood stove. "I think this kid's got hypothermia."

"What is that unholy *smell?"* Hap demanded, his keen green eyes sweeping over the new arrivals and lingering on the squirming, urine-soaked bundle in the woman's arms. "Oh, Jesus H. Christ, I ain't believin' this."

"Blankets, Hap," Aaron reminded him.

"I'm really, really sorry to trouble you—" the woman began, eyeing Hap with dismay.

"Don't be silly," Aaron cut in. "We'll get everything sorted out shortly. I'm Aaron, by the way, and that miserable old fart over there is Hap."

"I'm Sandy," the woman said. "That's Lucas, and this is my cat, Wilbur. Can I put him down, please? I think he'll be much happier on the floor."

"Of course you can put him down. But you better change clothes, too, quick as you're able. You may not be in as bad a shape as Lucas here, but you're not looking so good, either."

As he talked he stripped off the boy's coat, hat, mittens, boots, and socks and tossed them aside, then proceeded to unbutton the boy's flannel shirt. Lucas tried to help with the buttons but his hands were shaking badly, and it was obvious he could barely stand. "Best let me do it, son," Aaron said. "It'll go faster."

"Shit, there's snow all over my damn floor," Hap complained.

"Hap. Hurry."

Hap wandered out of the room, muttering, then wandered back in a moment later with an armful of blankets from the linen closet. By that time Aaron was tugging Lucas's half-wet, half-frozen shirt off the boy's thin shoulders and Sandy was unwrapping Wilbur on the floor. Wilbur hissed and spat in fury when first set free, but as he tried to run away his hind legs betrayed him and he sprawled out flat in front of the wood stove.

"What the hell's *wrong* with that mangy thing?" Hap asked nervously as Wilbur lurched over to cower beneath the table. "His whole damn face looks like it got caught in a lawnmower."

"He cut himself on a tuna can this afternoon," Sandy said. "I think he's still loopy from the shot the vet gave him."

Aaron reached out to claim one of the blankets from Hap, but before he could wrap it around Lucas's naked, freckled shoulders, Sandy—who was behind the boy—gasped.

"What on earth happened to your back, Lucas?" she asked. "Are all those bruises from when you fell in the ditch?"

Lucas stared at her blankly. "I have bruises?" He tried to look over his shoulder at his back but gave up. "My back hurts but I don't know why."

Aaron turned the boy around to see what had caught Sandy's attention. From the boy's waist to the base of his neck he was mottled with black, blue, and yellow bruises; his pale skin stood out in vivid contrast to the contusions. He looked as if he'd been beaten—badly—with a stick, or maybe a belt. "Damn," Aaron murmured, draping a blanket over the trembling boy. He looked over at Hap and shook his head.

"Them bruises been there awhile," Hap said, turning to study Sandy with a less-than-pleasant expression. "And he sure didn't get 'em by fallin' in no ditch."

Sandy's eyes went wide as she realized what Hap was suggesting. "Lucas and I only just met a couple of hours ago!" she protested. "He was walking on the road and I swerved to go around him, then I went in the ditch and he came to get me out of the car. That's all I know about him, except he says he doesn't remember where he's from, or how he got on the highway."

Hap's scowl grew as he turned his glare on the boy. "What do you mean, he don't remember?" he demanded. "Is he simple?"

"No, I'm not simple." Lucas's cheeks reddened. "I just can't remember anything right now. I don't know why, but I can't."

Hap snorted. "No offense, son, but you seem plenty simple to me." He glanced at Aaron. "Might be you and this boy are related, pinhead."

"Hush, Hap. Lucas has been through enough for today. You can pick on him when he's feeling better, okay?"

Hap's expression softened before he swung his attention back to the cat under the table. The cat hissed at the scrutiny, and Hap's eyes narrowed.

Aaron asked Lucas if he could manage his wet trousers and underthings by himself. Lucas nodded, his teeth chattering like a maraca as he fumbled with his belt buckle, then he remembered Sandy was in the room and glanced at her with a pleading look. Sandy turned away and shrugged out of her coat while Aaron held the blanket around Lucas, helping the boy keep his balance as Lucas pushed his pants and shorts down around his ankles. He stepped out of them awkwardly, too cold and tired for embarrassment, and Aaron wrapped him tightly in the blanket, noting that, in spite of his trembling, his color already seemed better; maybe he didn't have hypothermia after all.

"Things could be a heck of a lot worse, Lucas," he said, inspecting the boy's fingers and toes for signs of frostbite, mur-

muring reassurance when he found none. "We just need to get you warmed up again. I'll run a hot bath for you in a minute and find you some dry clothes." He turned to watch Sandy discard her coat—she wasn't as plump as he'd first thought—and shook his head when he noticed she was wearing sneakers instead of boots. "I think Lucas got away without any lasting damage," he told her, "but you might not be so lucky with those shoes of yours. We better take a look at your feet and make sure you're okay."

"I'm okay," Sandy said, shivering. "I'll warm up in a minute."

She wasn't pretty, exactly, Aaron thought, so much as unusual, with elfin features and big blue eyes that made her appear far younger—and more trusting—than she probably was. Her face could pass for that of a twenty-year-old, but something about the way she carried herself told him she was closer to thirty-five, and no stranger to hardship.

Hap snorted again. "Don't be daft, girl. Freezin' your toes off ain't nothin' to screw with, 'less you want to spend the rest of your life hobblin' around like a damn penguin." He settled a blanket roughly around her shoulders. "Sit your ass down in that chair over there and get those shoes off right this minute."

As Sandy moved to obey him, Hap stepped close to Aaron and leaned down to whisper in his ear. "Best they drink lots of water, too, son. They'll be dehydrated as all hell."

Aaron grinned. Hap put on a good show but could never quite manage to hide his innate decency. "I'll see to it," he said.

Hap stood up straight again, scowling. "Damn cat stinks to high heaven," he said loudly. "How 'bout we toss it in the tub with the boy?"

Lucas appeared to be reviving a bit and was looking slowly around the dining room. Aaron noticed the boys' green eyes lingering on his own reflection in the mirror, then on the enormous, thick-legged oak dining table next to the wall and the ancient, hand-crafted mahogany china cabinet with glass doors sitting in the corner. His gaze swept over the three separate entrances to the room and what they each led to—a large kitchen, on his right; a long, dark hallway with a wide staircase straight ahead; to his left, the bright, clean entry hall where they'd come in—and fleetingly took in the polished wood floor, glowing in the light from the overhead chandelier. The warmth of the fire seemed to draw his attention the most, however, and he stared fixedly at the hot burning coals and the red and orange flames in the open door of the wood stove.

"I've been here before," he murmured.

Interlude: Sandy

Sandy Satchell was neither promiscuous nor careless, and when she and the first true love of her life, Wally Wolfington—a skeletal, doe-eyed, distant cousin of the wealthy, frozen food Wolfingtons—fell for each other their junior year in college and decided to have sex, she'd made him wear a condom, of course, but just to be on the safe side she'd also insisted he withdraw his penis before ejaculating. Wally was her sole sexual partner at the time and the only boy she'd gone all the way with, and the staggering unfairness of her getting pregnant—just because Wally became too excited and prematurely orgasmed while wearing a faulty rubber—bordered, at least to Sandy's way of thinking, on an anti-miracle, a sort of satanic Wyoming version of the Christmas story, minus the camels and the manger, and yes, okay, technically *also* minus the virgin, even though Sandy was the next best thing, really.

Wally reacted terribly to the unwelcome news: His heart turned out to be colder than a Wolfingtons' frozen entrée, and he refused to believe that the baby in her belly was his. He also refused to submit to any test that might prove otherwise.

"If you think I'm such a big slut, why are you so afraid of getting tested?" Sandy had screamed. "I thought you loved me!"

"I did," Wally told her, and that was the last time they ever spoke.

She was twenty-one, and the idea of caring for a baby as a single mother while still in college was no part of what she'd planned for her life. Nonetheless, she did what she believed was right: She told her parents and friends she was pregnant, and prepared herself for months of raised eyebrows and snide comments on her college campus as she grew larger and larger. She spoke to an adoption agency and agreed, after the baby was born, to give it to somebody who truly wanted it; she went to counseling to help her deal with all the emotional turmoil.

And in her second trimester the baby, a boy, died. The miscarriage broke her heart, but at least it spared her the guilt of handing over the child—something she had begun to feel more each day was the wrong decision—to a stranger. She recovered from the ordeal in time, becoming only slightly less cheerful of a person than she'd been before she met Wally, although from then on she couldn't help but stare at any child she met who happened to be the same age as the boy she'd carried would've been.

The next time she fell in love was the year after graduating college. She was waiting tables at a German pub in Cheyenne called "The Bavarian Haus," where she met a slim, hairy, handsome, Italian bartender named John Sorelli. John made the best Bloody Mary's—brimming with fresh horseradish and marinated pickles—she'd ever tasted. He also did things to her in bed she'd never dreamed of, introducing her to her first multiple orgasm. Sadly, he likewise introduced her to gonorrhea, chlamydia, and a second broken heart, when he told her he was gay and tired of pretending otherwise.

She eventually recovered from John, too, becoming only slightly less cheerful of a person than she'd been before meeting him.

The third time she fell in love was perhaps the worst relationship of her life, though it certainly didn't start out that way. Andrew Newton loved many of the same things she did: Lasse Hallstrom's movies (they were particularly fond of *My Life As A*

Dog), Stephen King's early novels, pepperoni pizza with green olives, dry Riesling wines, lazy, naked Sunday mornings in bed making love, dozing off together and waking again to more love-making. But after two years of living together, things deteriorated. Andrew's streak of cruelty—he told her once about taping a sign to his half-Cherokee, ex-girlfriend's back that said "My Indian name is Many Blowjobs"—began to surface more and more, manifesting at first in cutting remarks about her weight—she'd gained eleven pounds in their time together—and the grating sound of her laughter—"Did you know you always laugh in threes? HA HA HA. It gets old."—but then moved on to more overt abuses: Mimicking her when she spoke on the phone, yelling at her when she got on his nerves, coming home drunk and surly more often than not, deliberately breaking things she loved, like her favorite coffee mug or her Best of the Eagles CD. When he slapped her one night during an argument, however, it was the final straw: She slapped him back hard enough to make him yelp; he was still cradling his mouth and spitting blood in the sink as she walked out the door.

She got over Andrew, too, but it took longer than she would've liked, and left her considerably less cheerful than she'd been before meeting him.

She often reminded herself that she had much to be thankful for in her life, in spite of her less than stellar romantic history. She had a mother and father who doted on her; she also had several close friends who loved her dearly and called her often, so she seldom felt lonely. Soon after her breakup with Andrew, she returned to her hometown of Wheatland and got a job as a receptionist for a dentist; she volunteered at the local food bank in her spare time and drove a car for Meals-On-Wheels. She went on dates occasionally but never allowed things to progress too far, wary of her own judgment when it came to choosing boyfriends. She learned to cook, she bought a stair-step machine and exercised half-heartedly, she gained a few more pounds, she got a cat from the A.S.P.C.A. and named him Wilbur. She was content with her routine, mostly, though sometimes she felt as if she was only existing on the surface of things instead of truly living. She hadn't completely given up on the possibility of one day rediscovering joy, but neither was she overly optimistic about her chances.

And then one cold January day in the year 2014, Wilbur the cat had stuck his head in an empty tuna can and sent her out on the highway in a blizzard…

Chapter Two

Lucas rested his head on the edge of the claw-footed bathtub and closed his eyes, luxuriating in the steaming water that went all the way up to his chin. Just a short while ago he thought he'd never be warm again, but the feeling had slowly returned to his fingers and toes—with a tingling that was initially quite painful—and he'd stopped shivering, and now all he felt was relaxed and tired, and very, *very* grateful to be alive and out of the storm. There was a pile of dry, soft clothes on top of the hamper by the tub, and Aaron had told him that as soon as he finished bathing there would also be freshly-baked bread and a hot bowl of beef stew waiting in the dining room. The nightmarish part of the day when he and Sandy had gotten lost in the blizzard now seemed like nothing but a distant memory.

It was also, unfortunately, his *only* memory.

He opened his eyes and frowned, racking his brain for at least the hundredth time since he'd met Sandy to recall how he'd come to be on the highway, but once again all he could summon up were a few vague images—staring out a window at a gray sky, closing a door and stepping into the cold, walking down a dirt road as the snow began to fall—images that weren't helpful in the slightest, because they were devoid of context. All he knew for sure was that his name was Lucas, and he was fourteen years old, and that he attended school in Wheatland, Wyoming. It seemed absurd he didn't know anything else: How could he *not* know his own last name, or how he'd gotten the ugly, stinging bruises on his back? Why did this old ranch house seem so familiar to him, when he was fairly certain he'd never laid eyes on either of the men who lived in it? Where was he going when he first saw Sandy's car in the blizzard, and how long had he been walking?

After telling Aaron and the others by the fire that he'd been here before, they'd all stared at him like he'd lost his mind. Sandy said he probably had a fever and maybe she was right; maybe he wasn't thinking clearly. He didn't feel sick, though, and when Sandy put her hand on his forehead, she said he didn't seem hot.

He sank in the water and let it cover his head. He found himself wishing he had gills instead of lungs and could just stay this way forever—warm and safe—with nowhere to go and nothing to do. Once he got out of the tub and returned to the others he knew he'd be asked a lot of questions he had no answers for, and he also knew he'd feel helpless and stupid—maybe every bit as stupid as the foul-mouthed, cranky old geezer named Hap already thought he was.

A knock on the door startled him to the surface again.

"You still alive in there?"

Lucas relaxed; it was Aaron. He instinctively liked and trusted the bald, soft-spoken man. It seemed odd that Aaron and Hap shared the same house and were clearly good friends; it was hard to imagine two human beings more unalike. "Yeah, I'll be right out," he responded, pushing his hair behind his ears. "Does Sandy want a bath, too? The water's still pretty hot."

There was a long pause on the other side of the door and when Aaron spoke again his voice sounded strange. "No need," he said. "She already took a shower in another bathroom."

"Oh." Lucas shifted in the tub. "Okay, I'll go ahead and pull the plug, then."

Aaron told him to give a holler if he needed anything. Lucas heard his footsteps receding down the hall, back to the dining room; he dipped under the water again for as long as his lungs allowed, then reluctantly pulled the plug with his toes and rose to dry himself as the bathtub emptied. As he reached for a towel, his stomach growled at the thought of the beef stew he'd been promised; he wondered how long it had been since he'd last eaten. He looked down at his body as he patted himself dry and was ashamed by how skinny he was, with his ribs sticking out and not a scrap of either fat or muscle anywhere on him. Whatever else might turn out to be true about where he was from, it was a safe bet precious little food had been involved.

Precious little food, and if his back was any indication, more than a fair amount of pain.

He suddenly wasn't sure he wanted to know any more about himself than he already did.

*

Sandy sampled her first spoonful of Hap's beef stew and her eyes widened. The bowl in front of her looked as if it held simple enough fare—chunks of beef, potatoes, carrots, parsnips, and onions; there were mushrooms as well, and she could taste red wine, garlic, thyme and lots of black pepper. But the beef was astonishingly tender, the vegetables delicate and savory, and the broth so rich and creamy she embarrassed herself by giving an involuntary moan of pleasure.

"Oh, my goodness," she said to Aaron, who was smiling at her across the table. "I'm a fair cook myself, but this is one of the most amazing things I've ever tasted in my whole life!"

"Hap made it," Aaron said. His pleasant round face was ruddy from having been outside a few minutes before, tending to the cows. "The old fart sure can cook, can't he?"

Sandy gaped over her shoulder at Hap, who was sitting in a rocking chair by the wood stove, looking cross. She was starting to catch on to the old man's tough guy act but was still shocked to discover that the prickly old cattle rancher was such a marvelous chef. "This is *wonderful,* Hap," she said. "Whatever did you put in it?"

"Oh, a handful of this, a pinch of that," Hap grunted. "I don't pay no heed. I just grab whatnot off the shelf as I go and toss it in the goddamn pan."

Lucas came into the room, freshly scrubbed and much less pale, though with dark rings under his eyes that betrayed his exhaustion. He was wearing a blue flannel shirt and a pair of beat-up jeans several sizes too big for him. Aaron had dug out some old things of his for the boy but Lucas was considerably shorter and less stocky than Aaron and had been forced to roll up the sleeves and the pant legs a few inches to make the clothes fit. His red hair was still wet and looked as if he'd attempted to comb it with his fingers; Sandy guessed when it was dry it would be quite curly, but at the moment it was long, straight and uneven, tucked behind his ears on the sides and covering his forehead all the way to his eyebrows. He glanced around the room and smiled shyly as Sandy and the two men all looked him over.

"About damn time, boy," Hap growled. "Stew's gone stone cold and there ain't hardly none left."

"Hap's pulling your leg, Lucas," Aaron said, grinning at the look of dismay on Lucas's face. "He's got your supper simmering on the stove and there's enough left to feed half the state. Sit down and I'll bring you a bowl."

He rose from the table and Sandy drew out the chair next to her and patted the seat, waving Lucas over. After their shared ordeal in the snowstorm, she felt oddly close to the boy, in spite of knowing next to nothing about him. What she *did* know was enough: He'd been both brave and uncomplaining when they were out wandering on the road, and he'd helped her keep going, just as much as she'd helped him.

"You look a whole lot better, kid," Sandy said, reaching out and touching his sleeve as he stepped up beside her. He had a sensitive, sweet face and alert green eyes. "Welcome back to the land of the living."

"Thanks," he said, smile restored. "You look good, too." He settled into the chair cautiously—his back was clearly bothering him—and looked around the room. "Where's Wilbur?"

"I'd like to know that myself," Hap said. "The only thing worse than havin' that damn devil beast in my house is not havin' him right where I can see him."

"He's hiding under a bench in the hall," Sandy said. "He's afraid of strangers but I'm sure he'll come out in a while."

She offered Lucas some bread from the basket in front of her. He accepted a slice gratefully and began wolfing it down the instant he had it in his fingers. Aaron returned to the room and set a big bowl of stew in front of the boy, warning him it was hot. Lucas ladled up a spoonful of the stew, blew on it a few times then eagerly shoveled it in his mouth. Sandy and Aaron laughed and even Hap wasn't able to hide a satisfied grin as a look of ecstasy crossed the boy's face.

"Wow," Lucas said. "Oh my *gosh,* wow."

For a few minutes there was very little talking. Aaron and Hap had already eaten and seemed content to watch in silence as Sandy and Lucas attacked their food; Sandy wasn't quite as famished as Lucas but she held her own, devouring two bowls to his four and also helping him dispose of the entire basket of bread. Lucas finally pushed back from the table with a happy sigh and Aaron asked if he felt better.

Lucas nodded. "I guess I was kind of hungry."

"That makes two of us," Sandy said, wiping her mouth on a napkin. "Aaron and Hap, I can't thank you enough for taking us in like this. I don't even want to think about where we'd be right now if we hadn't seen your mailbox on the highway."

"Jesus H. Christ," Hap said to Aaron, "the boy eats like a goddamn dingo, don't he? We shoulda just thrown a cow carcass on the table and let him have at it."

Lucas flushed but Sandy found herself smiling at the twinkle in the old man's eyes. "Thank you especially, Hap, for that fabulous meal," she said.

"Oh, you're mighty welcome, girl," Hap said mournfully, rocking in his chair. "That big ol' pot of stew was supposed to last a whole week, but now Aaron and me'll just have to make do with crackers and beans."

“There’s more food squirreled away in the pantry than we know what to do with,” Aaron told her, “and the old liar’s already got your breakfast planned. He *loves* cooking for company.”

“Yeah, but nobody never visits ‘cause you’re such a dimwit,” Hap said.

“Our breakfast?” Sandy asked, praying she was hearing Aaron correctly and he’d just offered her and Lucas a roof over their heads for the night. She hadn’t wanted to presume, but she’d had no idea how she was going to get herself and Lucas back to Wheatland while the blizzard was still raging. “So you don’t mind if we stay the night?”

“Don’t be silly,” Aaron said. He glanced over at the window, where a combination of freezing rain and snow was pelting against the glass pane. The sky had turned pitch black as night began to fall, and the wind was rising, causing the flames in the wood stove to flicker and flare. “You can stay as long as you need to. We’ve got plenty of room in this old house.”

“Plenty of room in the damn barn, too,” Hap said.

Sandy laughed. “Thank you *so* much. Both of you. I really don’t know how we can ever repay you for all this.”

Aaron waved a hand. “You’re doing us a favor,” he said. “This way Hap gets a chance to pick on new people, and *I* get a chance to talk to somebody who isn’t so full of piss and vinegar.” Hap cheerfully flipped Aaron the finger and began haranguing him in earnest, obviously enjoying himself, and Sandy used the opportunity to turn to Lucas.

“You okay with staying here tonight?” she asked. “I think we should.”

Lucas nodded, gazing out at the storm. “I want to stay,” he said quietly.

Aaron somehow heard this exchange over Hap’s diatribe. “Good, that’s settled,” he said, shushing the old man. “I’ll give you a tour of the place soon and get you fixed up for the night.”

Sandy had a thought, having seen a phone on the kitchen wall and remembering that her cell was useless. “Can we maybe call the sheriff in Wheatland? Lucas’s family must be worried sick, and I bet they’re out looking for him.”

Lucas looked uncomfortable at the mention of his family and Sandy abruptly remembered the bruises on his back. The boy's parents might indeed be worried sick, but it was also possible that one or both of them had beaten him half to death. She supposed he could have gotten in a fight with another boy or fallen prey to a bully—but if his parents *were* to blame, that would go a long way to explaining why he'd been out in a snowstorm by himself. Whoever the source of Lucas's injuries turned out to be, however, she resolved to alert the sheriff about the abuse as soon as she got the chance.

Aaron was shaking his head. "Our phone's dead. I tried to call while you were getting cleaned up but the storm knocked out the line."

"How about the internet?" Sandy asked. "Do you have a computer?"

"We've got a laptop, but it's useless without the phone line. This blizzard is making an unholy mess of things all over the state." Sandy squinted at the brightly lit chandelier above their heads and said it was lucky they still had electricity, and Aaron told her that was only because they had a gas generator, running full blast out back of the house.

"That's thanks to me, by the way," Hap said. "If it was up to Aaron we'd all be bumpin' into each other in the dark with only this dinky wood stove for heat. When we bought our gennie a few years back he said we didn't need one, but praise God I never paid him no heed."

"In case you and Lucas haven't already noticed," Aaron said to her, "Hap and the truth aren't very well-acquainted. All I said at the time was that we could've gotten by with a much, *much* smaller generator than the one we bought."

"And we woulda gotten cold much, *much* faster." Hap rose from his rocking chair, wincing; Sandy wondered if he had arthritis. "Stop bein' such a damn skinflint."

*

Hap stared into the kitchen at the woman and boy washing dishes after supper, trying to decide if he should make a fuss about having his kitchen commandeered. He and Aaron had gotten up after the meal to clear the table—in a leisurely ritual as old as their friendship, jibing at each other nonstop—but had been ordered back to their seats by Sandy, who'd insisted on doing the cleanup that night, with only Lucas's assistance.

"Tell me you're not happy to have a little female company for once, old man," Aaron said, interrupting his thoughts.

Hap shrugged. "I've had worse," he said, rocking slowly in his chair. "I expect you're on your way to fix up some beds for 'em?"

"Thought I would. You care which rooms I put them in?"

Hap shook his head and Aaron headed upstairs, whistling. Hap stared sightlessly into the fire in the wood stove, listening to the quiet, relaxed voices of the woman and the boy in the kitchen, talking as they worked. He couldn't make out what they were saying, but he guessed it wasn't anything important, just small talk between folks sharing a simple chore.

He'd forgotten how much he missed hearing a woman's voice in the house. The only females who'd been in the place for many, many years were the temporary cleaning ladies Aaron hired to help out every now and again, all of whom Hap had accidentally run off by speaking too gruffly when they became overly familiar—like the last one, an Indian woman named Daya, from Chugwater, who'd asked about the two wedding rings hanging together on a chain on the mirror of his dresser. He still felt badly for snapping at her, which was why he hadn't allowed Aaron to hire anybody else since: he'd told the younger man it was because he didn't need any help cleaning his own damn house, but the truth was he didn't want to risk seeing pain on another woman's face when he said the wrong thing.

He'd had more than enough of that with Ellen, thank you very much.

Sandy said something to Lucas in the kitchen and they both laughed. Hearing the boy laugh was nice as well, Hap supposed, but having a youngster in the place also stirred up a few things he'd just as soon not have stirred up at all.

He scowled, forcing his mind away from such thoughts. "Just don't break any of my things, goddammit!" he called out.

*

Lucas woke in the night, not knowing where he was. The room was pitch dark and all he could hear was the angry winter wind, rattling a window to the right of his bed. The air in the room was cold but he was marvelously warm, nestled beneath flannel sheets and several layers of thick, heavy quilts. As he returned to full consciousness a rhyme from a children's storybook suddenly came to him—*Clean and warm, and safe from the storm*—and he repeated it to himself several times, failing to recall the rest of the poem.

Hap Cobb and Aaron Littlefield's old ranch house: that's where he was. A small bedroom on the second floor. Sandy was in the room across the hall, presumably as snug as he was. He guessed Hap and Aaron were asleep, too, in their beds downstairs, so there was nothing in the world he needed to fret about—even Wilbur the cat was fine, no doubt curled up with Sandy. Lucas was surprised to find he was holding his breath; he released the air from his lungs and willed the muscles in his shoulders and neck to unknot.

Finding this big old house—the only place for miles with heat and electricity, running water and an abundance of food—had been a godsend. Neither he nor Sandy would have survived much longer in the storm, and just when they needed help the most, Sandy had run smack into that mailbox on the highway, as if she'd conjured the silly thing out of thin air to save their lives. It was like being in a fairy tale.

He rolled from his side onto his back and realized he had to pee. He didn't want to get up, though; it felt too good to be just where he was. Once he rose from the bed he'd be cold again, and he'd had enough cold to last a lifetime. He wished he hadn't had so much to drink before going to sleep, but Hap had made hot cocoa just for him, adding cinnamon and real whipped cream and topping it off with something called tequila. It was irresistible and made him feel wonderful, heating up his whole body and causing him to giggle at everything Hap said, and he'd had two huge mugs of it. Hap offered him a third, too, but Aaron objected, saying it was too much for a boy his age.

Aaron had given a tour of the house to him and Sandy after supper. The room he was in now had once belonged to Hap, Aaron said, when the old man was a boy. Hap was born in this house and had lived here his whole life. The bed—a sturdy brass-framed relic dating from the early 1900's—had been Hap's too, though it was even older than Hap. Lucas couldn't remember what kind of bed he normally slept in, but something told him it wasn't nearly as good.

It was strange to think of Hap as a boy, staring into the darkness at night just as he was doing. Picturing Hap as young was impossible; he had so many wrinkles and blue veins, and every slow, shambling step he took seemed to cause him pain. Lucas wondered if Hap could recall sleeping in this bed, wondered if the room had smelled the same all those years ago—like cedar wood, from a chest at the foot of the bed, and dust, and pinewood, too, from the old, smooth floors. A little desk in the corner and a wardrobe full of old clothes were the only other pieces of furniture in the room; Lucas assumed these had belonged to young Hap as well.

The house was groaning in protest as the wind assaulted it, but after each gust it stubbornly settled again, creaking, like an old soldier hunkering down for the next salvo. There was also a low-pitched, continuous hum he could feel through the bed frame; he decided it had to be the gas generator Hap and Aaron had talked about at dinner. He was pretty sure he'd never seen such a thing, and wondered how it worked. Maybe he could ask Aaron to show him tomorrow when they went out to feed the cattle; Lucas had volunteered to help with the chores.

An urgent twitch in his groin spurred him to move. He slid from beneath the blankets, grimacing as his bare feet made contact with the chilly floorboards. Generator or not, the house was *cold;* maybe Aaron and Hap were trying to save gas while everybody slept. Lucas groped around for his pants at the foot of the bed and pulled them on, shivering, then hurried to the door, not bothering with his shirt as he intended to be back right away.

It was much warmer in the hallway. There was more light to see by, too, owing to a nightlight in the bathroom down the hall. In that faint glow Lucas could see the closed door across from his own—the bedroom Sandy was sleeping in—and also four other doorways along the hall. The bathroom was at the far end, by the staircase, and he made his way to it, tiptoeing on the wooden floorboards. In the bathroom he didn't bother to turn on the overhead light; the nightlight was fine. He stood at the toilet, sighing with relief, and attempted to make out the faces of two people in what looked to be a very old, ornately framed photograph above the sink.

The photo was of a man with a big bushy beard and an enormous belly, standing beside a slim, short woman in a white dress, but the nightlight wasn't bright enough to see them clearly. He felt oddly drawn to the picture and after he flushed the toilet he almost reached for the light to see the faces better, but then decided not to blind himself when he could simply wait until morning. He stepped back in the hallway, yawning hugely.

He'd been in such a hurry to pee he hadn't noticed the open library door across the hall from the bathroom. He gazed into the dark room longingly, wishing he wasn't so tired and the night wasn't so cold. His spotty knowledge of himself aside, one thing he knew for certain was that he dearly loved books: When Aaron had shown him and Sandy the library earlier he'd cried out with delight to see so many treasures in one place. Aaron said that Hap's grandfather had been an avid book collector, and Hap and Aaron had continued the tradition, compulsively searching out every rummage sale in the area and often returning home with entire cartons of books to add to their stockpile. The library door had been closed when Lucas had passed it on the way to bed, but somebody else must've come along since, roaming around the house in the night just as he was doing now.

On a whim, he stepped through the doorway and turned on the light. The sudden brightness was painful and he flung up a hand to protect his eyes. He stood still for a moment, squinting and blinking, then lowered his hand and gaped in awe, just as stupefied as he'd been earlier. Floor-to-ceiling bookshelves lined every wall of the large room, and every shelf was jammed full. Waist-high stacks of books sprouted here and there on the floor—misshapen stalagmites in a warm, comfy cave—and a big, round oak table in the middle of the room was piled high, too. An overstuffed red leather chair in the corner made Lucas want to curl up and read for a hundred years: he couldn't imagine a more welcoming place in the whole world.

He took a closer look at the nearest shelf. Mixed with countless titles he'd never heard of he saw familiar classics: *The Prince and the Pauper, The Three Musketeers, Robinson Crusoe, Twenty Thousand Leagues under the Sea, White Fang, David Copperfield.* He ran a loving finger down the spine of *The Prince and the Pauper*, remembering the story vividly, and felt a thrill of surprise. Apparently his memory problem didn't extend to books; it was a tremendous relief to discover that at least he hadn't forgotten *everything* he'd ever known.

He wandered around, stopping every few seconds to tug out a book and read a page or two. He was barely aware of the thick red carpet under his feet, nor did he notice how many minutes ticked by; he only stopped when his knee collided with a tall stack of books and knocked it over. He squatted down to restore order, but he fell still again when his eyes skimmed over the bottom shelf of the bookcase he was crouched beside.

The shelf looked to be reserved for children's picture books; all the books on it had been pawed over a thousand times, their brightly-colored spines battered and ripped, held together more often than not with yellowed, peeling tape. He picked one at random—a dog-eared, ancient copy of *The Tales of Peter Rabbit*, by Beatrix Potter—and opened the cover, wrinkling his nose at the pungent odor of dust, mildew, and God only knew what else that had been left behind by small sticky fingers to molder between the pages. Lucas saw that a little kid had scribbled all over the text beneath the illustrations with a green crayon, rendering the words unreadable. He smiled for a moment, shaking his head at the mess made of a perfectly nice book, then the smile froze on his face and a shiver ran up his back that had nothing to do with being half-dressed in a cold house.

He flipped to the back of the book, his breath catching in his throat. On the very last page was another lurid sample of toddler graffiti, this time in purple and red crayon. The picture was crudely drawn, to say the least, but it was clearly meant to be a cowboy on a bucking horse. The stick figure cowboy looked more like a chimpanzee in a hat than a cowboy, and the circle-headed, club-footed horse more closely resembled a kangaroo, but Lucas still knew beyond any doubt what the drawing was supposed to represent. No one else on the entire planet could've said the same thing with any degree of certainty, but Lucas *knew* the truth of the drawing, as surely as he *knew* the identity of the two-year-old, cowboy-worshipping vandal responsible for it.

"This book is mine," he whispered.

Chapter Three

Aaron rapped sharply on Hap's bedroom door at 5:10 a.m., just as he'd done nearly every morning for more years than Hap could sometimes wrap his mind around. Aaron had been little more than a boy—not much older than Lucas—the first time he'd come to make sure Hap got out of bed all right: Hap's ankle was in a cast at the time and he'd given the newly-hired young man an earful for jostling him around overmuch while attempting to get him on his feet.

"You still alive and kicking, old man?" Aaron now asked, opening the door and sticking his bald head in the room. "Good Lord, Hap. How can you breathe in here?"

Hap liked to keep his bedroom toasty. According to his grandfather, Hap's great-grandmother Sarah had asked her husband Benjamin to build her a master bedroom with "lots of character," and Benjamin, an accomplished carpenter, had done his best to please her. The room was small but not cramped, with windows on three walls and a high ceiling. The south wall boasted a bay window and a magnificent window-seat with plush cushions to laze against; the north side of the room resembled a three-sided, cozy breakfast nook, but with built-in bookshelves and a handcrafted Colonial-style desk in lieu of table and benches.

Benjamin had also seen fit to install a neat brick fireplace for Sarah on the wall near the bed, but Hap had recently converted this to propane, tired of messing with wood and matches. Since the advent of the propane fireplace Hap kept the thermostat at eighty degrees from October thru May, and Aaron never failed to complain.

"Hold up right there," Hap said. He tugged off his reading glasses and set his book—*Moby Dick*—on the wooden chair that served as his nightstand. "You and your goddamn peppermint toothpaste are stinkin' up my personal space."

Hap seldom truly needed a wake-up call; he woke most mornings at 4:30 a.m., rose from his bed and went to the bathroom to wash his face and relieve himself, then returned to his room to read until Aaron came to check on him. Aaron's radio/alarm clock, dialed to a ghastly 70s and 80s classic rock station Hap couldn't abide—he was more of a Johnny Cash/Loretta Lynn kind of man himself—always went off at 5:00 a.m. in Aaron's room down the hall, blaring something hideous but mercifully brief; Aaron never took more than a few seconds to roll out of bed and shut it off. The younger man would then dress, complete his morning toilet and come to make sure Hap was up.

"You might want to think about brushing your own teeth now and then." Aaron stepped into the room in his stockings, carrying a well-worn pair of boots in one hand. "It smells like the wrong end of a skunk in here." He glanced at Hap's book as he sat on the foot of the bed. "Oh, crap, you only read Melville when you're feeling bloodthirsty." He leaned over Hap's legs to get the book and straightened again as he read aloud one of the many quotes Hap had marked: "'But heave ahead, boy, I'd rather be killed by you than—'"

"—than kept alive by any other man,'" Hap finished. "Yeah, Huck Finn was too tame last night so I went and snagged old Ahab. Now there's a man after my own goddamn heart."

Hap had long since lost track of how many times he'd read both *Moby Dick* and *The Adventures of Huckleberry Finn*. As a boy, he'd spent more time in the library upstairs than in any room of the house—even his beloved kitchen—and still never failed to cross its threshold without a certain hushed reverence, as if entering a cathedral.

"Whew." Aaron waved a hand in front of his face as he returned the book to the chair. "I'm serious, Hap. You need to brush your teeth today *and* take a shower. You're getting ripe."

Hap grinned. "Sad, ain't it? I used to wonder why this room smelled so awful when it was Granddaddy's, then one day I figured out it wasn't the room that stunk like a pig's anus, it was Granddaddy." He felt his good humor dissipating. "He made it all the way to ninety-three before he gave up the ghost. He was hard for most folks to stomach, but I loved the hell out of the old man and that's a fact. He always treated me like goddamn gold. There was this one time he took me down to Chugwater and..."

He suddenly noticed Aaron watching him closely and he groaned, realizing he'd just wandered into another unintended reverie that would likely end up upsetting Aaron.

"Know the real reason why old men stink so bad?" he demanded, vainly hoping to change the subject.

Aaron's sigh was patient as he tugged on his boots. "If they're all like you, Hap, then my guess is they don't put on clean long johns more than once a week."

"That's got nothin' to do with it. Old men stink 'cause our peckers are just too damn big for gettin' in and out of bathtubs. Mine needs an Olympic-sized swimmin' pool."

"Sounds like quite a cross to bear."

"I get by." Hap felt a flash of irritation at Aaron's ongoing scrutiny. "God*dammit*, Aaron, stop starin' at me! I'm *fine*."

"You sure about that? You were moping yesterday before Sandy and Lucas showed up, and you're still not looking too good."

"I'm eighty-two years old, son, with hemorrhoids the size of your whole damn head. That's all there is to it, so stop turnin' it into somethin' it ain't."

"Liar," Aaron said amiably, picking sleep from his eyes. "Something's eating you, old man, and I think you should talk to me about it."

Hap gazed over at the flames in the fireplace. "Don't you have some cows to tend to?"

Aaron sighed. "As a matter of fact, I do." He rose to his feet. "We'll be lucky if we didn't lose a few last night. They were okay when I checked on them before bed, but they were already standing in at least a foot of snow."

Hap shook his head, glad to be back on safe ground. "You got all the calves and their mommas in the barn, and the rest'll be cozied up in the corral. They'll be okay." He swung his legs out from under the covers. "You gonna get that youngster to help you?"

"I don't know how much help he'll be, but I promised I'd wake him."

"He'll do fine. You was as scrawny as him when you first got here, and you did pretty damn good."

Aaron raised his eyebrows. "Now I *know* something's wrong with you, old man. That's the first honest-to-God compliment I've ever heard come out of your mouth."

"What I *meant* to say was you did pretty damn good for a scrappy little halfwit." Hap shuffled over to his closet to get dressed. "That boy's back sure is a mess, ain't it? He looks like somebody tossed him in a blender and pushed the purée button."

"Yeah, he's had a pretty bad time of it. Think he's telling the truth about not remembering anything?"

"I wouldn't blame him a bit if he wasn't."

"Me either." Aaron rubbed at the stubble on his chin. "When he was taking a bath yesterday he asked me if he should leave the water in the tub for Sandy."

"No shit?" Hap paused, balancing on one leg like a stork as he wrestled himself into a pair of old Levi's. "I thought only old sons-a-bitches like me grew up sharin' bathwater. Boy's family must be dirt poor."

"That's what I thought, too, at first. But it's hard to imagine anybody hereabouts being *that* hard up."

Hap shrugged and finished pulling on his pants. "Lots of folks live rough. Remember that crazy Injun woman who was holed up in an old huntin' cabin outside of Chugwater a few winters back? They found her froze to death at her own goddamn kitchen table."

"That was more than twenty years ago, Hap," Aaron said, "but I take your point."

"It wasn't no twenty years. It was more like three or four."

"Whatever you say, old man."

"How in hell do you know how long it's been? You're so damn dumb you can't count to five without usin' your fingers." Hap glanced over at the bay window when the wind screamed against it. "Best bundle up today, son. That wind'll peel the meat right off your bones."

*

Sandy woke when she heard Aaron knock softly on Lucas's door across the hall. She rolled over in bed, stretching, then stiffened as Wilbur hissed and sunk his claws into her thigh, punishing her for disturbing the comfortable nest he'd made between her knees.

"Shoo, Wilbur!" she snapped sleepily, scissoring her legs.

Wilbur hissed again but then capitulated, jumping off the bed and landing on the floor with a thump. Sandy heard Aaron asking Lucas if he still wanted to help with the morning chores; Lucas's reply was inaudible to her but he'd apparently said "yes" since Aaron then said he'd meet him downstairs. She listened to Aaron's footsteps as he walked away, and a minute later she heard Lucas's lighter tread as he ventured out of his room and down the hallway.

It was pitch dark in her bedroom and she couldn't see her wristwatch, but she remembered Aaron saying the night before he'd get Lucas up around five. She groaned at the thought of going out to work in the cold at such an ungodly hour and closed her eyes again, praying she could fall back asleep, but then she heard Wilbur rooting around in the makeshift litter box—a washtub filled with shredded newspapers—that Aaron had devised for the cat.

"Oh, Jesus!" she exclaimed, catching a sudden whiff of what Wilbur had just seen fit to deposit among the strips of newspaper. "Jesus, Jesus, *Jesus!*"

Wilbur emitted the jubilant yowl he only made after relieving himself; he then proceeded to do a victory lap of sorts, careening around the small room in spastic fits and starts and hurling himself at every piece of furniture within reach. Sandy—unpleasantly awake now, with her eyes watering at the odor emanating from the litter box—kicked off her blankets and groped for the lamp on the nightstand beside her bed. A soft yellow light blossomed in the room.

"Ugh!" she cried, pinching her nose. She seized the litter box with her free hand and dashed to the door, yanking it open and hurrying into the hall. Wilbur scampered past her and raced for the stairs by the bathroom, where Lucas was washing his hands and face in the sink with the door open behind him. As the boy straightened to dry his face on a towel, the light by his head surrounded his thin silhouette with a bright corona.

"Make way!" Sandy warned, bustling down the hall. "Better hold your breath if you know what's good for you!"

Lucas stepped aside as she brushed past him but he didn't even glance at what she was carrying. He stood in the doorway to the bathroom, not moving as Sandy rooted through the cabinet beneath the sink.

"I can't flush newspaper down the toilet," Sandy explained by way of greeting. "I need a garbage bag, pronto." She tried a different drawer and grunted with triumph, brandishing a box of Hefty trash bags above her head. "Oh, praise the Lord!"

Only after overturning the litter box into an open garbage bag did she notice Lucas hadn't budged from the doorway. His face was pale and he wasn't looking at her; his eyes were fixed on an old black-and-white photograph hanging above the sink. The photo was of a stern-looking, bearded fat man and a short, thin woman, and judging from the clothes they were wearing—starchy, buttoned-up, ultra-modest formal wear—it appeared to have been taken a very long time ago.

"Hey, earth to Lucas," Sandy said from her kneeling position on the floor. "What's wrong?"

He blinked, startled, and looked down at her as if just realizing she was there. "Hi, Sandy," he said, smiling tightly before raising his gaze to the old photo. "I think I've seen this picture before, but I don't know how I could have. I think maybe..." He stopped abruptly.

"You think maybe what?" Sandy prodded, fighting a yawn.

He shook his head. "I'm just being stupid. I'm not awake yet."

"That's okay." Sandy got to her feet slowly, knees popping. "I feel a little stupid myself right now for ever believing it was a good idea to get a cat." She peered at her reflection in a small mirror beside the photo and grimaced at the state of her hair, reaching up to fuss with it. "So other than being half asleep, how are you this morning, kid? Anything coming back?"

"No. Not really."

The distracted tone of his voice caught Sandy's attention and she examined the picture more closely. She didn't see anything in it to explain his interest, other than its having been taken in Hap and Aaron's dining room; the antique china cabinet she'd been admiring last night at dinner was beside the woman in the photo, in the very same corner of the dining room it still stood in.

"So who do you think they are?" she asked. "Hap's parents? Grandparents?"

"Dunno." Lucas chewed on his lip. "It kind of seems like I *should* know, though. I swear I've seen them before."

"I don't see how," Sandy said. "Your memory must be playing tricks on you."

"Yeah, I guess," he murmured. Aaron called Lucas's name softly from downstairs but he studied the picture another few seconds before tearing his eyes away. "I'll be right down!" he called back.

*

Aaron led the way through the knee-deep snow behind the house and Lucas followed as closely as he could. His legs were shorter than Aaron's and it was hard to keep up, but he didn't want to ask the man to wait for him. It was still mostly dark outside; the only real light came from Aaron's flashlight, sweeping back and forth as they trudged toward the barn. Lucas could hear some cows lowing disconsolately in the corral, but they sounded far away.

"Watch your step," Aaron said over his shoulder, talking over the wind. The blizzard had finally ended but the wind was still savage, blowing stinging sheets of snow everywhere. "I lined Hap's garden with some railroad ties last spring and they're around here someplace." His boot struck something solid. "Found one," he said drily, turning so Lucas could make out his grin in the darkness. "Don't let Hap know I got us lost ten feet from our back door, okay? I'd have to beat the old bastard senseless to get him to shut up about it."

Lucas smiled back at him. It was impossible not to like Aaron; the man seemed so easygoing about everything. He reminded Lucas of an old pine tree—solid and patient, completely impervious to blizzards and tongue-lashings alike. They resumed plodding through the snow; some of the drifts were high enough to swallow Lucas whole but Aaron steered around them, making a zigzag course. Lucas was dressed in his own red coat and hunting cap, but Aaron had provided him with a pair of heavy-duty work gloves, several layers of sweaters and a wool scarf that felt wonderfully warm around his neck. Aaron himself was wearing insulated orange coveralls; he'd apologized for not having coveralls that would fit Lucas, too, but Lucas had assured him he'd be fine.

"Is Hap always....always so, you know, so, well, kind of... you know...like *that*?" he asked, wiping his nose on the sleeve of his coat.

A snort of amusement trailed out behind Aaron. "Yep, he sure is." He glanced back again. "It's all for show, though. He doesn't mean a word he says, and he's got a great heart." His grin widened. "Or at least that's what I tell myself to keep from strangling him in his sleep."

Lucas laughed and they resumed walking. After another twenty or thirty steps the door of the barn loomed up before them, illuminated by the roving beam of Aaron's flashlight. A shovel was leaning against the door, and Lucas could see where Aaron had cleared a spot in front of the barn the night before, though it looked as if another three or four inches of snow had since fallen.

Aaron handed over the flashlight and proceeded to clear the base of the door with the shovel. Lucas stayed out of the way and did his best to help with the light; Aaron worked quickly and was soon tugging at the enormous sliding door, forcing it open. As Lucas stepped out of the wind he was startled at how much warmer it was inside the unheated building. The potent smells of hay, cow dung and dozens of drowsing, warm-bodied mammals assaulted his nostrils, and he took several deep, appreciative breaths, knowing instinctively that odors like this were something he'd been around his entire life.

Aaron yanked the door shut again and flipped a light switch; a single bare bulb hanging from the ceiling allowed Lucas to turn off the flashlight and help Aaron tend to the animals—mostly a small army of cows and calves gathered together in the center of the barn, but also a few horses in stalls lining one wall and two milch cows in a separate stall by the back of the building. The barn was old but tidy, with a dirt floor everywhere save in one corner, where a big sink sat on a patch of concrete. The water to the sink had been shut off for the winter, so to fill the trough they had to use an old hand-pump by the rear door.

Lucas took to the chores with a sure hand, aware Aaron was watching him as they fed and watered all the animals, milked the cows, and mucked out the stalls. He was happy to find he knew what to do without having to ask, though it troubled him that he couldn't recall where he'd learned such things. He took off a glove and let a calf lick his fingers, enjoying the feel of its rough tongue and moist breath on his skin; he used his shoulder and hip to gently deflect an old cow who seemed to have a penchant for getting in his way.

"Well, one thing's certain," Aaron said as they finished up. "You're no stranger to work."

Lucas felt himself flush with pleasure at the praise. "I guess it feels pretty normal."

Aaron studied him. "Still can't remember anything?"

Lucas hesitated before shaking his head. It was on the tip of his tongue to say something about the eerie feeling he'd gotten staring at the children's book in the library the night before—and also about how unsettled the old photo in the bathroom had made him feel—but he was afraid of sounding crazy.

"You sure?" Aaron asked, raising his eyebrows.

Lucas looked at the floor and felt his frustration well up. "I don't know what's going on! Everything feels so...so, I don't know, I can't think of the word, but it's like...it's like I've seen your house and your barn a million times, but at the same time I'm on a whole new *planet*. How come I know how to do a lot of things when I don't even know where I *live*? How come I keep seeing stuff that almost makes me remember where I'm from but then it all goes away the second I start thinking about it? I feel so *stupid*!" His face suddenly felt hot and he fell silent again, keenly embarrassed by his outburst. He forced himself to meet Aaron's gaze, expecting a dismissive chuckle, but there was no mockery in the man's ruddy face.

"I think the expression you're hunting for is *déjà vu,*" Aaron said.

"Yeah, that's it! I couldn't think of it."

"I don't know what to tell you, Lucas. All I can say is I've never met you before yesterday. Hap and I hire a few hands every spring when things get busy, and every so often somebody brings along a kid brother or a son from town, but I've got a good memory for faces and I'd remember if you'd been here." He grinned as he pointed at Lucas's forehead, where a thick tuft of hair had escaped his hunting cap. "For one thing, that bright red stuff you've got on your head there sticks out a little bit."

Lucas found it easier to grin back than he would've thought. He didn't like hearing he was indeed mistaken about having been on Hap and Aaron's ranch before, but Aaron's easy humor made him feel as if it wasn't such a big deal, no matter what his gut was telling him.

"It's called hair," he said, glancing pointedly at the nylon cap Aaron was wearing over his bald scalp.

Aaron threw back his head and laughed. "So that's how you're going to be, is it?" He tugged his gloves out of a pocket and turned toward the door leading to the the corral behind the barn, where the rest of the cattle had spent the night. "You better steer clear of Hap Cobb, kid. You're starting to sound just like him."

*

"Good morning, Hap."

Hap jumped at the sound of Sandy's voice behind him in the kitchen, then wheeled around at the stove to scowl at her, brandishing a metal spatula. "God's balls, woman, you tryin' to give me a brain hemorrhage?"

"Sorry," Sandy said, smiling, "I didn't mean to startle you."

The heady smells of bacon, sausage, and coffee filled the house, making her mouth water. Hap's kitchen was brightly lit and spotlessly clean, with floor-to-ceiling white cabinets and an abundance of counter space. One countertop held a food processor, a blender, a crockpot, a rice cooker, and a toaster oven; another was home to what looked like a dozen or more wooden cutting boards of varying sizes. On one side of the stove was an impressive array of neatly-sorted knives in a rack, on the other was a doorless cabinet stuffed with what looked like every spice on earth.

She walked across the room and leaned against the sink, yawning. "It smells like absolute heaven in here. Can I help?"

Hap nodded, talking over the sputtering and spitting of the coffeemaker and the sizzle of the meat in the pan. "Set the table, if you've a mind. I ain't got a clue how long the pinhead will take diggin' out the cows this mornin'—especially considerin' he's got that sad little halfwit boy with him—but I figured I'd get everything ready for when they're done."

Sandy did as he asked, already knowing where things were after putting the dishes away with Lucas the night before. The table in the kitchen was small—a third the size of the massive table in the adjoining dining room—but Hap told her Aaron and he always ate breakfast in the kitchen. "Is your phone working yet?" she asked, digging silverware from a drawer by Hap's hip. "I should call my boss and tell him I'll be late today."

Hap turned to study her. "What's your work?"

"I'm a receptionist for a dentist in Wheatland."

Hap's face brightened. "Ed Marcy? That old buzzard's as dumb as a dog turd. The last time I was there he threatened to pull every tooth in my goddamn head and I ain't had the nerve to go back."

Sandy shook her head. "I work for Phil Vitek. He took over Ed's practice last year when Ed died of prostate cancer."

"Ed Marcy passed?" Hap looked stricken. "Hell. What a cryin' shame. I don't get no news from town 'cept for what Aaron tells me, and he didn't say a damn word." He turned back to the stove, falling silent for a minute before clearing his throat. "I ain't tried to call nobody yet, but you're welcome to try."

Sandy was taken aback by the sudden brusqueness in his voice and saw with surprise he was fighting tears; his thin shoulders were quivering. "Were you and Ed close?" she asked.

He didn't answer and she didn't want to press, wary of intruding into his grief. To give him time to recover she lifted the receiver on the wall phone and listened in vain for a dial tone; she replaced it in its cradle and perused some snapshots on the refrigerator door. Most of the photos were of Aaron and looked as if they'd been there a long time, judging by the thickness of the hair on his head and the thinness of his body. In one he was mowing the lawn, shirtless; in another he was on the roof of the ranch house, tearing off shingles. He'd been a beautiful young man, Sandy thought, with wild blonde hair and a face that was as still and unlined as a statue's—except when he was smiling, which was whenever he'd been aware the camera was pointed at him. Behind her Hap cleared his throat again so she guessed it was safe to resume their conversation.

"How old is Aaron in these pictures?" she asked. "He looks so young."

"Yep, he was just a little fartsniffer. That was the summer right after he moved in. I bought me a new camera that year but it broke when the little idjit started takin' pictures of me."

"He's changed a lot, but I'd recognize that smile anywhere. It's so sweet."

"*Sweet?*" Hap made a face at her over his shoulder. "Are you deficient, girl? He only smiles like that to get under my skin."

Sandy laughed. "Oh, he doesn't either, and you know it."

"Don't know any such thing." He turned back to the stove. "I shoulda told Ed Marcy when I had the chance that if he was lookin' to pull some teeth then Aaron's mouth was a fine goddamn place to start."

Wilbur suddenly appeared in the doorway between the kitchen and the dining room and mewed loudly. Hap jumped again and swore.

"Uh oh," Sandy said. "Looks like somebody's hungry. Do you have any canned tuna or chicken I can give him, Hap? I'll be happy to replace whatever he eats."

"I fed his highness a cup of milk and a big damn egg already," Hap said, nodding at an empty bowl on the floor by the counter. "I s'pose the the next thing he'll want is a mint on his damn pillow."

Wilbur made several violent gagging noises and spewed his breakfast on the linoleum floor.

"Son of a bitch!" Hap bellowed. "Tell me that didn't just happen right in front of my own goddamn eyes!"

Sandy apologized, scrambling for paper towels to clean up the mess as Wilbur fled the room. "He's got a very delicate stomach," she explained.

"My ass! The little cockbite did it on purpose!"

The outside door to the back porch that abutted the kitchen suddenly opened and Sandy and Hap both looked over at the sound. Through the glass pane on the interior door they saw Lucas step inside, wearing his red coat and his hunting cap; they watched as the boy bent to beat the snow from his legs. Behind him Sandy could see that the sky outside was now light gray instead of black; sunrise was still some time away but there was a hint of blue on the horizon.

Lucas clomped across the porch and stuck his head in the kitchen; his freckled cheeks red from the cold. "Morning," he said. His eyes flitted shyly over Hap and settled on Sandy. "Why are you on the floor, Sandy?" he asked.

"Wilbur had another little accident."

"Oh. Is he okay?"

"What do you mean, *another* little accident?" Hap interjected.

"Wilbur had a little problem in his litter box this morning," Sandy sighed, "but I already cleaned it up so there's no need to make a fuss."

"Jesus H. Christ," Hap moaned. "I don't know if I I should call an exterminator or a goddamn exorcist." He turned his scowl on Lucas. "Well, don't just stand there gawking, boy. Come inside and get some grub."

"I can't, yet," Lucas said, looking with longing at the frying meat in the pan. "Aaron just told me to let you know we'd be another fifteen minutes or so."

Hap asked if they'd lost any cattle to the blizzard and Lucas said Aaron didn't think so but was still checking. Hap glanced at the clock above the table. "Well, tell him fifteen minutes don't mean two damn hours like it usually does, hear? Food's gonna go cold."

Lucas looked over at Sandy again as she sopped up Wilbur's mess with paper towels. "You're really lucky to have such a nice cat, Sandy," he told her. "Honest."

She started to thank him, touched by his kindness, but then the corners of his mouth twitched and she realized he was teasing her. "You stinker," she said, laughing. She wondered at his change of mood since their earlier encounter in the upstairs bathroom. "I should've just run over you on the highway."

His grin grew broader as he headed back outside. "Seeya in a bit," he called over his shoulder.

Sandy shook her head. "He's sure getting sassy all of a sudden, isn't he?" There was no answer from Hap and she peered over at him; he was chewing on his lower lip and staring after the boy. She asked him what was wrong.

Hap stirred. "Nothing." A loud pop from the bacon in the frying pan called his attention back to the stovetop. "Boy reminds me of somebody. I just can't put my finger on who." He glanced over to check her progress. "Trash can's by the door when you're done cleanin' up after that mangy hell beast of yours."

Interlude: Aaron and Hap, 1984

A mud-spattered Mexican cowhand named Julio—grizzled, soft-spoken, and smelling strongly of sweat, coffee, and horses—dropped off Aaron Littlefield midway between house and highway on Hap Cobb's miles-long gravel driveway. "Sorry, kid," he said as Aaron hopped out of the beat-up Chevy pickup. "This is as close as I get to that son of a bitch."

There were no trees in sight and the earth was as flat as a cookie sheet, yet Aaron could barely make out the ranch house. He wished his feet weren't so sore. Ordinarily he wouldn't mind the hike, but he'd been walking for the best part of three days and was wearier than he'd ever dreamed he could be.

"This is great, thanks," he said. He leaned back in the cab to shake Julio's hand.

"Good luck," Julio said. "You're gonna need it."

"Is he really as bad as all that?"

"Nah." A sly grin broke out on Julio's face. "He's worse."

Aaron laughed and shut the door. He retrieved his backpack from the bed of the truck and watched Julio do a neat turnaround in the driveway, then threaded his arms through the well-worn backpack straps and hobbled toward the house, grateful the spring air at least had some warmth. Aside from the clothes he was wearing, everything he owned in the world was in his pack: a few clean shirts and underthings, thirteen dollars and seven cents in loose change, a winter coat and gloves, a towel, a transistor radio, two condoms, a toothbrush, and a dog-eared copy of *David Copperfield.* Ever since dropping out of the University of Wyoming at Christmas he'd drifted around the state, looking for work. He'd stopped by the Farmer's Co-Op in Wheatland that afternoon and learned a local cattleman had broken an ankle and needed a temporary ranch hand; he'd also been warned the man was an ornery bastard who kept firing—usually within hours—every worker he hired. Aaron was desperate for money, though, so he decided to give it a shot. Julio was at the Co-Op picking up feed and offered him a ride, saying he was passing right by the White Creek Ranch.

Aaron had just turned nineteen, and the single semester he'd spent in college had really only taught him one thing he valued: He'd rather die than be indoors all day. He'd grown up working on farms and ranches, and being caged in a place where he never had open sky above his head made him physically sick. He needed room to breathe and fresh air in his lungs; he needed hard work to keep his mind sharp and his body strong. Virtually everyone he knew told him he was a fool for abandoning college—he'd made the dean's list with zero effort and was adored by teachers and friends alike—but the moment he stepped off campus and stuck out his thumb for a lift, he felt he'd just been released from prison.

Unfortunately, life as a free man wasn't quite what he'd expected.

Steady outdoor work in the middle of a Wyoming winter was impossible to find. Everywhere he went he was told "Sorry, kid, try back next spring," or "I can only use you for a day or two." The little money he made was barely enough to keep him alive. He'd been estranged from his family for years and was too proud to mooch off friends, so he'd spent countless nights sleeping in bus stations and barns. He'd lost twenty pounds he could ill afford to lose, and there'd been times he was so cold and hungry he'd almost called his parents, but so far his pride had proven stronger than his need for food and shelter. Now that spring had finally come he hoped his prospects would improve, but the truth was he was exhausted, half-starving, and near the end of his rope. Four long months of hard living had taken a toll and he was beginning to feel like one of the hapless urchins in a Charles Dickens novel—a modern day David Copperfield in cowboy boots and a denim jacket, limping down Hap Cobb's lonely, beat-to-hell driveway in early April.

With his blistered feet it took the better part of an hour to reach the huge ranch house at the end of the drive. He knocked on the old oak door and stared around the yard, praying that Cobb, who he'd been told lived alone, was home. The property was showing signs of neglect: the barn and outbuildings were all in want of a fresh coat of paint; the fence around the corral was missing boards; a large vegetable garden between the barn and the house hadn't yet been cleared of tumbleweeds and debris from the long winter; the driveway at the base of the front walk was pocked with muffler-mangling potholes. Still, the house and barn were sturdy and imposing—though very old from the look of some of the paint-thirsty wood—and in far better shape than most of the ramshackle affairs Aaron had seen elsewhere in the past few months.

He became aware of a voice yelling in the house, but it sounded like it was on the other side of the world. The voice crescendoed as it came closer, but Aaron couldn't make out any words until the door flew open and he was suddenly face-to-face with a gaunt, leathery-skinned, unshaven man in his fifties. He was an inch or two short of six feet, and on crutches, with a soiled cast on his right ankle.

"You deaf, boy, or just a good old-fashioned retard? I've been hollerin' my fool head off for the last five minutes, saying *come in, come in*!"

Julio and the man at the Co-Op had told Aaron to expect a rude reception, but the level of hostility was still a shock. He wasn't easily intimidated, however—it was hardly the first time in his life he'd been yelled at for no reason—and he recovered quickly.

"Mr. Cobb?" he asked. "My name is Aaron Littlefield. I heard you might need some help around here."

"That so?" Cobb's glower lessened ever so slightly. "What idjit told you that?"

"Some tall guy with a beard at the Wheatland Co-Op. I didn't catch his name."

"Oh, Jesus, that's Lennie. He's been sending me one butt-pickin' jackass after another, so I hope you're not a full-on feeb, too." He narrowed his eyes. "What are you grinnin' at?"

Aaron couldn't seem to stop smiling. The last thing he wanted was to annoy the man further and screw himself out of a job, but it tickled him Cobb was so clearly enjoying playing the ogre: The more vitriol that spilled from his mouth the more pleased with himself he looked.

"Sorry," Aaron told him. "I didn't get much sleep and I guess I'm a little slaphappy."

"Well, snap out of it, pronto. You look like a degenerate."

Aaron was sure Cobb was right: He was definitely not at his best. He knew he smelled bad, for one thing; the last shower he'd had was almost a week before, and since then all he'd been able to do was brush his teeth and wash his face now and again, in public restrooms. Nor was he exaggerating about a lack of sleep. Since his last job six days before on a small spread up north, he'd been unable to afford a hotel room and was reduced to snatching a few minutes of shut-eye wherever he could find a warm place to doze off. He did his best to stop grinning—he really *was* feeling uncharacteristically goofy—and tried to think of something that might convince Cobb to give him a chance.

"I've worked on a lot of ranches, Mr. Cobb, and I've got a ton of folks who'll vouch for me. I just helped a guy put up a fence on his place north of Casper, and before that I was up by Cody, building a sheep shed. I'm not afraid of hard work, and I'll be glad to do whatever you need done."

"The last three jokers said the same damn thing, son, but all any of 'em did was pound their puds." Cobb sniffed. "I ain't opposed to pud-poundin,' mind you, but I'll be goddamned if I'll pay some halfwit to wiggle his weenie while my ranch falls down 'round my ears."

Aaron knew he was grinning like a fool again. "I think I can manage to refrain from doing that, Mr. Cobb."

Cobb studied him. "You don't talk like no ranch hand, boy. Where you hail from?"

Aaron told him he'd grown up just outside of Jackson Hole but offered no further information; he was afraid the details of his childhood—dropping out of high school and leaving home when he was sixteen—might cast him in a negative light. In truth, running away from his parents was an act of self-preservation, and quitting high school had only been common sense: His S.A.T. scores were so high he didn't need a diploma to get into college, so he'd decided his time would be better spent working odd jobs and saving money till he was eighteen. An older friend took him in and gave him a couch to sleep on in return for helping make ends meet; the same friend offered to take him in again when he left the university, but Aaron had refused, not wanting to impose more than he already had.

"Jackson Hole, huh?" Cobb asked him. "You still got kin there?"

Aaron nodded reluctantly. "My folks. But we're not in touch."

"Why the hell not?"

Aaron shrugged. "We just don't have much in common, I guess."

Sam Littlefield—Aaron's angry, humorless father—was a decorated Vietnam veteran and a semi-literate cattle rancher. He grouped all the souls in the world into two categories: Assholes and Stupid Fuckers. The Assholes were people who thought themselves better than Sam Littlefield; the Stupid Fuckers were those who didn't agree with everything Sam Littlefield had to say. He never physically abused Aaron, but his normal speaking voice was a shout, and Aaron grew up being berated—loudly—for everything from getting good grades in school and reading books (thus earning him a lifetime membership in the Asshole camp) to daring to have a mind of his own when it came to almost everything (establishing him as an honorary Stupid Fucker as well). Aaron's mother, Elsa, was a wisp of a woman who floated around the house like a ghost, seldom speaking and never contradicting Sam, even when he was making her only child's life miserable. As a young boy, Aaron had done his best to love both his parents—he was good at loving—but when he realized he no longer felt anything but pity for his mother and dislike for his father, he'd left home forever, never once looking back.

He was good at loving, and didn't want to become good at hating, too.

"How old are you, boy?" Cobb asked him. "You ain't no damn runaway, are you?"

Not anymore, Aaron thought. "I'm nineteen. I know I look younger, but I can show you my driver's license if you want."

"I best take you up on that. I ain't about to hire no juvenile delinquent."

Aaron shrugged out of his backpack and fumbled through it for his wallet. Cobb's lean face was impassive as he glanced at Aaron's license, but his stance relaxed somewhat after a moment, making him seem less forbidding. As Aaron waited, his fatigue suddenly got the best of him and he hid a huge yawn behind his hand.

"Am I keepin' you awake, son?" Cobb demanded, handing back the license. "Want I should fetch you a comfy pillow and a nice warm blanky?"

"Sorry." Aaron embarrassed himself further by yawning again. "Jeez, I'm *really* sorry. I don't know what's wrong with me."

Cobb's fierce green eyes swept over Aaron. There was an unblinking intensity to his gaze that reminded Aaron of a hawk. "You look like hell, boy. When's the last time you slept in a proper bed?"

Aaron could feel his face flushing; he didn't want to admit how squalid his living situation had become. He shrugged again. "Just last night," he lied.

"And the last time you ate a decent meal?"

Aaron's only meal that day—nine hours before—had been a donut and some coffee at a truck stop. He'd put his head down on the table afterwards and slept for twenty minutes until the waitress woke him and made him leave. He shrugged again. "Just a bit ago. I had a huge lunch today, in Wheatland."

"Bullshit." Cobb leaned heavily on his crutches. The hostile edge to his voice was gone, replaced by a matter-of-factness that—

while not exactly kind—was at least civil. "Look, son. I can see you been rode hard and put up wet, and if you wasn't such a skinny little flyspeck I'd be happy to hire you. Lord knows I need the help. If my neighbor and his boy hadn't come 'round the last few days my goddamn cattle woulda starved to death. But I need somebody with a strong goddamn back and some meat on his bones to handle things till I'm back on my feet, and that ain't you."

Aaron stood up straight, shaking off his fatigue. "I'm stronger than I look."

"Shit, son. I doubt you could even lift a pail of milk, let alone dig a few hundred postholes, or put up a load of hay. I can give you a bite to eat and maybe even find you a ride back to town, but that's all I can do."

Aaron heard both the pity and the finality in Cobb's tone and he dropped his gaze to hide an unfamiliar rush of bitterness. Even in his current condition he could outwork most men he knew, but Cobb wasn't going to allow him to prove it. The rejection was hard to bear and he was shocked to find himself near tears; he hadn't been aware until then just how fragile he was getting. He kept his face stony, though, and knelt to stuff his wallet in his backpack. As he zipped up the pack again his copy of *David Copperfield* fell out and landed at Cobb's feet, front cover up. He started to jam it back where it belonged but Cobb lifted the tip of a crutch to stop him.

"Hold up, now. What the Sam Hill are you doin' with a book like *that*?"

Aaron shrugged. He wasn't inclined to discuss his choice of reading material with a man who'd just refused to hire him, but the look on Cobb's face—unguarded and almost friendly—was so different than any previous expression he'd seen there, he couldn't help but be curious.

"It's the best book I've ever read," he said. "Have you read it?"

Cobb's narrow, stern face suddenly lit up with a smile; he banged his crutch on the ground and cried out: "Janet! Donkeys!"

Aaron laughed aloud, astonished. "That's one of my favorite parts! I also love when Betsey tells off the Murdstones."

"Yep, I'm partial to that bit, too. She sure sends them sons-a-bitches packin' in style, don't she?"

"She sure does." Aaron sobered at once as Cobb's unfortunate choice of words sank in. He, too, was being sent packing, and in his case it was no laughing matter. Cobb apparently realized the same thing because he grimaced and dropped his eyes. Aaron put the book away in silence and stood again, glancing involuntarily at the endless-looking driveway. He was tempted almost past bearing to take Cobb up on the offer of food and a ride back to town, but he was not so far gone yet that he'd stoop to begging. He could make his own way back to Wheatland, and once there he still had enough money for a hamburger. As he lifted the pack once more Cobb hopped out to stand beside him on the porch.

"See them goddamn potholes in my drive?" he asked brusquely.

Aaron looked where he was pointing and nodded, heart quickening.

"Well, there's a shovel and a wheelbarrow in that there shed, and a big-ass pile of gravel out back of the barn," Cobb said. "Get your ass to work. I'll scrounge up some grub for us and let you know when it's ready."

Aaron dropped the backpack and fairly leapt off the porch to obey, not knowing why Cobb had changed his mind but not about to let the miracle go by. Unfortunately, his feet betrayed him: try as he might to mask the pain that walking in his boots caused, all he could do was hobble.

"What the hell's wrong with your feet, boy?"

Aaron bit his lip, assuming Cobb was now going to rescind his offer. He couldn't really blame him, he supposed; he must look pathetic. "I've been doing a lot of walking lately, Mr. Cobb," he said, no longer able to keep a pleading note from his voice, "but I can still work, I swear."

Cobb locked eyes with him for what seemed an eternity, and Aaron could almost read his thoughts. Whatever else might be true about Hap Cobb, he was not the simple, crass man he pretended to be—at least not entirely. There was a loneliness and a vulnerability in his gaze that Aaron recognized all too well, and something else, too, that went far beyond all the bluster and blasphemy.

"You are one sorry little idjit," Cobb said at last, "and that's a fact. Get inside and bandage yourself up before you start on them potholes. You ain't no use to me crippled."

Aaron swallowed past a lump in his throat, moved by the rough kindness in Cobb's words. As he limped back to the porch he tried to say "thank you" but Hap cut him off.

"Any other goddamn afflictions I need to know about? I mean, besides chronic stupidity and an allergy to soap? Oh, Jesus Christ. Would you *stop* grinnin' at me like that?

Chapter Four

"Phone's still out," Aaron said.

It was midmorning and breakfast was over. The sun was glinting off the snow behind the house and it hurt Hap's eyes to have all that bleak, blinding whiteness glaring through the south window of his kitchen. Icicles hung from the gutters of the house, dripping and sparkling as the mercury gradually rose, but the wind whistling in around the window panes still made his bones feel as if they were coated with hoarfrost.

"I should move someplace where it's warm all the damn time," he murmured. "I'm sick to death of freezin' my ass off."

As a boy, Hap used to love winter—rising early in the mid-winter dark to do chores with his grandfather, riding his horse to school afterwards as the sun rose, snowball fights and sledding with friends when time allowed, ice fishing and skating on the pond north of the house, late nights out walking under a sky so vast and riddled with stars it took his breath away just to look up and see all that glory above him—but that was back when his blood burned hot and his hands and feet never, ever got cold. Now he huddled shivering under his blankets at night, listening to the wind howl outside his bedroom windows, and his fingers and toes always felt as cold as death.

As cold as Ed Marcy, now buried in some frozen patch of earth.

He and Ed Marcy went back a long, long way; they hadn't been particularly close, but they'd grown up together and had always enjoyed each other's company. It didn't surprise him that Aaron, ever the mother hen, had kept the upsetting news of Ed's death to himself—he had to have known about it, since he went to town on a weekly basis and always came back loaded with local gossip—but it seemed odd no one else had said anything, either. Granted, Hap hadn't been to town himself for ages, but he still couldn't believe no one had bothered to tell him.

"What'd you say, old man?" Aaron asked behind him.

Hap started, wondering how much or how little of what he'd just been thinking he'd actually said aloud. "I said there ain't gonna be no phone service for a long while yet. How about you clean out your ears?"

He went back to staring at the bright red barn and the canary yellow chicken coop (Aaron had painted both buildings last summer, and was overfond of vivid colors, in Hap's opinion) as Sandy finished cleaning up the dishes behind him. The pigheaded young woman had refused help from everyone in this task, including Lucas, saying "I'm the only one here who hasn't done any work yet today." Hap secretly approved of both Sandy and Lucas for not expecting to be waited on hand and foot, but he'd given them an earful, anyway, for making him feel useless. It was Aaron's prerogative if he wanted to say things like "Thanks for helping," but if God were to die one day and leave Hap Cobb in charge of the universe, good manners would be at the top of the list of pointless, aggravating things he'd abolish for all eternity, second only to winter.

Winter, and goddamn *cats.*

The boy had vanished shortly after breakfast, saying he wanted to poke around the library. (Hap was impressed by this, too, having assumed Lucas would be like every other damn kid in America, playing video games with one hand and diddling himself with the other.) Lucas had also insisted before going upstairs that Aaron let him know when he was going outside again; he seemed unduly fascinated by their gas generator and wanted to tag along and watch Aaron tend to it.

"Son of a bitch," Hap muttered. "Here we go *again.*"

The niggling sensation he'd been experiencing all morning was back, triggered by Lucas's interest in the generator. This was the umpteenth time Hap had been teased to distraction by the mystery of why the boy seemed so familiar, but the sensation passed once more, flashing by like headlights on the highway. He couldn't for the life of him figure out why Lucas's face and manner were ringing a big damn alarm bell in his mind, but they sure as hell were, and if he didn't solve the puzzle soon he was going to give himself an aneurysm.

"I must be getting senile," he mumbled.

"You're talking to yourself again, Hap," Aaron told him. "Sandy's going to think you belong in a nursing home."

"I won't either," Sandy said, smiling at Hap. "I read somewhere once that talking to yourself is a sign of a high IQ."

"Huh," Aaron said. "I thought it was a sign of dementia."

Hap gave the younger man the evil eye. "Shut up and check the phone again, would you? I want to find out who that boy upstairs belongs to."

"I just checked two seconds ago," Aaron said, but he picked up the receiver anyway, listened for a dial tone, then hung up once more, shaking his head.

Hap pursed his lips and turned back to the window. "Does the little dimwit remind you of anybody? I keep thinkin' he looks awful goddamn familiar."

"Really?" Something in Aaron's voice made Hap look at him again. "Lucas said in the barn that he kept feeling he'd been here before. I told him I'd never seen him, but was I wrong?"

"Nah, he ain't been here. He just reminds me of somebody I can't rightly place."

Sandy cleared her throat by the sink. She was standing with her hands in the soapsuds in the sink, her shoulder-length blonde hair pulled back into a ponytail. "Lucas and I had a strange conversation this morning, too," she said, wiping her forehead on her sleeve. "He thought he recognized the people in that old picture in your upstairs bathroom."

Hap frowned, nonplussed. "That's my grandma and granddaddy, and they've both been dead for more'n half a century." He turned to Aaron again. "Think the boy might've busted out of that crazy farm in Torrington?"

"Lucas isn't crazy," Sandy said. "His mind is just playing tricks on him. For all we know, he might be remembering something he saw on a television show."

Hap snorted. "In other words, he's batshit *crazy*."

"He's not the one standing around talking to himself," Aaron said. "And as far as memory problems go---"

"There ain't nothin' wrong with my memory!"

"Don't get so riled, old man. I was just going to say that whatever's going on in your thick skull probably doesn't have anything to do with Lucas."

"I never said it *did*. Jesus God in heaven, son, you get dumber every day. It's a wonder you still know enough to scratch your butthole when it itches."

An almost imperceptible flush slowly crept up Aaron's neck and cheeks. "For Pete's sake, Hap. We've got a lady in the room with us, or didn't you notice?"

Hap could scarcely believe his eyes and ears; it was the first time in years he'd managed to discomfit his normally unflappable housemate in the slightest. Before he could begin probing the contours of this chink in Aaron's armor, however, the phone rang, spoiling the moment.

"Well, hell," Hap protested. "Why'd they have to go and fix the damn phone right this second?"

*

"Lucas?" Sandy stood in the hallway outside the library on the second floor, wondering where the boy could have gone. He wasn't in the library or his bedroom; the bathroom was unoccupied, too. "You still up here, kid?"

With the phone working again, she'd reached her boss and been given the day off, and Aaron had called the sheriff's office in Wheatland. Lucas's identity was still a mystery, but the sheriff was now looking into it and either he or somebody from social services would come for the boy as soon as the roads allowed. Sandy called again, louder, closing the library door.

There were four bedrooms off the upstairs hallway, including her own and Lucas's. She poked her head in the spare rooms, but there was nothing to see, save for a lot of old, musty-smelling furniture, draped in sheets. Aaron had showed her and Lucas the whole house last night, but she'd been so frazzled from her ordeal in the snowstorm she hadn't paid much attention. She now noted, however, that the room next to Lucas's must've belonged to a woman; she could make out the shape of a dressing table with a large mirror set against one wall. The other bedroom had served as a nursery, with a crib in the corner and light blue and yellow paint on the walls, now looking faded and forlorn; there was also an old wood stove, not currently in use, near the door.

It struck her as odd that Hap's family had lived in the same house for generations, yet aside from the photo of his grandparents in the bathroom, she'd seen no pictures of Hap's forebears anyplace. In fact—save for the snapshots of Aaron on the refrigerator—there were no photographs in the entire house. There wasn't much in the way of artwork, either, aside from a couple of Old West-themed watercolors in the dining room and a print of Picasso's *Don Quixote* in the downstairs hallway. She supposed that was what happened when you had two single men living in the same house for years on end without a woman to soften things up.

Not that Hap and Aaron didn't do all right on their own. The old ranch house was lonely in some ways, but the two men's oddball friendship was appealing, as was their book-stuffed library and Hap's aromatic, inviting kitchen. There was also something about Aaron that intrigued her, something reassuring and lovely, but she couldn't quite put her finger on it. He gave the impression he'd never wasted a second of his life wishing for more than what he had, and his apparent peace of mind made her envious.

She shut the door to the nursery and headed back downstairs, telling herself Lucas was probably just using one of the first floor toilets, but when she reached the bottom of the staircase she checked both bathrooms and found them empty.

"Lucas?" she called again.

Aaron's room had a television, but Lucas didn't strike her as the sort of kid who would just invade someone's bedroom and plop himself down in front of the TV. She checked anyway, opening Aaron's door and sticking her head in. The small room was just as she'd seen it last evening: tidy and spartan, with only a computer desk, a bed—the bedclothes tucked into neat hospital corners—a dresser, a nightstand piled high with books, and on a small chest at the foot of the bed, an ancient, neglected-looking television. All four walls, once again, were bare. She closed the door and continued her search, but the other rooms along the hallway were likewise unoccupied. It abruptly occurred to her she hadn't seen Wilbur, either, ever since the cat had vomited on the kitchen floor. She frowned, looking up and down the empty hall.

"Wilbur? Lucas?"

She returned to the kitchen, perplexed. Hap and Aaron were—predictably—in the middle of an argument.

"You're hallucinating, old man."

"The hell I am. Ain't no call to be ashamed, son. Matter of fact it's about damn time as far as I'm---"

They broke off when they saw Sandy.

"Lucas didn't come back in here, did he?" Sandy asked, wondering at the blush on Aaron's face. "I can't find him or Wilbur anyplace."

Aaron asked if she'd checked the library and she nodded, saying she'd looked everywhere. She suddenly remembered Hap mentioning a cellar earlier and asked if she should search there, too. Aaron told her the only entrance was outside and he pointed to Lucas's red coat hanging on a coat tree on the porch and his boots over by the door; the boy wasn't likely to be wandering around in the snow in his shirtsleeves and stocking feet.

"Ain't no call to worry," Hap said. "Lots of nooks and crannies in this old house. Boys his age always get scarce when grownups get to talking."

"Especially if one of those grownups is a vile old fart," Aaron added.

"You're just sore 'cause I figured out that you—"

"I guess he could be up in the attic," Aaron said loudly.

"There's an attic?" Sandy asked. "I didn't see a door for it."

Aaron nodded and told her there was a trapdoor with an attached ladder in the ceiling of the nursery; he said it was possible to pull the trapdoor up from the attic, and hard to hear anything in the rest of the house once that was done. "Maybe Lucas saw the rope pull in the nursery and decided to go exploring."

"Ain't nothing worth seein' up there," Hap said. "Just a load of crap that's been stowed away ever since Moses popped his first goddamn pimple."

"Sounds like the perfect place for a bored teenager," Sandy said, brightening, "and *also* for a nosey thirty-four-year old woman who loves poking around in other people's things. Mind if I go look?"

"Suit yourself." The coffee-stained smile Hap gave her was startlingly sweet; in that moment he reminded her more than a little of Aaron. "I played up there all the time when I was a youngster. Hell, I even stayed a whole day once when my granddaddy was after me with his belt for ruining a good pair of boots. I tied the trap shut so he couldn't get at me but I finally got hungry enough to come back down. Granddaddy'd worn himself out screaming at the goddamn nursery ceiling all day, though, so he didn't have more'n a couple of good swings left in him."

Sandy blinked, not sure what kind of a response was called for, but Aaron grinned and came to her rescue. "Most of Hap's stories about his granddaddy are more heartwarming."

"Damn straight," Hap agreed. "As long as you didn't cross him Granddaddy was a goddamn saint." He turned to Aaron. "Listen, son, you best go get the driveway plowed so the sheriff can come by and get the boy later. The catwoman and me can check the attic."

Aaron raised an eyebrow. "You better let Sandy go by herself. You're too old to be climbing that ladder."

"And you're too damn dumb to be tellin' me what to do in my own house."

"I mean it, Hap." Aaron pointed a thick finger at a footstool in the corner. "Remember what happened when you got on that thing and tried to grab your grandma's china bowl instead of waiting for me to help you?"

"You were takin' too long to get your ass in here. I only fell 'cause I was a mite dizzy from a head cold."

"You didn't have a head cold, you old liar." Aaron turned to Sandy. "He ended up breaking his wrist in three places, and things didn't go so well for his grandma's bowl, either."

"Fine," Hap snapped, flushing. "I'll just show Sandy how to work the ladder." He sniffed petulantly. "Even though I'm so goddamn *feeble* I may have a heart attack between here and there."

Aaron rolled his eyes. "Whatever you say, you big baby. Just stay off that ladder."

*

"You up there, Lucas?" Sandy called, staring up at the closed trapdoor in the nursery ceiling. She reached for the rope pull above her head when there was no answer.

"Best use both hands," Hap ordered. "Damn door's heavy."

Sandy obeyed, tugging hard on the rope, and the trapdoor swung open with a creak. A storm of dust and debris came raining down, causing both Sandy and Hap to throw up their hands in front of their faces, coughing. Sandy squinted up with watering eyes into the black hole above them.

"Okay, I think it's safe to say he hasn't been up there," she said as the dust settled. The bright sunlight pouring through the nursery windows revealed all the motes still in the air, floating around like ghosts. "Where on earth *is* he?"

"More'n likely camped out in some closet, playin' hide-the-sausage with a whole goddamn troupe of imaginary friends." Hap stepped forward and put his hand on the folding ladder attached by a wire to the trapdoor. "That boy ain't right in the head."

"Lucas is too old for an imaginary friend, Hap, and I don't think he's avoiding us on purpose. He's a pretty levelheaded kid."

"Well, he's deaf, then, not to hear all the hollerin' and carryin' on you been doing." Hap unfolded the hinged ladder from the trapdoor, dropping its wooden feet to the floor of the nursery. "I wonder if the light still works up there," he said, peering into the attic.

Sandy wasn't listening. After Hap and Aaron had told her about the attic, she'd been sure she'd find Lucas there, but now she didn't know what to think. Wilbur's absence was troubling her too, but not as much; in her two-bedroom condo in Wheatland, the cat had once managed to evade her for an entire afternoon, finally turning up behind a suitcase in her closet just as she'd begun to despair of ever seeing him again. But Lucas was a five-foot-something, one-hundred-fifteen-pound teenager, who—unlike her psychotic cat—had thus far displayed no antisocial tendencies.

"I sure hope he's okay," she said.

"He'll turn up soon as I put more chow on the table. Don't fret yourself."

Sandy abruptly became aware that Hap was now halfway up the attic ladder; his feet were almost level with her head. "Hap! Aaron told you not to climb up there!"

"Aaron can kiss my ass."

Between the cuffs on Hap's pants and the tops of his black socks Sandy could see a network of blue spider veins in the nearly translucent skin of the old man's calves. His ankles looked puffy enough to be painful, yet he was climbing the ladder spryly enough, one rung after another. Left with little choice, Sandy scampered after him, praying if he slipped that she'd be able to catch him before he could inflict too much damage on himself.

"Jesus H. Christ, somethin' stinks to high heaven," Hap said as his feet reached the top of the ladder. "Where's the goddamn light chain?" He stuck out an arm and flailed around in the darkness. "I can't see a damn *thing*."

"Be careful, Hap!" Sandy begged, bracing him with a hand on the back of his stick-like thighs.

"Whoa there, girl!" Hap's face was in the shadows so she couldn't make out his expression. "Ain't nobody touched me down there in more years'n I can count."

"I'm sorry!" She quickly withdrew her hand. "I just didn't want you to fall."

"I already got one goddamn nanny, thank you very much," Hap huffed.

Sandy's temper flared. "Oh, for pity's sake, Hap! Why do you always have to be such a crabby old *pill*? I'm only trying to help!"

A long silence followed, broken at last by Hap clearing his throat.

"Ain't no call to get all het up." He shifted his weight on the ladder. "Anyhow, I shoulda figured you wouldn't be able to help fondlin' my nether regions. I can't hardly keep from touchin' myself down there, neither."

Sandy flushed and began to stammer, then realized he was only teasing her. "Oh, ha ha ha. Next time I'll let you break every bone in your body. How would you like that, wiseass?"

His giggle sounded so much like a schoolboy's that Sandy was hard-pressed to stay irritated. She sighed and told him to hurry up and turn on the light; he found the chain and pulled.

"Jesus, would you look at this goddamn mess!"

Hap grasped a wooden rail attached to a wall and stepped from the ladder to the floor of the attic, grunting with exertion, and Sandy climbed the last few rungs to join him. As she stepped off the ladder she wrinkled her nose at the stench of dried urine; mice had apparently taken over this part of the house. A cardboard box near the trapdoor had a jagged hole in its side, stuffed with shredded, yellow newspaper and bits of cloth; the floor around the box was spattered with droppings.

"Oh, no!" she said. "I hope there was nothing valuable in that box."

"Nah, it's all horseshit." Hap looked around the attic, his eyes roving over dozens of boxes, chests, and an assortment of well-worn furniture. "I'll make the pinhead haul it outside today and set some traps for those furry little sons-a-bitches."

The attic was larger than Sandy had thought it would be; she guessed it was at least thirty feet long and twenty-five or thirty feet wide. The ceiling was low and slanted on both sides, however, making the space seem much smaller than it was, and because there was only the one bare light bulb—dangling like a lynched man from a cord in the rafters—the room was full of shadows. She spotted a child's pogo stick leaning against an old rocking chair with a broken arm; she smiled at an enormous, glassy-eyed buffalo head propped against one wall, with a man's derby hat hanging rakishly from one horn.

"I don't know why we ain't thrown all this crap out years ago," Hap said. "Some of it's been here my whole damn life."

"Really? You may have a fortune up here and not even know it."

He snorted, bending over to pick up a rickety footstool. "Nah. Everything's junk." He set the footstool on a battered chest of drawers and nudged a box with the toe of his shoe. "This here box, for instance, ain't nothin' but pictures of dead folks who don't matter to nobody. I showed 'em to my granddaddy once and asked if any was of my parents or my big brother, but he just said "no" and to put 'em back where I found 'em."

Sandy stared at him. "You didn't recognize your own family?"

"They all up and died in a fire when I was two years old. I ain't never even seen a picture of 'em." He nudged the box again with his toe. "Leastwise not if Granddaddy was telling the truth about these here snapshots just being distant relations and such."

"Why on earth would he lie to you?"

"Dunno. He never talked about my folks, other than to say he didn't see eye to eye with 'em about anything on God's green earth. I couldn't get him to say nothin' about my brother, neither, and my grannie was just as zipper-lipped as he was."

"But that's terrible!" Sandy protested. "You had every right to know about your family!"

Hap smiled at her indignation on his behalf. "You'd a thought so, wouldn't you? Anyway, that's why I hung on to these damn pictures. I keep thinkin' one of these days I'll look through 'em again and see somethin' I ain't seen before." A cabinet by the buffalo head caught his eye. "You like to sew, girl? I got my grannie's old sewin' stuff over there. It's probably all crap, too, but you can see if there's anything you want."

*

Aaron reached the top of the steps to the second floor and paused at the sight of the open nursery door midway down the hallway. He thought he could hear Hap talking, but it sounded as if the old man was in another county. Aaron sighed.

"Of *course* the old jackass went up the ladder," he muttered.

He'd been outside for the past hour, plowing the ranch's long driveway. It was now possible for a car to get from the highway to the house, but the highway itself was still impassable; the county plows hadn't yet found the time to get out their way.

He wandered into the nursery and gazed up through the open trapdoor into the attic. The light was on up there; he could see the bare wooden beams of the ceiling from where he stood, but nothing else. Hap's voice was louder here but Aaron still couldn't quite make out what he was saying. The old man sounded more lively than he had in some time, however, and Aaron was thankful to hear it. No doubt he'd cornered Sandy and Lucas where they couldn't escape from him; nothing ever made the old man happier than a captive audience.

"Hap!" Aaron called up.

"God's almighty balls!" Hap bellowed back after a moment of silence. "You scared the bejesus outta Sandy and me!"

Aaron paused. "Just you and Sandy? Where's Lucas?"

"Oh, my Lord!" Sandy's head popped into the space above Aaron. "Hap and I got chatting and I lost track of time. Lucas still hasn't turned up?"

Aaron shook his head and she said she'd come help him look.

"Ain't no call for that," Hap objected plaintively. "There's still lots of stuff to show you."

"I'd love to stay and poke around some more with you, Hap," Sandy said. "But we really should go find Lucas first, don't you think?"

"Aaron can hunt for the boy. He's a goddamn bloodhound when you give him something to track. There was this one time—"

"If you want to stay with Hap, Sandy, that's fine," Aaron broke in. He found himself wishing he'd left them alone for awhile longer to allow Sandy more time to keep working her good mojo on Hap's spirit. "Just don't let the miserable old sourpuss talk your ear off."

"No, I better come down. I should've been looking for Lucas this whole time. I can't imagine where he's gone."

"Hap best come down with you, then," Aaron said, surrendering to her wishes. "I don't want him near this ladder by himself."

"You and that goddamn *ladder!"* Hap hollered. "I got up here just fine, didn't I?"

"Yeah, but I bet Sandy was right behind you the whole way, wasn't she, just in case you fell?" Aaron smiled at Sandy. "Did you bother to thank her for that, by the way?"

Hap's voice was somewhat more subdued when he answered after a few moments. "She only did it 'cause she was hankerin' to get her hands on my backside."

"Oh, for heaven's sake," Sandy snorted. "Here we go again."

The yowl of a cat from somewhere behind Aaron interrupted them.

"Wilbur!" Sandy cried, leaning down. "What have you gotten into now?"

Aaron stepped over to the doorway. "Wilbur?" he called. Wilbur yowled again from somewhere down the hall, sounding as if he were asking a question. "I think he's in the library."

Aaron was sure he remembered the library door being closed when he first came up the stairs but it was standing wide open now.

"Oh, no!" Sandy said. "He's got like this weird fetish-thing about paper! He'll tear up your whole library!"

"He'll do *WHAT?"* Hap yelled with genuine panic. "Aaron! Get that little son of a bitch away from my books right this goddamn second!"

"I swear I closed the door earlier when I went in there!" Sandy protested. "I don't know how he got in!"

Aaron sighed as Sandy's feet appeared on the ladder; Hap was swearing up a storm and yammering at her to hurry, sounding as if he intended to climb on her shoulders if she didn't get out of his way. *So much for good mojo,* Aaron thought.

"Just slow down, the pair of you," he commanded, raising his voice to carry over Hap's cursing and Sandy's fretting. "Sandy, please make sure Hap gets down safely. Hap, calm yourself before I put a muzzle on that vile old mouth of yours. I'll go rescue your books, okay?"

He paused long enough to make sure Sandy, at least, would follow his instructions, then hurried down the hall, shaking his head at yet another obscenity-laced outburst from Hap. Stepping into the library he saw Sandy's maladjusted yellow tabby standing stiffly, tail twitching, near a pile of Hap's beloved books—thus far undamaged—and Aaron relaxed.

"Good boy, Wilbur. You've earned yourself a reprieve from the executioner."

Wilbur didn't seem to notice he was there, even after Aaron yelled out to Hap that everything was fine. The cat's green eyes were focused with single-minded intensity on the red leather chair in the corner. The chair was empty, but on the floor in front of it was an open book, lying face up. Aaron stared curiously at Wilbur and wandered over to the chair for a closer look, wondering why the cat was so transfixed. Squatting down to pick up the book, he put a hand on the seat of the armchair to steady himself and was surprised to find the overstuffed leather seat was warm to the touch, as if somebody had been sitting on it.

Aaron pursed his lips, mystified. "Lucas?" he called out.

There was no answer.

He supposed Wilbur himself might have hopped out of the chair an instant before, but the back cushion was warm as well. He raised his voice. "Lucas? Where are you, son?"

Was Hap right about the boy hiding from them? The idea made no sense to Aaron—it would be a childish stunt to pull, and seemed deeply out of character—but what other explanation was there? The chair cushion hadn't heated itself, nor could a teenage boy like Lucas simply evaporate like condensation on a cold window.

At a loss, Aaron picked up the book before him—*The Tales of Peter Rabbit,* an old children's book he himself had loved as a little boy—and saw it was open to its last page. The page had been badly defaced with purple and red crayon: A small child's cryptic portrait of something that really could have been just about anything. Aaron closed the book and ran his hand absently over the cover, chewing his lower lip. He looked at Wilbur again and found the cat staring back at him.

"Okay, Wilbur," Aaron said, oddly unnerved by the cat's unblinking regard. "What's going on?"

"Rrowraoor?" Wilbur demanded in return, then hissed and ran from the room, yowling.

Chapter Five

Hap answered a loud knock at the front door and found Glenn Nixson—Wheatland's perennial, unexcitable sheriff, in the job for nearly forty years—standing on the stoop, looming over him and blocking the early afternoon sunlight. The outside air was crisp and clean, but so sharp it hurt Hap's lungs.

"Hap, you contrary old bastard," Glenn rasped, extending a gorilla-like paw for Hap to shake and baring his crooked, yellow teeth in an affectionate smile. "I was truly, *truly* hoping you'd gone to your eternal rest."

"Glenn, you sad sack, sorry-ass son of a whore." Hap gripped the other man's gigantic fingers tightly in his own. "Jesus God, boy, it's a wonder your poor heart ain't exploded into a million tiny pieces of lard. I didn't think it was possible for a man to get any fatter than you already was, but I'd swear on a stack of goddamn Bibles you went and did just that."

It was true: Glenn Nixson was extraordinarily obese. His brown uniform coat was unzipped despite the weather, and the buttons on his white and brown shirt beneath looked as if they were mere seconds away from popping off the man's enormous belly. His heavily jowled face was an unhealthy, beet red and the wooden step under his feet sagged beneath his weight.

"Shut up, Hap," Glenn responded, still earnestly shaking Hap's hand. "I've got something important to say." He leaned forward to speak in a more confidential tone; his warm breath—-turning to mist in the frosty winter air—-reeked of onions and cooked beef. "I've been doing some thinking, and I finally decided the Lord God seriously *fucked* up by allowing a hateful old windbag like you to live so long. It's a crying shame, and that's all there is to it."

"It's also a cryin' shame for a man to weigh more than a damn school bus," Hap countered, shivering as a frigid gust of wind blew past the sheriff. "Don't just stand there grinnin' like an idjit. Come in outta the cold, Glenn. I just put on a fresh pot of joe."

Glenn shook his head regretfully. "Believe it or not, there's nothing I'd rather do than sit a spell with you, old man, but I've got too much to do today. I only came out to pick up that boy Aaron called me about."

"You ain't heard the news? I told Aaron to call you back so's you wouldn't make the trip all the way out here for nothing."

"What news?"

"The boy's gone missin.' I told the bald pinhead to call you."

Glenn sighed. "He probably did, but I didn't get the message. Our new dispatcher has shit for brains."

"Well, he'll fit right in with the rest of us then, won't he?" Hap stepped back and gestured imperiously. "Get your ass in here before I freeze to death."

"How in hell did you and Aaron lose track of the kid?" Glenn asked, surrendering. He closed the door behind him and wiped his big feet on the rug. "I mean, *you'd* lose your own dick if it wasn't attached, but Aaron's usually right on top of things."

Hap shrugged as he led the other man down the hall toward the dining room. "The boy's just hidin' out somewhere. Aaron and Sandy say he ain't, but they're both deficient."

"Who the heck is Sandy?"

"The girl who showed up yesterday with that dimwit boy. Drove her car into a ditch durin' the storm. Says she works for some new dentist in Wheatland who took over for Ed Marcy." Hap fixed a stern eye on the sheriff. "By the by, how come you didn't let me know Ed passed? I just found out."

"Are you kidding me? Sorry, Hap. It never crossed my mind to think you didn't know. You never go to funerals anyway, so when you weren't at Ed's, I figured you were just being your usual spiteful old self."

"Was Aaron there? At the funeral, I mean."

Glenn studiously avoided Hap's gaze. "I can't recall. Anyway, that girl you're talking about is Sandy Satchell, and she's a sweetheart. Went to school with my niece." They passed through the dining room into the kitchen, the floor groaning beneath Glenn's feet. "Place looks good," Glenn said, panting as he seated himself at the table. "Still looks just the same as when Daddy first brought me out here on his rounds. How long ago was that? Sixty years? Sixty-five?" He paused, watching Hap slice a loaf of freshly-baked banana nut bread on the counter. "You were already older than God is all I remember."

"And you were a snot-nosed little brat, peekin' at me from behind your daddy's legs. I still miss your daddy somethin' fierce. He was dumber'n a hardboiled egg and mouthy as a goddamn lapdog, but he was a damn fine man, and that's a fact." Hap finished slicing the bread and stepped over to the fridge to fetch a stick of cream cheese from the dairy drawer. "He was also the only goddamn cattle vet 'round these parts worth a shit."

"He liked you, too, Hap." Glenn eyed the bread as Hap brought it to the table on a plate, along with a mug of coffee. "He always told me you were the stubbornest, nastiest, and most useless man on the face of the earth, but every time he got to come out here he laughed his ass off all the way home. Where's Aaron, by the way?"

Hap glanced at the wall clock. "Shoulda been back by now. He took Sandy out to the highway an hour or so ago to see if they could dig her car out of the ditch."

"It's still real bad out there. They'll be lucky to even find the thing."

"Nah, I bet the meathead's already got it hooked up to his goddamn pickup and is tryin' to pull it out. I told him to take the tractor but he always thinks he knows best."

"That's 'cause he does." Glenn reached for a slice of bread. He chewed with relish, breathing heavily through his nose. "He's way smarter than you, Hap, and everybody knows it. Hell, even *you* know it. I don't have a clue how you ever talked him into working for you all these years."

Hap scowled. "I should've kicked his uppity ass out a long time ago. Just this morning he was bossin' me around like he was Captain Kingshit Bligh and I was his goddamn cabin boy."

"Well, what dumbass thing were you doing? He only bosses you if you got it coming."

"It's my own damn house and I can do whatever I want!"

"Whatever you say, Hap." Glenn paused to reflect. "It's too bad Aaron never knew Ellen. The two of 'em together might've had a fighting chance of turning you into a halfway decent human being."

Hap swallowed hard and looked away. Until that moment, the pleasure of Glenn's company had actually made it possible to think about something *other* than Ellen, who had been on his mind for days now, in a way she hadn't been in years. Now she was back with a vengeance, stomping around in his heart like a jackbooted thug. He couldn't understand why hearing her name spoken was so much harder to take than when he just kept his memories to himself: as much as she'd been haunting him lately, it really shouldn't make a lick of difference to him whether or not someone else brought her up.

But it did. Oh, yes indeedy, you bet your sweet old ass it did.

"Sorry, Hap." Glenn stared sheepishly at the table. "It's been so long since Ellen passed I didn't figure you'd mind talking about her. Guess I was wrong."

"It don't matter none," Hap said, fighting to keep his voice steady.

*

Aaron put his pickup in reverse and the rear wheels skidded all over the icy road as he made his third attempt to drag Sandy's car from the ditch. He'd chained his front bumper to the rear tires of the car.

"I can't tell you how glad I am Hap isn't here." He pitched his voice to carry over the whine of the straining engine and the strident screeching of the tires, spinning out on the pavement. "He'd sprain his tongue saying I told you so."

Sandy was perched in the passenger seat of the pickup, bracing her hands on the dashboard. She shook her head cheerfully, clearly enjoying herself. "I won't tell if you won't."

Aaron eased up on the gas and brought the truck to a halt, drumming on the steering wheel with his fingers. Sandy's car was now nose-down in the ditch instead of on its side—its rear end protruding a couple of feet above the lip of the embankment—but thus far that was the extent of what he'd accomplished. He'd spread a veritable beachhead of sand on the highway for traction, but every time it seemed they were just about to succeed in dragging the car onto the road, his rear tires would slip.

"Can you drive a stick?" he asked Sandy, glancing at the gear shift by his knee.

"Not very well." Apprehension crossed her face. "What do you have in mind?"

"Well, I was thinking we might do better with me in your car. If I can get your engine started—and you can keep me from sliding back into the ditch—we might be able to just back the thing up onto the highway."

Sandy looked dubious. "I better drive my car. I totaled my ex-boyfriend's jeep the last time I tried to drive a stick. Nobody was hurt, but the way he carried on you'd have thought I'd killed a busload of puppies. I've never had anybody scream at me like that in my whole life."

The vulnerability in her voice touched Aaron. "I know how you feel. I wrecked my dad's car when I was sixteen and he yelled so loud I almost went deaf. I ended up running away from home just to get away from him." He smiled. "Then about three years later I moved in with the proud owner of the biggest, meanest mouth in the West. Guess I'm a slow learner."

She shook her head. "Hap definitely has a mouth on him, but he was as sweet as could be when we were up in the attic. I can't imagine him ever being as hateful as my ex."

"That's the first time I've heard the words "sweet" and "Hap" used in the same sentence. Did he sneak something in your Kool-Aid?"

"I'm serious. He kept trying to give me things, like his grandmother's sewing kit and his great uncle's squirrel gun. He looked so disappointed when I kept refusing that I almost felt guilty for not accepting anything."

Aaron stared at her. "Did he really offer to give you some of that old stuff?" He waited for her nod before emitting a low whistle. "Hap acts like everything up there is junk, but it's all he has left of his family and he usually guards it like an old dragon watching over a pile of gold. He must've really taken a shine to you."

"Wow, I had no idea he felt that way." She blushed. "About his things, I mean. He *did* call it all junk, and a whole lot worse than that, too. Now I know how he really feels about it, though, I'm so glad I didn't take anything."

Aaron fretted at his lower lip with his teeth. Hap Cobb was a packrat, down to his dusty old bones; the closets were full of things like empty Kleenex boxes and maple syrup jars, and he still occasionally wore the same clothes he'd had on when Aaron first met him. That he was suddenly willing to part with his attic treasures made no sense. Sandy asked if something was bothering him and he sighed.

"Something's wrong with Hap. I'm worried he may be sick or something and isn't telling me. He's been pretty blue for the past couple of months, and he's starting to show his age in a big way. I can't help but wonder if he's wanting to give stuff away because he doesn't think he'll be around much longer."

"Surely he'd tell you if there was something really wrong with him, wouldn't he?"

"Not a chance." Aaron stared out the side window. "Hap hates talking about anything to do with death or dying. It terrifies him. For all I know his whole body could be one gigantic tumor by now but he'd never breathe a word. He'd just stick his head in the sand and pretend it wasn't happening."

"Oh, no, now I feel awful. I told him this morning that Ed Marcy died of prostate cancer, and I could see it really got to him."

"Oh, hell," Aaron groaned. "That's my fault. I knew Ed died but I kept it from Hap. I even went to the funeral but I lied about where I was going because I didn't want to risk upsetting him until he was in a better frame of mind. The last time somebody he cared about passed away he sat around for weeks, just staring at the wall in his bedroom."

"I'm so sorry. I didn't know."

"There's no way you could have." A falcon in the sky caught his attention and he watched it hover, wings outstretched, far above the snow-shrouded prairie. "I guess I can't really blame him for taking things to heart. He's not a religious man, to say the least, and I think he just can't stand the thought that when people are gone, they're gone forever. I don't know if he told you, but his folks and a big brother died in a fire when he was a baby. He doesn't remember them, but how they all went at once like that haunts him." The falcon plunged to earth in a breathtaking burst of speed and seized on a hapless rabbit running across the highway. "Things never really got much easier for him, either, I don't think. At this point in his life he's lost just about everybody he's ever loved, or who's loved him."

"Everybody but you," Sandy said quietly.

"Yeah," he agreed. "Everybody but me."

He abruptly fell silent, embarrassed to talk like this with someone he really didn't even know—all the more so because when he turned back to Sandy she seemed at a loss for words.

"Well," she said at last, "for what it's worth, he seemed to recover from the news about Ed pretty quickly." The corners of her mouth twitched. "And as far as him showing his age, you should've seen him scoot up that attic ladder. A chimpanzee couldn't have climbed it any faster."

Aaron laughed in spite of himself. "Yeah, I bet. The sneaky old fart was probably in a big hurry to get up there before I could show up and spoil his fun."

"He *did* have a few choice things to say about you. I'm a little surprised your ears didn't catch fire, the way he was carrying on."

Aaron was grateful to her for trying to lighten his mood but it wasn't really working. Hap had always been close-mouthed and prone to bouts of sadness, ever since they'd met, but this business with the attic was something else. He could just feel it. He resolved to sit the old man down that very night and not let him up again until he explained himself.

Sandy's smile had become uncertain and he realized he wasn't being very good company. He apologized, making himself return to the present with an effort.

"So are you game to try out my master plan?" He gestured at her car. "If we have to go back for the tractor I'll never, *ever* hear the end of it."

*

The voices were faint, but Lucas could hear Hap saying goodbye to somebody downstairs in the entryway. Curious, the boy rose from his chair—gently dislodging Sandy's purring cat, Wilbur, from his lap—to look out the window of the library. He was in time to see a massive, mottle-faced man in a uniform waddle out to a Platte County Sheriff's car parked in the driveway. He watched the big man squeeze himself behind the steering wheel, wave back at the house, then close the car door. Lucas kept watching as the sheriff executed a tight three-point turn between snowbanks and drove slowly away, vanishing down a narrow corridor through the snow that Aaron must've plowed after breakfast.

Lucas frowned, wondering why Aaron hadn't bothered to tell him he was going back outside. It worried him to think the man might not really have wanted his help. He also wondered why the sheriff had come to the ranch, but decided it must not have anything to do with him since no one had come to fetch him.

Wilbur rubbed against his calves, behaving like a different creature now it was just the two of them. Lucas reached down to pick him up and stared out the window, holding the cat to his chest. The sky was a vivid, ethereal shade of blue, but almost everything on the earth below was marshmallow-white. Aside from the brown and gray of the plowed gravel driveway, the only spots of color he could see were a few Calvary-like telephone poles on top of a hill in the distance; Lucas assumed these ran parallel with the highway, though he couldn't make out the road itself from his current vantage point. A startling flash of red suddenly shot by the window—a lonely cardinal, extremely rare for Wyoming, especially in the winter—and Wilbur stiffened in his arms, hunter's instinct awakening.

"He's moving too fast, Wilbur," Lucas murmured. The cat relaxed at the sound of his voice and began purring again. "He'd only make a fool of you if you tried to catch him."

"JESUS CHRIST, BOY! WHERE IN *HELL* HAVE YOU BEEN?"

Lucas spun around. Hap was planted squarely in the door of the library; his craggy old face bright red with anger. Wilbur leapt from Lucas's arms and hightailed it from the room, darting between Hap's legs; Hap bellowed in outrage and aimed a feeble kick at the cat's hindquarters. Wilbur was far too nimble for him, however, easily evading his foot and vanishing down the hallway.

"Yeah, you'd better run, damn you!" Hap howled, then spun back to Lucas. "What do you think you're doin,' lettin' that devil beast loose in my library again?"

"I'm sorry!" Lucas squealed. "I didn't know you didn't want him in here!"

"Horseshit! You hid your scrawny little ass someplace we couldn't find you, but you still heard every word we was saying!"

Lucas gaped. "I wasn't hiding!" he protested. "I asked at breakfast if I could come up here and you said yes. I've just been sitting here reading, waiting for Aaron to come get me."

"Breakfast was six *hours* ago, boy, and we was all in this very room right before lunch, huntin' for you. I guess you musta been invisible."

Lucas's mind went blank. "Six *hours?* But that's not...that isn't...I mean, that's *impossible.* I've only been up here an hour or so, and I've been alone the whole time. Except for Wilbur, I mean."

His unfeigned shock seemed to blunt Hap's anger. "How dumb do you think I am, boy?" he asked. "It's past two o'clock in the goddamn afternoon. Look outside if you don't believe me." He gestured at the window. "Sun's in the west, headin' down."

Lucas wheeled about and gasped. He didn't know how he'd missed it when he was watching the sheriff leave, but Hap was right: the sun was well past its zenith. When he'd come upstairs after breakfast dawn had just broken; he'd watched the sunrise for a few minutes before settling in the red leather armchair with a few books. He met the old man's eyes as best he could and tried to say something, but his tongue wasn't working.

"Spit it out, son," Hap growled. "I ain't got all day."

Lucas swallowed, tried again. "I know you think I'm lying, Mr. Cobb, but I'm *not.* I haven't left this room once since I came upstairs. Not even once." He threw up his hands. "Not even to use the darn *bathroom.*"

"Look here, son." Hap's face was no longer red, but he looked as if he'd eaten something unpleasant. "You're spoutin' foolishness. Somethin' ain't right with you, and we need to get you to a doctor, pronto."

Lucas could think of nothing to say that would make a whit of difference—especially because he wasn't sure at all that Hap wasn't right. In the barn that morning, talking to Aaron, he'd felt crazy enough, but this was far worse.

"The sheriff was just here to pick you up, but we didn't know where you was," Hap told him. "We best go downstairs and call him back."

Lucas's heart sank at the prospect of being forced to leave, but he held his tongue and nodded. As the old man turned back to the hall, Lucas looked around the room at all the books; his gaze lingered on the tattered copy of *The Tales of Peter Rabbit,* resting on the floor by the armchair. The old storybook was the first thing he'd picked up that morning when he'd stepped in the library; he'd wanted another look at the crayon drawing on the last page to confirm that he hadn't been imagining things the night before, and he hadn't.

He *hadn't*, dammit.

He cleared his throat. "That book is mine," he said as firmly as he could. He pointed at the storybook as Hap glanced back. "I remember drawing a picture in it when I was a little kid."

Hap squinted to see the book's cover and shook his head. "I've had that there book my whole life, son. Granddaddy read it to me when I was just a knee-high little fartsniffer, but you're welcome to it." He paused, and when he spoke again his voice was surprisingly gentle, as was his sudden smile. "Just don't go droolin' all over the pages when they give you a goddamn lobotomy."

Lucas blinked, taken aback at first by Hap's insensitivity, but then in spite of everything he gave a shaky laugh. The old man's tactless humor abruptly reminded him of somebody, but he didn't have any idea who. He searched Hap's face, trying to wring some sort of answer out of the rancher's weathered, leathery features, but after several long seconds he realized any such effort was futile: His memory was still locked tight.

"I'm sorry," he said, realizing Hap had just said something else. "I wasn't listening."

Hap repeated that he'd rustle up some grub for him, guessing he must be starving since he'd missed lunch. Lucas shook his head and said he was still stuffed from breakfast, but the words were no sooner out of his mouth than they struck him with revelatory force.

"*Wait*!" He put a hand on his own normally nonexistent stomach and felt the muscles stretched taut over the mounds of bacon, eggs, pancakes, and toast Hap had served for breakfast that morning. "If I haven't eaten anything for six hours I should be hungry, but I'm *not*. Not even a little bit!" He hitched up his shirt. "Look, Mr. Cobb. My stomach is still so full I look pregnant!

"What the hell?" Hap snapped as Lucas trotted over and seized one of his liver-spotted hands, forcing the old man to place a palm on his belly. Hap's eyebrows shot up and he jerked away. "Jesus H. Christ, boy, leave me be!"

"I'm *not* crazy, Mr. Cobb," Lucas said. Whatever Hap said, he could tell the old man was startled by what he'd felt. "I swear I'm *not*. I only ate an hour ago, just like I said, and that's all there is to it. I'm *not* crazy."

"Just 'cause you got food in your belly don't mean you ain't also got a whole goddamn *flock* of bats flappin' 'round your belfry." Hap rubbed his temples. "Merciful Christ, would you stop grinnin' like a nitwit and cover yourself? How about we go back down to the kitchen so I can get me some aspirin? I ain't lettin' you out of my sight till the sheriff comes to collect you."

Lucas sobered again at the mention of the sheriff, but as he nodded and followed Hap from the library he still felt nearly limp with relief. He knew the fullness of his stomach would never be taken as evidence by anybody else, yet it was the first tiny shred of proof he had—for himself, at least—that he wasn't completely unhinged.

"Listen up, boy." Hap closed the library door behind them. "You being a lunatic and all, maybe you *didn't* hear me before about not lettin' that cat loose in my library. But consider yourself warned from here on, 'less you want your balls roasted over a hot goddamn fire. Got it?"

"Got it." Lucas's smile returned in spite of Hap's gravity. "I won't let him in again, Mr. Cobb. I swear."

Hap sighed. "And stop Mr. Cobb-ing me. Just call me Hap." He led the way to the staircase and started down, gripping the handrail. "I ain't never had no use for my last name no how, not since I was a kid. Every joker in school called me 'Corncob,' and it was pure misery, I kid you not, 'cause folks hereabouts was still usin' corncobs back then to wipe their butts."

Lucas clapped his hands over his mouth and Hap glanced at him with narrowed eyes.

"You got something to say, boy?"

Lucas shook his head, keeping his hands firmly in place.

"Good, because I guarantee you wouldn't think it was so funny if *your* last name was as stupid as mine." Hap tilted his head to the side and cracked his neck. "The only name I hated worse than Corncob was 'Hapalong Assity.' Oh, for Christ's sake, go ahead and get your tee-heein' over and done with before you bust a rib."

Lucas complied.

Chapter Six

Aaron and Sandy came into the kitchen and found Hap and Lucas sitting across from each other at the table, playing cribbage. Aaron was surprised to see how relaxed both the old man and the boy seemed to be with each other, but what surprised him far more was Hap playing any kind of game at all: in their three decades of living together he'd never once seen Hap pick up a deck of cards, let alone shuffle and deal like a professional gambler.

"*There* you are, Lucas!" Sandy exclaimed. "Where on earth did you go?"

"Oh, sweet Jesus, don't get the little idjit wound up again," Hap rasped, glancing over at Aaron before returning his attention to the card game. "Not 'less you want to rub his goddamn Buddha-belly for luck, that is."

"Beg pardon?" Aaron said.

"I was in the library," Lucas said, flushing. Sandy raised her eyebrows but he cut her off before she could dispute his claim. "I know you looked for me there, but that's where I was."

"The nimrod just keeps sayin' the same thing over and over," Hap said. "He *thinks* he was in the library the whole time he was missing, and he also thinks he was only in there for an hour instead of half the damn day."

"I *was* in the library, and it *was* only an hour or so," Lucas asserted.

"And I'm Betty butt-sniffin' Crocker."

Aaron looked at Sandy, then back at Lucas. "I guess I'm not following you, Lucas. We were all in the library right before lunch, and you weren't there."

Lucas made a helpless gesture. If the boy was lying, Aaron thought, he was a *very* good liar; his eyes were clear and unblinking and there was no hint of deception in his manner. "I can't explain that. All I know is I went up to the library after breakfast, and I didn't leave until Hap came to get me."

"I don't understand." Aaron suddenly remembered how the seat of the armchair in the library had been warm to the touch when he'd gone to check on Wilbur that morning. He mentioned this to Lucas and the boy simply shrugged.

"I can't explain that, either." He watched Hap moving a peg on the cribbage board and sighed in exasperation. "Hap. You're cheating again."

"I ain't neither. You just can't count for shit."

"Look." Lucas snatched Hap's cards away and spread them on the table. "Fifteen-two, fifteen-four and a run of three makes *seven.* You moved your peg for twelve, see?"

"I didn't neither."

"I'm moving it back."

"The hell you say."

They both clawed for the peg in question but Lucas was faster.

"I ain't believin' this," Hap said forlornly to Aaron. "Give me one good reason I shouldn't kick his little ass all over the damn kitchen."

Aaron stepped over to the sink and took two glasses from the dish rack, telling Hap they'd gotten Sandy's car out of the ditch. Hap snorted and reminded him if they'd taken the tractor like he'd suggested they would have been home an hour ago.

"Maybe," Aaron conceded. "But what counts is we didn't *need* the tractor after all. I was right, old man."

"First time for everything, I s'pose."

Sandy sat down in the chair next to Lucas and asked if he'd taken a nap when he was in the library, suggesting maybe he'd been sleepwalking or something when they were looking for him. Aaron saw she, too, found it difficult to believe Lucas was capable of lying so convincingly.

"I'm pretty sure I didn't fall asleep." Lucas ran a hand through his messy red hair. "But even if I *did*, that still doesn't explain my stomach being so full."

"Oh, Jesus," Hap said, rolling his eyes at Aaron, "here we go again."

Aaron didn't know what the boy and Hap were talking about, but he thought Sandy's theory of sleepwalking was unlikely. He didn't say so, though, because—if Lucas *was* telling the truth—the only other explanation for his story Aaron could come up with was that Hap had been right all along about the boy having some sort of mental illness. The likelihood made him sad: Given the bruises on Lucas's back, the poor kid had clearly been through plenty without also having to deal with psychological fallout.

"Glenn Nixson's comin' back to fetch the boy around dinner-time," Hap said, breaking into his thoughts. "You was out lollygaggin' in your damn pickup when he stopped by."

"Glenn was here?" Aaron walked over to hand Sandy her water. "How come he didn't just take Lucas then?" He smiled at Lucas. "Not that I'm not happy you're still with us."

Lucas smiled back at him. "I'm happy to be here, too."

"The little looney didn't show up till Glenn had come and gone," Hap explained. "I called and told him to come back but he said he can't get out this way again for a few hours." He shook his head. "That sorry-ass excuse for a sheriff ate a whole loaf of my banana bread, and a whole goddamn stick of cream cheese, too. Jesus God, that man can *eat*."

"The sheriff doesn't have to come all the way out here again," Sandy said. "I can take Lucas back to Wheatland and drop him at the sheriff's office before I head home." She turned to Lucas. "I mean, if that's okay with you, Lucas?"

"Nah," Hap objected. "Ain't no need for you and the boy to go runnin' off. You best stay put for a spell and have a bite of dinner." He darted a glance at Aaron and flushed. "Quit grinnin' like a jackass."

"Sorry," Aaron said. "I was just thinking it sounded like you might be sorry to see Sandy and Lucas leave us."

"I just hate seein' good grub go to waste." Hap ignored Sandy, who was smiling at him, too. "I'm makin' a big batch of chili and rice for dinner."

Lucas looked hopefully at Sandy. "I *love* chili."

Sandy glanced at the clock on the wall. "You really don't mind if we stay a little longer?" she asked Aaron. "I'm not in any rush to get back home, but I don't want to keep imposing if you're sick of us."

"Ain't no imposition for *him,"* Hap grumbled. "He ain't the one havin' to cook for a pack of damn jackals."

"Hap means he'd love to have you stay for dinner," Aaron translated, watching the corners of Hap's lips quirk up against his will. Lucas beamed, and Sandy looked nearly as pleased. Aaron patted Lucas's shoulder and asked if he'd like to help feed the cows and gas up the generator.

"Sure!" Lucas said. "Just give me a second to whup up on Hap again. I'm going to peg out this hand, anyway."

"Keep right on dreamin', son," Hap grunted.

Lucas showed Hap his cards. "Fifteen-two, fifteen-four, fifteen-six, fifteen-eight, and a double run of three makes fourteen." He moved his peg and grinned broadly; he had crooked teeth but it was a sweet grin. "You lose again, old man."

"Well, ain't you the mouthy little nutjob," Hap said, folding his hand.

*

Glenn Nixson phoned as they were finishing supper in the dining room. Aaron took the call in the kitchen and came back to say the sheriff wasn't going to return that night after all; there'd been a major semi-trailer accident on the highway, and Glenn and all of his deputies were busy. Glenn asked if Sandy could bring Lucas to the sheriff's office that evening instead; he'd made arrangements for a woman from social services to meet them at 6:30 and take Lucas off their hands. Sandy readily agreed—although she refused to leave until she and Lucas had finished helping with the dishes—and Aaron insisted on following them to town to make sure they got there safely.

"I s'pose you might drop by sometime, if you're out this way," Hap said to Sandy in the hallway by the door. "But if you bring that damn cat near my house again I swear to God I'll shoot you."

Sandy laughed as she lifted Wilbur in her arms. "You're not fooling anyone, Hap Cobb. You talk tough, but you're really just an old softie."

"Oh, sure, you betcha, Hap's as sweet as they come," Aaron said, putting on his boots by the door. "Just like arsenic."

"Shut up, pinhead." Hap offered his hand to Lucas. "If you ever bust out of the booby hatch again, boy, come see us. I'll put you to work."

Lucas shook his hand, grinning, but Hap was touched to notice that the boy's grin looked strained; he was obviously unhappy to leave. "Thanks, Hap." His grin slowly became more genuine. "I'm really, *really* glad I whupped you so bad at cribbage."

"Kiss my ass, son." Hap squeezed Lucas's hand one last time before releasing him. "Make sure the nice men in white suits give you a good clean straightjacket, hear?"

Hap stood in the open doorway, shivering, and watched the boy and the woman walk out to Sandy's car. Sandy cradled Wilbur tightly against her coat and took small, careful steps on the icy driveway, Lucas followed closely behind her in his red coat and hunting cap, keeping an eye on her. Aaron stepped around Hap on his way out the door.

"They'll be okay, Hap. I'm sure we'll see them again soon."

"Good riddance," Hap grunted. "Now if I could just get shed of *you*, I'd be happy as a two-twatted whore in a roomful of Siamese twins."

Aaron shook his head, laughing, and went to get in his pickup, parked next to Sandy's car. Sandy got behind the wheel of her car and Lucas climbed in the passenger side. Before Lucas shut his door, Hap could see—in the glow of the car's dome light—Sandy handing Wilbur over to the boy across the front seat. The door closed a moment later and the light went out.

Hap sighed sadly, grateful no one could see his face clearly from that distance.

There was a metallic clicking sound from under the hood of Sandy's car, and two seconds later, the identical sound came from Aaron's pickup. Neither engine was turning over. The clicking resumed in both the car and the pickup a moment later, then ceased altogether. Hap's eyes went wide as he stood listening in the doorway to the silence of the winter night. Clouds drifted across a full moon, making it harder to see, but there was still some illumination from a yellow overhead light on a pole in the driveway, directly above where Aaron always parked.

"What the hell?" Hap breathed.

Sandy opened her door just as Aaron opened his. "My car won't start," she called out. "I think my battery must've died."

"Mine too," Aaron called back, sounding amused but also puzzled. "I'll be damned."

Hap stepped out on the porch. "The girl's battery has juice," he hollered to Aaron. "I just seen her dome light pop on a second ago."

Sandy turned to look through the open door of her car; Hap could barely see Lucas and Wilbur sitting in the dark. "Well, it's not working now," Sandy said.

"Neither's mine," Aaron said, "and I just put a new battery in my truck a month ago." More clouds drifted across the face of the moon as he crawled back in his pickup. He emerged a moment later with a flashlight and popped the hood on his truck to poke around in the engine. Lucas got out of Sandy's car, too, still holding Wilbur; both the boy and the woman walked toward Aaron.

"What's the holdup, Aaron?" Hap demanded, unaccountably edgy. He let go of the screen door and stepped off the porch. "Do I have to show you what a goddamn battery looks like?"

"How about you go back inside where it's warm?" Aaron asked. "You're going to freeze to death standing out in this cold without a coat."

"Aaron's right, Hap," Sandy scolded. "You really shouldn't be outside."

"Don't you start bossin' me, too, girl! I know when I need to put on a damn coat!"

In truth, it *was* more than a bit nippy out—Hap doubted it was any colder in Siberia that night; he could already feel the snot freezing solid in his nose—but there was no way in *hell* he'd let himself be bullied.

Aaron sighed. "Sandy, do you mind babysitting? If you can get the old fart out of our hair, Lucas and I will stand a better chance of sorting things out."

"Oh, that's a jim-dandy plan there," Hap said as Lucas passed Wilbur to Sandy. "You and that chucklehead of a boy ain't got but half a brain between you. He'll be slurpin' battery acid through a straw while you're busy electrocutin' yourself, mark my goddamn words."

Sandy came back up the walk to Hap. "How about we go inside where it's warm, Hap?"

"I ain't cold," Hap said, shaking as if he had a case of ague.

"Well, *I'm* cold, so how about being a gentleman and keeping me company?" She took his arm with her free hand and Wilbur hissed, not pleased at having to share his mistress's affection.

"I wonder what cat meat tastes like," Hap growled.

A light freezing rain started to fall. Hap gaped at the sky, cringing as ice pellets struck his face. He'd listened to the weather forecast on the radio less than an hour before; there'd been zero chance of precipitation. The late afternoon sky had been a heartbreakingly limpid shade of blue, without a ghost of a cloud on the horizon, and Hap would have sworn it was going to be a dry night.

"What in the name of Christ is goin' on?" he asked.

"Welcome to Wyoming in winter," Sandy said, too complacently for Hap's liking.

"My *ass!* Winter or no, we ain't *s'posed* to get any rain tonight! We wasn't even s'posed to get any *snow* for the next goddamn week!"

The rain fell harder and Hap threw up his hands, grudgingly allowing Sandy to herd him inside. With the door closed behind them and the warmth of the house once again enveloping them, he watched Sandy set Wilbur down on the floor without really even noticing what she was doing. "That's just all damn *kinds* of wrong," he said.

"It won't be long, Hap, I promise. Aaron and Lucas will get things figured out in a jiffy and you won't have to put up with Wilbur anymore."

"I ain't talkin' about that mangy critter of yours, girl." He stared at the closed door and chewed on his lip. "Somethin' goddamn *peculiar* is goin' on out there tonight, and I don't like it one little bit."

*

Lucas was soaked to the skin and freezing—again—but this time he didn't mind it one little bit. This time he was a mere thirty feet away from shelter, safety, and warm, dry clothes; this time he knew he wasn't going to die in the cold on the side of the road, not having a clue where he was or how he'd gotten there.

"Okay, this is weird." Aaron detached the voltage meter from the battery in Sandy's car, scantly illuminated by a flashlight resting on the radiator. He lifted the battery and stepped away from the car, raising his voice above the din of the heavy sleet falling on the tarp Lucas held over them. "Sandy's battery doesn't have any more juice than mine, so her alternator must be on the fritz, too. But how in heck did our batteries get drained so fast, with no warning at all?"

Lucas closed the car's hood then fell in beside Aaron as they trudged back toward the barn in the freezing rain and the darkness, crunching through the fresh layer of ice on top of the knee-deep snow. Lucas was in charge of the flashlight and the tarp, but try as he might he couldn't keep the sleet off Aaron and himself; he wasn't tall enough to wrap the tarp around both of them. He asked what kind of warning they should've gotten and Aaron explained when a battery was on its last legs things like the engine taking longer to turn over and the turn signals getting slower were warning signs. "But Sandy's car and my truck *both* ran fine this afternoon," he said, "and I don't get how they could've died so soon."

Lucas was listening—the gaps in his memory had swallowed anything to do with auto mechanics, and the inner workings of engines fascinated him—but he couldn't hide a delighted smile. Whatever the cause of the mechanical failure, it was a godsend. Aaron had told him recharging the truck's battery would take quite a while, and with Sandy needing a recharge, too, there was no way they could get to Wheatland that night to meet the social worker at the sheriff's office. Moreover, the ice storm now pelting down on them would also prevent anybody from town coming out to steal him away, until at least the following morning.

Which meant, of course, he got to spend another whole *night* at White Creek Ranch.

He still didn't have any idea where he came from, but he knew he didn't want to go *back*. Where he wanted to be was here, right now, on this ranch, with Aaron and Hap and Sandy. Hap's library and the small, quiet bedroom at the end of the second floor hallway; talking to Aaron while doing chores and sitting down beside Sandy for another of Hap's magnificent, gut-busting breakfasts; curling up with Wilbur in a chair for hours; sprawling in front of the wood stove at night with nothing and no one to fear, cradling a mug of Hap's glorious, tequila-infused hot cocoa in his hands: Where else could he go that would feel more like home?

He glanced at his companion, remembering something he'd been wanting to ask ever since they'd met. "How come you never got married, Aaron?"

Aaron half-turned to see him in the rain. "I thought we were talking about batteries."

Lucas feared he might have hit a sore nerve. "Sorry."

"It's fine. You just caught me by surprise." Aaron paused to adjust the grip on the battery. "There's no big mystery, I guess. I've just never met the right lady, simple as that."

"Never?"

"Nope." Aaron steered Lucas around a stump-shaped mound of snow that the flashlight revealed in their path. "I was engaged to a nice gal in Chugwater for a while when I was younger, but it didn't work out, so we parted ways." He snorted. "My recollection is she skedaddled the second she met Hap."

Lucas asked him if he ever thought he'd find anybody else.

"Maybe, but my expiration date is running out, if you know what I mean. I turn fifty in a couple of months."

Lucas didn't believe for a second Aaron would have trouble finding a woman. He was smart, funny, and kind; he was also good looking—at least for a middle-aged bald guy—and strong as a bull elephant. What wasn't to like?

"Don't you get lonely sometimes?" he asked.

"Sure." Aaron's voice was wry in the darkness. "But I'm pretty sure getting hitched to the wrong person is a whole lot lonelier."

Lucas mulled this over. "What about Hap, then? How come *he* never got married?"

Aaron hesitated. "Maybe we should go back to talking about batteries."

The sudden cautious note in Aaron's voice piqued Lucas's curiosity. "That's fine." He bit his lip to keep from asking more questions. "It doesn't matter."

Aaron snorted again. "Liar."

Lucas laughed in spite of himself, and Aaron joined in. They walked the rest of the way to the barn in an amiable silence, plodding through the snow. The tarp was growing heavy with ice and Lucas's hands felt frozen and clumsy in his gloves by the time they finally reached the barn door. Aaron handed over the battery to Lucas and wrestled the door open; they stumbled into the relative warmth of the barn with relief. They'd left the light on earlier, and the thirty or so calves and their mothers inside the building stirred sleepily, a few of them pressing against their pen to get a closer look at them.

Aaron shut the door and took back the battery, walking over to set it beside the charger where his own battery was re-juicing. "Hap was married a long time ago," he said quietly. "But it was before I came along, so I can't tell you much about it."

Lucas didn't know what startled him more: that Hap had been married, or that Aaron had chosen to confide in him after all. "Really? What happened?"

"No one knows for sure—not even the people who knew Hap way back then—and Hap won't talk about it. Not even to me." Aaron wiped his nose on the back of a glove. "All I know is his wife died in childbirth at a hospital in Cheyenne, just a couple of months after she and Hap separated. I gather Hap wasn't with her at the time."

Lucas asked if the baby died, too; Aaron nodded but didn't say anything else. Lucas digested this, then asked if Hap was the baby's father.

Aaron eyed him. "You don't miss much, do you?" He stepped over to the cattle pen and rested a hand on a calf's bony back. "I've been told there was a lot of gossip about Hap's wife, but I've never had the heart to ask him about it." He grinned. "By the way, let's keep this conversation to ourselves, okay? I'd rather not get castrated in the middle of the kitchen."

Lucas nodded solemnly and Aaron looked back at the calf and patted its flanks; the calf leaned against the pen and gazed up at him with dumb adoration. "Hap's not overfond of most people," Aaron said, giving the calf one last pat, "but he sure warmed up in a hurry to both you and Sandy. In fact, the only other soul on earth I've ever seen him take a shine to like that is me."

"Really?" Lucas struggled to remove his gloves; they were frozen solid and didn't want to come off. "He's sure got a funny way of showing it."

"Yeah, he's about as warm and cuddly as a hyena." Aaron took pity on him and stepped over to help, tugging at his fingers until his gloves at last peeled off. "I probably should've kept my mouth shut about his wife, but Hap likes you and Sandy so much, I guess I thought it couldn't hurt to tell you. Truth be told, I'm kind of hoping you might be able to help me figure out what's going on with him."

Lucas blinked. "I don't understand."

Aaron picked up the tarp from the ground and shook it hard; a layer of ice on the fabric shattered like glass, falling to the earth in paper-thin shards that reflected the light from the bulb above their heads. "I didn't think there was anything Hap could do that would surprise me, but with you and Sandy here, he's acting really strange. Take that cribbage game this afternoon. In all the years I've known him, I've never once seen him go near a card table. I didn't even think he knew how to play Go Fish, let alone cribbage."

Lucas recalled how Hap had asked him out of the blue if he wanted to play cribbage with him. He shared this with Aaron, and also how surprised he'd been when it turned out he didn't need Hap to explain the rules because he already knew them.

"Really?" Aaron raised his eyebrows. "Even with your memory out of whack?"

"Yep. Pretty dumb thing to remember, huh?"

"What else did Hap say? Anything seem funny?"

"Nope. He just told me he used to play all the time when he was growing up. He said his grandfather taught him."

"Huh," Aaron said. "I never knew that." He studied Lucas's face, speculating. "What else did you guys talk about?"

Lucas thought back to the card game in the kitchen. Hap and he hadn't really said much while they were playing; they'd only chatted about this or that while shuffling the cards between hands. He did recall Hap's voice as maybe being a trifle shaky when he'd asked if Lucas knew how to play the game; he also remembered the old man's thin, veined fingers lightly—almost lovingly—tracing the edges of the cribbage board when he first set it on the table. Lucas wasn't sure that meant anything, though, so he shook his head.

"Not really. We just played cribbage, and gave each other a hard time. It was really fun."

"Huh," Aaron repeated. "You had fun with Hap." He nudged Sandy's battery with the toe of a boot and shook his head. "Just when I thought things couldn't get any stranger."

Chapter Seven

Sandy was the first to go to bed that night. Aaron, Hap and Lucas all watched her scoop up Wilbur in her arms on her way out of the dining room; the cat had been drowsing peacefully on the floor next to Lucas and the fire. Sandy was weaving slightly from having one too many mugs of Hap's potent hot cocoa—the fumes alone were enough to wake the dead—but Aaron was glad to see she wasn't embarrassed. She wiggled her fingers at them as she said goodnight.

"Careful on the stairs," Aaron called after her. "Hap's cocoa has been known to cause folks to trip over their own feet."

Hap snorted. "It's also caused 'em to wake up bare-ass naked on the porch."

"Oh, my." Sandy giggled. "I guess I'd better chain myself to my bed, just to be safe." She vanished up the stairs but another giggle floated down a few seconds later, along with what sounded like a hiss from Wilbur. "Bad kitty," Sandy's voice admonished.

The fire in the wood stove was dying, and the only other light in the room was a small lamp on a table in the corner. The orange and red firelight cast flickering shadows on the walls and made Aaron feel like he was in a warm, dry cave, listening to the sleet fall outside. It wasn't even nine o'clock yet, but it had been a long day and he was having a hard time staying awake. He glanced over to see how Hap was faring and was surprised to find the old man fully alert, his green eyes bright and clear as he gazed into the open door of the wood stove.

Lucas was stretched out on his side in front of the fire with his head propped on his hand, blinking at the flames. He'd only been allowed two mugs of cocoa—as compared to four for the rest of them—yet he clearly wasn't feeling deprived. Aaron was sitting on a chair beside Hap's rocker; he patted the old man's knee as Lucas rolled on his back and closed his eyes.

"Nice work, Hap. You're the one who gets to carry him upstairs if he passes out."

"He's just restin' his eyes, ain't you, boy?"

"Yeah," Lucas agreed. "I'm just resting my eyes."

Aaron shook his head and Hap grinned. "Toss a blanket over him and let him be. A boy his age don't mind sleepin' on the floor."

"Not when he's had a snootful of tequila, at least." Aaron yawned. "All I can say is you better hope there's a teen chapter of Alcoholic's Anonymous in Wheatland."

"Don't be such an old woman. A hot drink on a cold night never hurt nobody."

An angry gust of wind outside rattled the window behind them; Aaron felt a draft of cold air on the back of his neck and Hap shivered as well, looking uneasily over his shoulder. "Damn radio weatherman ought to be horsewhipped. Clear and dry all week my ass."

Aaron was inclined to agree. This ice storm was a doozy, and had really caught them with their britches down. With so much wide open space around, they could normally see a storm coming for miles, and when Aaron had stepped outside earlier that night to take a gander at the stars—only an hour or so before Sandy and Lucas were preparing to leave—there'd been no hint of bad weather. He told Hap he'd never seen a storm come in so fast.

"Me neither." Hap's face grew somber. "We'll lose a quarter of the herd if this keeps up. Maybe more."

Aaron nodded bleakly, knowing Hap was right but also knowing there was nothing more to be done. It was a part of ranching that both of them hated, this feeling of helplessness when the weather took control out of their hands. All they could do was wait the storm out, and pray when Aaron went outside in the morning he wouldn't find dozens of frozen carcasses in the corral behind the barn. The two men remained silent for a while, watching the sleeping boy and the dying fire. Aaron had intended to confront Hap about his recent odd behavior but found he was too tired. He yawned again and the old man stirred.

"Best get to bed, son. With all the ice and snow out there tomorrow's gonna be a bitch of a day."

Aaron grinned. "Not for you. You'll just sit around playing cribbage."

"Nah, I'll be too busy for such foolishness. Besides, you'll have the boy with you. He needs to earn his keep around here if he expects to get fed."

"No worries there. I worked him like a mule today."

"Good. When he's worn out he ain't such a mouthy little goat turd." Lucas didn't even stir and Hap sighed. "Well, hell. Ain't no fun callin' him names when he ain't even listening."

Aaron got to his feet and bent down to gently shake Lucas awake, telling him it was time for bed. Lucas's eyes fluttered but that was his only response, so Aaron lifted the boy in his arms. As he stood up straight, Lucas's limbs dangled lifelessly in the air and his head fell back on Aaron's shoulder, as if he didn't have a muscle or a bone in his body.

Hap grunted. "Boy reminds me of that Raggedy Andy doll in the attic, red hair and all."

"Yep," Aaron said, smiling. "He's really dead to the world, isn't he?"

Hap watched with an oddly pensive look on his face as Aaron lugged the boy toward the stairs. "Don't drop the little fartsniffer."

Aaron paused in the doorway, recalling something Hap had said a minute before. "You'll be too busy doing what?" he asked.

"Come again?"

"You said you'd be too busy to play cribbage tomorrow. What've you got lined up?"

"Oh, this and that. Nothin' important."

"Don't be coy, Hap."

Hap gestured at Lucas's inert body. "You gonna stand there all night with that boy?"

"Hap."

"Oh, for Christ's sake. I'm gonna put things to rights in the attic." Hap shook a finger at him. "And don't you go throwin' another hissy fit about that goddamn ladder."

Aaron frowned. "Okay, Hap, spill." He shifted Lucas in his arms, grateful the boy didn't weigh much. "About the attic, I mean, and the cribbage game."

Hap stared at him. "What are you goin' on about?"

"You're more attached to that stuff in the attic than to the rocks in your head, but you tried to give Sandy whatever she wanted. How come?"

"It ain't like we're ever gonna do anything with any of it. Quit makin' a goddamn mountain out of a molehill."

Aaron wondered for a moment if that was indeed what he was doing. It was clear Hap didn't really know why he wanted to give his old possessions to Sandy; maybe it was nothing more than a passing whim. "Okay, fine. What about that cribbage game this afternoon, then? You *hate* card games. You told me so yourself."

"I never said that," Hap protested. "I just said they was a waste of time."

"But now they're not?"

"Lord have mercy, Aaron, you're actin' like I been sneakin' rabbit turds into your raisin bread. What's wrong with you?"

Aaron heaved another weary sigh and turned to go. "Okay, if you won't talk, you won't."

"That boy's gettin' too old to be carted around," Hap called after him, his voice mellowing. "He'll likely be all hot and bothered when he wakes up in the mornin' and finds out he got put to bed like a babe."

Aaron looked down at Lucas's sleeping face; he could feel the boy's steady, quiet breathing against his own chest. He abruptly remembered the bruises on Lucas's back and he wondered yet again what kind of person could do something like that to a kid—especially a kid like the one he held in his arms. It made no sense to him, no sense at all. "I get the feeling this boy hasn't had much in the way of folks looking out for him. It might be about time somebody tried, don't you think?"

He glanced back at Hap and found the old man watching him with an unwontedly soft expression. Hap quickly looked away, embarrassed. "Suit yourself."

*

It was nearly midnight.

Hap built up the fire in the wood stove again and sank down in his rocker with a groan, wondering why he wasn't in the least bit sleepy. This was the first time in years he'd been up so late. He'd said goodnight to Aaron three hours ago, when Aaron had come back downstairs after putting Lucas to bed. Aaron asked if he was planning on turning in soon, too, and Hap told him yes, he'd be on his way to bed directly. It wasn't a lie, either; he truly hadn't planned to stay up much longer. He'd just known he wanted a little more time by the wood stove—he had the propane fireplace in his room, of course, but tonight he was in the mood for the smells and sounds of a real fire—and he didn't want Aaron fretting more than he already was.

"Peabrain," Hap muttered. "I ain't never met such a damn mother hen in all my days."

He'd been minded all evening to take the younger man to task for not telling him about Ed Marcy's death, but was afraid he'd lose that argument: Aaron would just say he thought staying silent was for the best, given Hap's history when it came to hearing about old friends dying. Hap couldn't in all honesty deny this; Tommy Leighton's passing four years ago had sent him into a black depression for weeks, frightening Aaron out of his wits.

Hap reached down for the bottle of Bushmill's Irish whiskey by his rocking chair. He knew he was drinking too much but didn't care. Tonight was his to do with as he chose and tomorrow could go straight to hell. *"Build me a castle, forty feet high,"* he sang to the flames. *"So I can see her, as she rides by."* Ellen had always liked his voice. He had a much more limited range these days but the handful of notes still left to him were true enough, he supposed, if a trifle gravelly. The fire popped and a glowing ember shot out on the patch of tile surrounding the wood stove. Hap watched it slowly burn itself out, pulsing red then black several times, as if gasping for air. The black prevailed in the end, of course, but Hap kept staring at the ember anyway, hoping for one more flare of red. *"As she rides by, Lord, as she rides by,"* he sang, *"so I can see her, as she rides by."*

He was thinking about how Aaron had grilled him for playing cribbage with Lucas. Asking the boy to play *was* a mite strange, he conceded, considering how long it had been since the cribbage board had seen the light of day. The last time would have been almost forty-five years now, back when Ellen was still living with him.

Ellen again. Lord have mercy.

He missed her so much sometimes he could hardly stand it: Her hoarse, rich, smoker's laugh, the spill of her long black hair down her back, how she used to sidle up to him when they were sleeping, the scary look she got in her eyes whenever he riled her, the honey-and-cream smell of lotion on her skin. These days he even missed their fights, missed how they always made up afterwards, sooner or later, no matter how bad it got.

And it did get bad, sometimes. Oh my, yes, it surely did. They never fought about the small things that vexed many couples; neither of them gave a damn about the best way to scrub a pot or fold a shirt. They never even fought about finances—though in their first years money was often tight, and both had reason to blame the other's thriftlessness. No, their fights were always about two things, and two things only: Hap's mouth, and Ellen's propensity for flirting with other men. (She'd done more than flirt, too, on at least one occasion Hap was aware of—with Harry Goddamn Gunther, no less—but whether it had gone beyond a little slap and tickle was still an open question.) Ellen could no more walk down the street without batting her eyes at every Tom, Dick, and goddamn *Harry* than Hap could keep from running his mouth about everything and everyone in creation. Jesus, what a sorry pair they'd been, at least half of their time together.

The other half, though, was another story altogether.

He took a long pull on the bottle of Bushmill's, loving the burn of the whiskey in his throat and chest. He held the bottle up and gazed through the glass at the fire, admiring how the flames gave the golden liquid a reddish-amber hue. "Good thing I kept you all for myself," he said fondly to the bottle. "You woulda kicked that poor youngster's butt, and then some."

Thinking of Lucas rekindled his earlier unease. Just what was it about the boy that was so familiar? He couldn't put his finger on it and the mystery was getting on his last nerve. Was it his freckles? His voice? The way he walked, the way he cocked his head when he listened? His crooked teeth when he smiled?

"I have *seen* that child before." Hap set the whiskey back on the floor with a thump. "I swear to Christ I have."

The freezing rain outside had finally stopped an hour or so ago. After it stopped, he'd flipped on the porch light and stared out the window at the frozen wasteland in front of the house; it looked like there was at least a half-inch of solid ice on top of the previous day's snow. The cows in the corral were having a godawful, miserable night, and he didn't want to think about how many of them would be dead by morning. He suddenly recalled an old saying of his grandfather's: *Do what you can, and blame what you can't on the first asshole you meet.*

"You were a genius, Granddaddy," Hap said ruefully. "And that's a fact."

Jacob Cobb, his grandfather, had lived long enough to see Hap and Ellen married, but just barely. The old man took a bad spill in the basement five days after their wedding; he'd broken his hip and a couple of ribs, and after that he caught pneumonia and died. Hap never cried harder in his life than he did at Jacob's funeral; the old man was Hap's only remaining family, and the two of them had been alone together ever since Hap's grandmother passed away when he was fourteen. Until that moment, there was a part of him that had never believed his grandfather would truly ever leave him. Jacob Cobb was a difficult man but also a loving one; Hap still missed listening to him rant about their neighbors and the government and everything else under the sun; he missed the sly way the corners of the old man's mouth would twitch whenever he was pulling someone's leg.

Just as Lucas's mouth had twitched that very morning in the kitchen, giving Sandy guff about her damn cat puking on the floor.

"Granddaddy," Hap breathed. He suddenly sat up straight in his rocker. "Son of a *bitch*."

He felt foolish for having spent most of the day trying to figure out who the boy reminded him of: He should've remembered that telltale lip quirk of his grandfather's right away. It meant nothing, of course; it was only a trifling coincidence. Aside from that one peculiar similarity Lucas didn't resemble Hap's grandfather in the slightest.

Except for the fact that they both had bright green eyes.

"Hell, that don't mean shit!" Hap objected. "Lots of folks got green goddamn eyes!"

Like Hap himself, for instance.

He chewed on his lip for a long minute then shook his head and snorted. It was a night for seeing ghosts, and the whiskey surely wasn't helping. He picked up the bottle once more and took a long swig; a fair share of the liquor missed his mouth and slopped on his shirt, and he gazed down with dismay at the mess.

"Well, hell," he said. "That's a waste of some good goddamn booze."

Interlude: Hap, Ellen, and Jacob, 1956

"Ain't you tired of bein' a jackass, son?" Jacob said. "Deal the damn cards."

"Hold your horses, Granddaddy." Hap was demonstrating a new one-handed shuffle he'd taught himself. "Watch close now." All the fancy ways he'd learned to shuffle were enjoyable to him—he'd worked hard to acquire the dexterity involved—but they also had the side benefit of irritating Jacob. He executed a three-way split with the cards involving several intricate contortions of his fingers.

"Just deal the goddamn cards," Jacob growled.

"Stop tormenting the poor man, Hap." Ellen was sitting by the open door of the back porch, shelling beans into a pan and smoking a cigarette. It was a hot August afternoon, but there was a sharp breeze coming through the open windows and doors, keeping the house livable. "Show your tricks to me later, okay? I promise to be impressed."

"Nah," Hap said. "Granddaddy's more fun."

The ranch was at its best in August, at least in non-drought years, like this one. They'd had an unusually wet summer, and the prairie surrounding the house was alive with wildflowers of every imaginable color and variety: Yellow balsamroot and barberry, white thimbleberry, orange daylily, delicate blue quamash and chicory, green fiddleneck. The mornings were especially easy on the eyes and the soul, before the heat of the day, and Hap and Ellen had gone fishing in the creek almost every morning that month, after chores, watching the sunlight play on the surface of the swift, chatty water and lingering as long as they liked in the cool shadows of a narrow canyon where the trout were plentiful—and privacy was easy to come by, after fishing lost its allure.

Jacob shoved back from the table and hobbled over to the stove to refill his coffee mug. "I'd think twice about marryin' this asshole if I was you," he said to Ellen. Hap was saddened to see how much pain the arthritis in Jacob's joints was causing him, but the old man's vain attempt to hide his discomfort from his soon-to-be daughter-in-law was so typical it made him smile.

Ellen blew a cloud of smoke out the door and gave Hap an arch look. "If I get a better offer in the next twenty-four hours, I'll be out of here before he knows what hit him."

"I ain't worried," Hap said. "Nobody but me is dumb enough to ask you to get hitched."

"It's a damn miracle she said yes, boy." Jacob sat back down and gathered up the hand Hap had finally dealt. Ever since Hap was a child the two of them had played cribbage whenever they had a free moment, and Ellen was now addicted, too. "But if she had a lick of sense she'd poison your flapjacks tomorrow before you head to the courthouse."

"Hell, you got nobs," Hap said as Jacob turned up the jack of spades.

Jacob took his extra point on the cribbage board. "I ever tell you 'bout the time I asked your grandma to marry me?"

"Only every day of my life."

"Shut up, Hap," Ellen said. "Go ahead, Jacob, I'm listening."

Jacob turned in his chair to talk to Ellen. "When we was kids, Hap's grandma was a sight to behold. I was s'posed to meet her that day on the front steps of the library, back when it didn't have no more'n ten books or so on the shelves." He sipped his coffee and seemed to drift off for a moment. "Her hair was as black and pretty as yours, just not so long."

Hap knew Ellen was a sucker for love stories, plus she had a soft spot for Jacob and was smart enough to see how much the old man missed his wife. "I sure wish I could've met her," she said quietly.

"Me, too, darlin'. She woulda taken to you like a wetback takes to a taco. Fifteen-two, fifteen-four, and a pair makes six."

"Jesus, Granddaddy," Hap said, "don't go around sayin' *wetback*, okay?" No one sane had ever accused Hap himself of being overly enlightened, but Jacob's bias against Mexicans upset him. "Carlos gets mad as a hornet when he hears you talk like that. Fifteen-two and a run of three makes five."

Carlos was one of the men from town Jacob and Hap hired every spring to help them brand cattle; he was also Hap's closest friend.

"I ain't talkin' about Carlos, idjit. I'm talkin' about the rest of 'em."

"It still ain't right to call 'em wetbacks. It's your deal."

"Quit your fussin.' I was talkin' to Ellen anyhow." Jacob shuffled and dealt, then looked back at Ellen, who was waiting patiently. "So like I was saying, there was Becky—Hap's grandma—comin' out the door and stuffin' a book in her coat 'cause it was startin' to rain cats and dogs. I swear to God when she spotted me, though, I stopped thinkin' about the rain and everything else, too, 'cause her face was shinin' like the goddamn sun. She always looked real nice, a'course, but I ain't never seen nothin' like what she looked like that day and I won't never see it again, neither. I just stood and gawped at her till we was both soaked to the skin, and the first thing that popped out of my mouth was to ask her to get hitched." He took another sip of his coffee and glanced down at his cards. "Funny thing is I never knew I was goin' to ask. I was more surprised than she was."

Hap shook his head. "The last time you told that story you said Grandma was comin' out of the telegraph office, not the library. Fifteen-two, fifteen-four, and a run of three makes seven."

"I never said no such thing. Fifteen-two, fifteen-four, fifteen-six, and four hearts is ten."

"What if Grandma heard you call Carlos a wetback, Granddaddy? S'pose she'd have married you then?"

Jacob's eyes narrowed. "I swear to God, son, you're gettin' on my last nerve." He turned back to Ellen. "Anyhow, she said yes, a'course, and we went and did it that same damn day, right at the courthouse."

"That's a sweet story, Jacob," Ellen told him. "Very romantic."

"You should hear the one he tells about the wetback tooth fairy," Hap said.

Jacob snorted. "Okay, fine, I won't say that word no more if you'll shut the hell up and give me some goddamn peace. Ellen, trade places with me before I throttle this asshole."

Ellen dropped her cigarette in an empty beer can by her feet and did as he asked, handing over the pan of shelled green beans and taking a chair across from Hap at the table. Hap told her it was her deal and she took the deck from him. Their fingers touched and Hap impulsively pulled her over to his lap.

"This time tomorrow," he said, "you'll be Mrs. Hap Cobb. How 'bout them apples?"

"Ugh. Let's change your name to mine. Mr. and Mrs. Watson sounds a whole lot prettier than Mr. and Mrs. Cobb."

"Girl's got a point," Jacob said as he lowered himself with a grimace into the chair in the doorway. "Besides, every Cobb 'cept me is an asshole."

Hap winked at Ellen. "That include my ma and pop, Granddaddy? Or my big brother?"

"Never you mind," Jacob snapped, predictably, and Hap and Ellen exchanged a look that was half-amused, half-exasperated. Questions about Hap's family were off-limits, but that didn't keep Hap from asking now and then in hopes the old man might one day let something slip. It was the only thing Ellen ever took Hap's side on, because she was as curious as he was about why Jacob never said a word about his son, daughter-in-law, and grandson, all unknown to Hap and dead now for nineteen years.

"Oh, for heaven's sake, Jacob," Ellen said mildly. "Hap's got a right to ask about his own flesh and blood. Come to think of it, so do I, now we're getting married."

"Ain't nothin' to talk about."

Hap could see the stiff-necked resistance rising in his grandfather. "Best let it go," he murmured in Ellen's ear. Jacob didn't hear well enough anymore to catch anything much below a shout. "He ain't gonna tell us nothin' anyway."

Ellen, he knew, was of the opinion they should drag the information out of Jacob no matter how bent out of shape he got, but she'd never seen how unreasonable Jacob could be when pushed too hard. She shook her head against Hap's shoulder in frustration but then sighed and leaned back to whisper in his ear. "Fine. But one of these days I'm going to sit him down and make him answer every single question I have."

"You may as well speak up," Jacob declared loudly. "I can hear every goddamn word."

"Bullcrap," Hap and Ellen said at the same moment. They burst out laughing as Jacob glanced over his shoulder, scowling.

Hap still couldn't believe his luck. Every time he looked at Ellen his heart sped up; every time he touched her he still trembled. Her eyes were as dark as her coal-black hair, her olive skin was as smooth and unblemished as a nectarine, and her lithe, long-limbed body—with soft, small-nippled breasts that fit perfectly in his hands and an ass that could make Oscar Wilde rethink his preferences—had been known to cause happily married men to behave like absolute fools. He still couldn't understand what a beauty like the woman now sitting in his lap had ever seen in a skinny roughneck like him.

"What did I ever do to deserve you?" he blurted.

"I guess you caught me at a weak moment."

"I'm serious." Hap nuzzled her neck. "You could've had anybody. Hell, both Jack Colyer and Harry Gunther would like nothin' better'n for me to drop dead so they'd still have a shot at you. Why'd you pick me?"

He'd never had the balls to ask her to explain herself before. He didn't even know why it was suddenly important to him to hear what she had to say, but it was; now that they were so close to tying the knot, he couldn't shake the feeling Ellen herself wasn't completely convinced she'd made the right choice. They'd been courting ever since she'd moved to Wheatland thirteen months ago, yet he suspected that before he proposed to her she hadn't exactly been an angel every time he wasn't around. He knew she wasn't the full-on hussy some people in town made her out to be, but she *was* a wildcat, and he'd heard a few rumors that gave him pause until he decided most of it was nothing but wishful thinking. Now the question was out in the open, however, he almost regretted asking, and not just because Jacob was sitting there in the room, listening.

Ellen shifted in his lap, raising her eyebrows as she realized he was in earnest. "Lord, you're slow," she said. "Do I really have to spell it out for you?"

"Best show him lots of pictures, too," Jacob said over the pan of green beans.

"Remember what you were doing the first time I met you?" Ellen asked.

"Sure. Watchin' fireworks at the fairgrounds on the Fourth of July and goin' "ooo" and "ahhh" with every other idjit in America."

"You could've cared less about the fireworks. You were sitting in the top row of the bleachers all by yourself, reading a book with a flashlight."

Hap shrugged. The book he'd been reading was Steinbeck's *The Winter of Our Discontent,* and he couldn't put the damn thing down. He'd caught grief from everybody he knew that night for being antisocial, but it wasn't his fault John Steinbeck was infinitely more interesting to him than the whole population of Wheatland, Wyoming.

"Anyway," Ellen continued, "when I first saw you sitting there I thought you were just putting on airs. But the girl I was with—Alice Lindsey—said no, she'd known you your whole life and never once seen you without a book in your hands. She said even though you dropped out of school you'd probably read more books than the whole town put together.

I watched you for a while then finally decided to see what you were like up close."

When Ellen first sat next to him at the fairgrounds Hap hadn't even noticed her until she'd started talking. Then, when he saw how pretty she was, he'd been stricken dumb, terrified of making an ass of himself. She persisted in talking to him, however, so he finally set his book aside—albeit reluctantly; it *was* a damn fine book, after all—and found his tongue again. He asked where she was from and what brought her to Wheatland; she told him about growing up in Bozeman and never meaning to leave, but then she heard Wheatland was in dire need of a math teacher so there she was, talking to Hap Cobb on the bleachers. Hap, for his part, told her about the ranch and his granddaddy, and about growing up an only child and quitting school after his grandma died; the two of them were still sitting there chatting long after the fireworks were over and the rest of the crowd had left the fairgrounds.

It was now Hap's turn to raise his eyebrows. "You told me you only came to sit by me 'cause you didn't like bein' stuck in the crowd."

"I lied. Anyway, I kept trying to talk to you but I couldn't get any more than a few caveman grunts out of you to start off with. You didn't care about me any more than you did about the fireworks. You just wanted to read."

Hap shrugged. "It was a damn good story, see," he said, "and I was close to the end."

Ellen laughed. "That's my point, Hap. I'd never had to compete with a book for a man's attention." She patted his hands to get him to release her, then returned to her seat, shuffling the cards and dealing them almost as proficiently as Hap could do himself. "I'm sick to death of men like Jack and Harry falling all over themselves every time I walk by. You're the only man I've ever met who cares about what I *think* more than what I look like." She leaned over the cribbage board and kissed him on the forehead. "Does that answer your question?"

"Yep." Hap paused for a minute, then grinned. "But I wouldn't give a rat's ass what you was thinkin' if you didn't look so damn good."

Ellen narrowed her eyes; she had a quick temper—almost as quick as Jacob's—and Hap usually managed to set her off at least once or twice a day. "Don't you go spoiling a nice moment, Hap Cobb," she warned.

Jacob snorted. "That's like tellin' a goddamn duck not to quack."

Chapter Eight

Lucas woke in the night again, needing to pee.

He lay still, listening to the wind outside the house and wondering how he'd ended up in bed. The last thing he remembered was stretching out by the wood stove in the dining room; he'd been listening to Hap and Aaron talk but not really paying attention to what they were saying. He just liked the sound of their voices, liked hearing the nonstop verbal jousting that seemed to be the only way the two men knew how to talk to each other. Aaron's voice was deeper and quieter than Hap's; Hap's was a little scratchy but had an almost musical quality to it, a kind of hectoring lilt that seemed eerily familiar—just like the house itself, creaking and bellyaching as the wind sought a way through its walls.

Aaron must've carried him upstairs: Hap was too old and Sandy had already gone to bed. He was still wearing his jeans under the blankets but his torso and feet were bare. Aaron must have removed his shirt and socks before tucking him in. He blushed in the darkness, praying his feet hadn't stunk to high heaven when he was being undressed. He'd have to tell Aaron first thing tomorrow he was sorry he'd needed to be taken care of like a little baby.

Aaron's act of kindness made him feel like crying. He didn't know why, really, yet found himself wishing he'd been conscious when the man picked him up, wished he could've heard what Hap and Aaron said to each other at the time. The bed creaked beneath him as he rolled on his side, wincing; the bruises on his back were still painful. He wondered again who'd hurt him; it frightened him to think somebody could hate him so much. The house protested loudly as the ever-present wind renewed its assault, and he shivered, wishing he didn't have to make his way down the cold hallway to the bathroom. He told himself it could be worse: he could have to go outside and use the outhouse.

He suddenly sat upright in bed.

In his mind, there was an actual *memory* of an outhouse: A tiny building on a barren patch of earth, plain as day. He could picture the knotted pine of the wooden frame; he could almost smell the acrid aroma of quicklime masking fouler odors. He waited tensely in the blackness of Hap's old bedroom for other memories to return, but after half a minute passed, he snorted in frustration.

"Perfect," he muttered. "All I remember is a stupid *outhouse.*"

He shoved aside his covers and rose from the bed, trembling in the cold. He groped around at the foot of the mattress for his shirt but couldn't find where Aaron had put it. He gave up looking and made his way to the door as best as he could, marveling at how dark it was; he couldn't even see his hand when he held it an inch in front of his face. He stubbed his left big toe on the brass frame of the bed and hopped around on one foot, holding his toe.

"God*dammit*!" he yipped, eyes watering.

He found the door and hobbled into the hall, stopping when he saw it was nearly as dark as his bedroom. He thought at first the nightlight in the bathroom had burned itself out, but then he noticed a tiny edge of light at the bottom of the door and realized someone—-most likely Sandy—-was using the toilet. He grimaced, hoping she'd be quick; the cold air made the discomfort in his bladder worse. He made his way down the hall toward the sliver of light, fingers brushing the wall. As he neared the bathroom door he heard a moan of misery coming from the other side. He tapped on the door and the moan tapered off.

"Sandy?" he asked. "Is that you?"

"Lucas?" Sandy's voice was a lot weaker than usual. "I'm sick as a dog."

"Oh." Lucas stood still, not knowing what else to say.

"You need to use the bathroom?"

"Sort of."

"Okay, I'll be out in a min—-" A retching sound stopped her mid-sentence and there was a brief silence before she continued. "Oh God, Lucas, I feel so bad. You better go downstairs."

"Okay." He hesitated. "You all right?"

"Yeah. I just drank too much of Hap's stupid cocoa." She retched again. "Oh, dear Jesus. Please, *please* kill me."

Lucas felt he shouldn't leave her alone but the pressure in his bladder was making him hop from foot to foot. He told her he'd be right back and hurried to the stairs. At the bottom of the steps he was surprised to see a fire still burning in the wood stove in the dining room: Hap was sitting in his rocking chair, just as he'd been hours earlier. Lucas didn't know what time it was but he imagined it was late. Hap was awake and upright, rocking back and forth; he apparently hadn't heard Lucas's footsteps in the hallway. Lucas couldn't put off peeing any longer, so he hastened to the bathroom and relieved himself. When he returned to the dining room the old man was still slowly rocking, oblivious to all but the fireplace and his own thoughts.

"You okay, Hap?" Lucas asked softly.

Hap jumped. "God*damn*, boy! You tryin' to make me soil my britches?"

Lucas apologized, then told him about Sandy being ill in the upstairs bathroom.

Hap grinned. "I ain't surprised, the way she was beltin' down my cocoa. You better take a glass of water up and tell her there's aspirin in the medicine cabinet."

Lucas went to the kitchen to get a glass of water, then returned to warm himself by the wood stove before returning upstairs. Hap was staring at the fire again; his wrinkled, narrow face looked ancient and careworn in the shadows cast by the firelight.

"What's wrong?" Lucas asked.

Hap's eyes drifted up to meet Lucas's own. "You'll catch your death runnin' around half-naked in the cold, boy. The pinhead always turns the furnace down too damn low when he goes to bed. I keep tellin' him I ain't no damn polar bear, but he does it anyway."

Lucas belatedly saw the nearly empty bottle of Irish whiskey on the floor by Hap's rocking chair. The front of the old man's red flannel shirt looked wet, too, and when Lucas sniffed the air, his nostrils flared at the smell of alcohol. "How much did you drink, Hap?" he asked, afraid for the old man.

"That's a damn fine question." Hap glanced down at the bottle. "I ain't sure."

"I better go get Aaron."

"Don't you dare, son!" Hap barked, head snapping up. "I ain't in the mood for a lecture from the bald fusspot right now, thank you very much."

"But don't you think you need—"

"I don't *need* a thing, 'cept for you and those green goddamn *eyes* of yours to leave me in peace!" Hap snatched the whiskey bottle off the floor; his papery-looking hands shook as he took another drink. "Jesus God, why is it so *cold* in here tonight? Ain't you about to turn to ice, son? I'm two feet away from a hot damn fire and I'm still freezin' my balls off."

Lucas wondered why Hap had chosen to single out his eyes for abuse but decided it didn't matter; the old man probably had no idea what he was saying. He was right about the house being cold, however; it seemed to be growing more frigid by the minute. He wanted to run back to bed and crawl under the covers, but he couldn't just leave Hap alone; he might break his neck if he tried to stand on his own. Lucas set the water on a table and headed for the hallway. Hap would no doubt be furious with him for waking Aaron, but he didn't know what else to do.

"I'll be back in a second, okay, Hap?" he called over his shoulder.

"Just go to bed, boy," Hap muttered. "I can't hear myself think with you in the same damn vicinity."

*

Aaron woke to a knock on his door and he rolled over and blinked at his bedside clock, shining softly in the darkness of his room. It was 2:37 a.m.

"Hap?" he called out, bleary and disoriented.

"It's Lucas. Hap's in trouble."

Aaron snapped awake. He lurched out of bed—-almost blacking out from getting up too fast—-and stumbled to the door in his flannel long johns. He yanked the door open, startling Lucas in the hallway. The boy was only wearing a pair of jeans, but Aaron barely noticed. "What's wrong with Hap?" he demanded.

"He's in bad shape. He's in the dining room."

Aaron barreled past him. "Did he fall?" he asked over his shoulder, Lucas on his heels. "How badly is he hurt?"

"He's not hurt, he's just really drunk. I thought I better tell you."

Aaron stopped walking so abruptly that Lucas bumped into him.

"He's just drunk? Lord, Lucas, you scared the crap out of me. I thought he was dying."

Lucas looked abashed. "I didn't want to leave him by himself," he said quietly.

Aaron grimaced. The boy was right, of course; Hap couldn't be trusted not to do something stupid when he'd been drinking. "It's good you came to get me." He ran a hand over his head and sighed again. "Well, hell, let's get this over with."

"Well, looky here," Hap said from his rocker as they entered the dining room, "ain't this a sight for sore eyes." He waved his arms as if shooing a mosquito. "I told that skinny halfwit of a boy there behind you to let me be, but look what the little tattletale done. He brung old Nervous Nellie herself to ruin my damn night."

Aaron came to a halt a few feet away from the old man. Lucas hadn't been exaggerating: Hap was profoundly drunk. His eyes were bloodshot and unfocused in the light from the fire, and he was swaying in his chair, responding to some internal rhythm. His speech was unaffected but that didn't surprise Aaron; Hap's tongue was always the last thing to stop working.

"That's a nice little dance you've got going on, Hap." Aaron eyed the empty bottle of Bushmill's on its side on the floor next to Hap's chair. "What do you think you're doing?"

Hap stopped swaying and leaned forward to stare at Lucas. "Boy, you best stop makin' that goddamn *face* right this minute. You're givin' me the heebie-jeebies, and that's a fact."

Aaron glanced at Lucas, nonplussed, and Lucas, too, seemed taken aback. "What are you talking about, Hap?" Aaron asked. "Lucas isn't making faces at you."

"No, but that's the same damn *face* my granddaddy used to make whenever he was gettin' ready to give me a piece of his mind. I'd know it anywhere."

"See the face *I'm* making, Hap? It's my *I'm-looking-at-a-drunken-old-fool* face."

"That's as may be, son, but what I'm tellin' you, if you'll just listen, is that there boy's mouth is the same as my granddaddy's, and so are his goddamn *eyes.*" He shook a finger at Lucas. "Somethin' ain't right about you and I want an explanation."

Aaron saw Hap's scrutiny of Lucas was unnerving the boy, so he stepped between them and squatted down in front of Hap. "It's about time for bed, Hap, don't you think?"

"No, I *don't* think, and I ain't goin' to bed until I figure it all out, neither."

"Figure all *what* out?"

Hap rolled his eyes. "I swear to God, son, you're the dumbest genius I ever met." He pointed at Lucas again. "I'm *talkin'* about that poor little red-headed stepchild right there, and also about that pretty catwoman pukin' her guts out upstairs. The pair of 'em just showed up out of nowhere last night, in the middle of the worst goddamn blizzard in livin' memory, and you don't think that's even a *little* out of the ordinary? The boy don't know which end of his pecker to pee out of, and the girl's got a goddamn *cat.*"

Aaron tried to interrupt—wondering if Sandy was indeed ill upstairs and how Hap knew about it—but Hap waved him to silence.

"The boy's clothes are hand-me-downs from before Noah took his first crap on the ark, and he claims he's been in our damn house before when he *ain't*. He disappears for half the day, and only shows up again *after* Glen Nixson damn near eats the handle off my fridge and heads back to Wheatland. Then your truck and that girl's car—the girl with the goddamn *cat,* in case you forgot—both break down the same damn second, just in time for a hellacious ice storm that ain't even *supposed* to happen." He beckoned Aaron closer and dropped his voice. "But that ain't the half of it, neither. Want to hear what's *really* crazy, son?"

Aaron rocked back on his haunches to escape the old man's breath, trying to determine how much of Hap's earnestness was booze-inspired and how much was genuine distress. "Okay, Hap, sure, I'll bite. What's really crazy?"

"What's *really* crazy, nutsack, is I could *swear* I knew that boy standin' right there when I was still in goddamn diapers!"

Lucas made an odd noise in his throat. "I'm only fourteen, Hap," he squeaked.

"Oh, sweet Jesus, son, don't be an idjit. I ain't sayin' it was *you* I knew back then. I'm just sayin' you *remind* me of someone I knew. Someone 'sides Granddaddy, I mean. Someone goddamn important, too, only I can't recall *who*."

Aaron rubbed his temples. "Glad that's settled." Drunk or not, he knew Hap wouldn't be carrying on like this if something wasn't really bothering him, but he also knew there was no way to figure anything out until the old man sobered up. "Can we all go to bed, now?" he asked, reaching for Hap's hand to hoist him from his chair.

"Leave me be, Aaron!" Hap cried. "I have *got* to figure this out, can't you see that?" He beat violently on the arms of his rocking chair. "Christ have mercy, son, can't you just *feel* somethin' brewing in the air? Somethin' real goddamn *bad*?"

"Hap!" Aaron seized Hap's wrists to prevent him from injuring himself. "Settle down!"

Lucas touched Aaron's shoulder, startling him. "Hap's right." Lucas's voice was quiet, but something in his tone made Aaron feel as if a cold finger was slowly gliding down the length of his spine. He glanced back at the boy and was shocked to see his skin had turned from pale to albino-white.

"Lucas? What's wrong?"

Lucas's eyes rolled up in his sockets and he pitched forward, falling to the floor.

Chapter Nine

Sandy made her way down the stairs slowly, wondering why the house was so quiet.

Her head ached and her stomach was still queasy. The rising sun was streaming through the east windows; the polished wood floor at the base of the stairs was a blinding, hurtful shade of gold wherever the light found it. She reached the bottom of the steps and wandered gingerly through the empty, almost deathly-still dining room into the kitchen, where she was surprised to find no signs of life, either. The coffeepot was clean and ready to go but hadn't yet been turned on; Hap's countertops were sparkling but bare, and her nose detected no trace of any recent cooking. She put her hands on her hips and looked around, uneasy.

"It's like a tomb in here," she murmured.

There were no dishes in the sink nor on the table; there was no sound at all save for the steady hum of the gas generator outside, keeping the house warm. She bit her lip, knowing it was nearly seven o'clock in the morning and hence a couple of hours past Hap's and Aaron's normal rise-and-shine time. Had the two men and Lucas already completed the morning chores, eaten breakfast, cleaned up after themselves, and then gone someplace else, all without her hearing—or smelling—a thing?

A cat mewed plaintively somewhere in the house.

"Wilbur?" Sandy called out. After vomiting in the bathroom last night, she'd returned to her bedroom and—too sick and drunk to chase him down—accidentally let him loose into the house. "Where are you, baby?"

Wilbur mewed again, much more loudly, his cry echoing through the hallway on the other side of the dining room.

"SHUT THE HELL UP, YOU MANGY LITTLE PRICK!"

Sandy scurried out of the kitchen and through the dining room, emerging in the hallway at the base of the stairs just as Hap came storming from his bedroom, dressed in red long johns and glaring wildly around until his gaze fell on Wilbur, who was laying on the floor, midway between Sandy and Hap. A few inches from Hap's bare, blue-veined feet was a small, neat mound of cat feces; Sandy saw it before Hap did, but she wasn't quick enough to prevent the old man from stepping in the mess as he lunged toward Wilbur. He slipped and nearly fell, shrieking.

"Yaarrowww," Wilbur said, stretching languidly.

"SON OF A BITCH!"

"Oh, Hap, I'm so, so sorry!" Sandy said. "It's all my fault!"

"THERE'S *CAT SHIT* ON MY FOOT!" Hap hopped toward a closet. "WHERE'S MY DAMN SHOTGUN?"

Wilbur at last appeared to realize the bellowing old man bouncing up and down on one leg in the hallway constituted an existential threat. The cat flew toward the staircase—dodging Sandy's grasping hands—and disappeared up the steps.

"THIS AIN'T OVER!" Hap screamed at the ceiling, slapping the wall. "COME BACK HERE AND TAKE YOUR MEDICINE LIKE A MAN!"

The sight of Hap standing in his long johns with one foot in the air and glowering vengefully at the ceiling was too much for Sandy; to her own horror she heard a noise emerge from her mouth like a lapdog's high-pitched bark. Hap gawked at her and she spun away, burying her face in her hands and doing her utmost to keep her shoulders from shaking. She tried to squeal out another apology but her words were lost in a semi-hysterical bray.

“I had best not be hearin’ what I think I’m hearin’,” Hap said.

Sandy bent over helplessly, holding her belly and gasping as Hap threw up his hands and hopped to the nearest bathroom, mumbling. By the time he returned, Sandy had cleaned up Wilbur’s mess with paper towels and had nearly recovered from her laughing fit, too, but she still couldn’t look at Hap, and her stomach was aching almost as much as her head.

“I’m really, *really* sorry,” she said. “But you looked so—”

“Oh, shut up, girl, and help me with breakfast. I need some damn coffee, pronto.”

Sandy followed him into the kitchen. The old man was walking unsteadily and she realized she wasn’t the only one who’d had a rough night. When Hap flipped on the overhead light she saw how sickly-white his skin was; there was also a sheen of perspiration on his forehead and cheeks, and as she stepped close to him at the counter the pungent stench of alcohol and dried sweat coming from his pores made her wince.

“Yeah, I know.” Hap got the coffee brewing and wandered over to the pantry to dig through a bag of potatoes. “I smell like a dead mutt’s butt. But I overslept a mite and I ain’t got time for a shower till I get grub on the table for Aaron and the boy. I expect they’ll be comin’ in any second.”

“They’re outside?” Sandy walked over to the back door to gaze at the barn. The glare of the sun on the ice-crusted snow made her head throb, so she quickly gave up trying to catch a glimpse of Aaron or Lucas and returned to the counter. “I didn’t hear them get up.”

“Me neither. Aaron always sticks his head in my room first thing, but he must’ve caught a whiff of me today and gave me up for dead.” Hap handed Sandy four large potatoes to peel, then opened the refrigerator and filled his arms with red bell peppers, leftover corn, and a carton of bacon. “Seems a bottle of whiskey kicked my ass good and proper.”

“Ugh, don’t mention alcohol in my hearing. I was up sick half the night.” Sandy retrieved a paring knife from the rack and went to work on the potatoes. “Don’t ever come near me with any of that so-called ‘hot cocoa’ of yours again.”

Hap grinned. "Don't be such a sissy. You and the boy both need more practice holdin' your liquor."

"Lucas was sick, too?"

"Passed out cold in front of Aaron and me. Scared the righteous piss out of us." Hap was expertly slicing garlic on a cutting board as he spoke—preparing what looked to Sandy like some kind of bacon and vegetable hash—but all of a sudden his hands faltered and he glanced at her, troubled. "I can't recollect much, but now I think back on it I mighta brought on the boy's spell. Suppose he might still be in bed, feelin' poorly?"

Sandy saw the unspoken request in his eyes and patted his arm. "I'll go check."

He looked away with a sniff and reached for another clove of garlic. "Suit yourself."

*

"Poor old girl." Aaron gazed down at the fourth rust-red carcass he and Lucas had discovered that morning after separating the living cattle from the dead. The ice storm had not been gentle with the older animals. "There wasn't enough meat left on her bones for a night like that."

The rest of the herd was now on the other side of the corral, staring at them with wide, startled eyes, like gawkers at the site of a road accident. The sun had only been up for a short while but the glare from the snow was already enough to cause Lucas to squint as he studied Aaron's unusually grim face.

"At least you didn't lose too many," Lucas offered, not sure how to interpret the man's mood. "That's good, right?"

Aaron nodded but remained silent. Lucas knew that ranchers like Aaron and Hap dealt with the death of livestock all the time, and he was sure this wasn't the first time a winter storm had taken such a toll. Nor did he think Aaron was likely to be overly sentimental about individual cows; ranchers couldn't afford to be too tenderhearted about animals destined to be sold as meat. Aaron stirred and glanced shrewdly at him, as if reading his mind.

"Hap always says I'm too soft for this line of work. When I first moved in with him I was so squeamish about slaughtering cattle I used to puke afterwards." He sighed. "I eventually got used to it, but this is different."

Lucas blinked, not understanding.

"Freezing to death is a hard, slow way to go," Aaron said. "At least when we slaughter them it's over quick."

Lucas told him he'd read once that freezing to death was supposed to be kind of peaceful, at least for people; after a point you supposedly stopped feeling the cold and simply fell asleep.

"Maybe so, but what happens *before* you stop feeling the cold?" Aaron said. "That's the part that worries me."

Lucas remembered being lost in the blizzard with Sandy, and he shivered. He'd been profoundly miserable—every bone in his body had ached with the cold and his mind had been awash with exhaustion and fear. He wouldn't wish that experience on anybody, human *or* animal. There might be peace at the end, but Aaron was right: It was a bad way to go.

Aaron walked toward the water tank in the corral and Lucas followed. In spite of his memory problems, he somehow knew he hadn't grown up around people who thought about such things as animal suffering. He wanted to believe he was sensitive like Aaron, but he wondered if that would turn out to be true. His memories might come back attached to a whole different Lucas—a Lucas who didn't share Aaron's values, and might not even *like* the man. It didn't seem possible at the moment, but who knew what would happen once he remembered who he really was?

He'd already been awake when Aaron came to get him out of bed; Aaron had been visibly relieved to find him alert and healthy. Lucas had apologized for forcing Aaron to carry him upstairs not just once but twice in the same night; Aaron had waved aside his apology with a smile, telling him at least he hadn't needed to be dragged to bed kicking and screaming like a certain eighty-two-year-old infant of his acquaintance.

It doesn't matter what I end up remembering about myself, Lucas realized as he helped Aaron break the ice on the surface of the water tank. *I'll always really like this man.*

He just wished he could be as certain Aaron would still like *him.*

*

Sandy knocked on the door to Lucas's bedroom, then stepped inside and flipped on the light when her knock went unanswered.

"Yikes," she muttered. "It's freezing in here."

The room was clean and spare, but it was at least thirty degrees colder than her own, just across the hall. The lovely brass-framed bed in the center was made and the blue-checkered flannel shirt Lucas had worn the day before was hanging neatly on a post of the bed frame; the boy must've tidied the room before going outside. A large cedar chest sat at the foot of the bed; there was a child's desk in the corner and a tall wardrobe against one wall. Sandy had been in the room twice before—once on her initial tour of the house with Aaron and Lucas, the other when Lucas had gone missing and she'd tried to find him—but this time she paid closer attention, puzzled why it was so cold.

There were two windows in the room, on the east wall, but both were shut tight. A faint draft was coming in around the frames yet it wasn't enough to explain the frigidity of the room; she could actually see her own breath when she exhaled. She found the heating vent on the floor by the wardrobe and leaned down to make sure it was open. It was, and warm air was flowing through it. She straightened, shivering.

A sudden explosive noise from somewhere nearby—sounding like the chest-pounding *WHUMP* of a bass drum in a marching band—startled her so much she jumped, screeching. No other sounds followed but she remained paralyzed, listening to the frantic beating of her heart. It occurred to her Wilbur might have gotten up to more mischief and she rushed back into the hallway.

"Wilbur? What are you doing, you naughty little monster?"

Nothing was amiss in the hall, so she checked her own room first, praying she wouldn't find anything to fan the flames of Hap's antipathy toward her demented cat. Her bedroom was as she'd left it—reeking, to her chagrin, like a hobo's den from her binge the night before—and she moved on to the nursery. She stepped in the room and turned on the light, and was surprised to find the trapdoor to the attic hanging open, its attached ladder fully extended to the floor. The attic was pitch black above her, and the open trap unnerved her.

"Hello?" she called up into the darkness. She herself had folded the ladder and securely closed the trapdoor yesterday: She was sure of it. "Anybody there?"

She guessed the noise she'd heard could've been the trapdoor swinging open by itself, but then she remembered how difficult it had been to pull it down. She didn't think even someone as strong as Aaron could open it with enough momentum to explain what she'd heard; it would probably take an elephant jumping on it to get it to move so fast.

She put her hand on the ladder, biting her lip before forcing a laugh at her own uneasiness. There was nothing to fear in this old house; the very idea of any harm coming to her in Hap and Aaron's attic was absurd.

"You've seen too many horror movies, missy," she scolded. "Just who do you think might be up there waiting for you? Freddie Krueger?"

She climbed the ladder.

*

"Goddamn idjit!" Hap raged.

He stood at the kitchen sink with his hand under the cold water tap, cursing his own carelessness as he watched blood from his left index finger dribble from a deep, angry-looking cut and run down the drain. He'd gotten distracted chopping an onion and his knife had slipped, slicing into his finger as easily as if it were biting through soft cheese.

"The *stupidity* around here is as contagious as the damn clap," he declared, snatching at the paper towel roll above the sink. He calmed down and studied the cut, deciding it wasn't as bad as he'd first thought. It might require a few stitches but that was all; in his long life he'd been stitched up more times than he could count—often doing the stitching himself—and he figured yet another go-around with needle and thread wouldn't kill him. He wrapped the finger and held it.

The outer door on the back porch banged open and he looked up to see Lucas, stamping his feet on the porch rug. The boy entered the kitchen, red-faced from the cold, and bent down to remove his boots. Hap was relieved to see him up and around, and—judging from the broad smile on his face—clearly not holding a grudge. Hap couldn't recall much of the conversation he'd had with Aaron and Lucas by the wood stove, but he knew he hadn't been kind.

"Morning, Hap," Lucas said. "Aaron said to tell you he'll be ready for breakfast in about fifteen minutes."

"He may have to cook it himself. I near just cut off my whole goddamn hand." He showed the boy the blood-soaked paper towel on his finger.

"How bad is it?" Lucas asked. "Should I get Aaron?"

"Nah, it's too late for that. Best just dig a hole in the ground and toss me in."

"Really?" Lucas seemed to consider this for a moment then surprised him with a grin. "Where do you keep your shovel?"

"Wiseass." Hap turned back to look at his breakfast preparations on the counter. "I don't cook so good with only one hand. Aaron still need you?"

"Nope. He told me to come in and get cleaned up." He hung up his coat on the tree by the door. "Is Sandy still asleep?"

Hap blinked, realizing Sandy should've returned long since. "She was down here a bit ago. Every damn time I turn around in this place someone else goes AWOL."

"I'm here." Sandy entered the kitchen carrying a shoebox Hap recognized instantly; it was the box he'd shown her yesterday in the attic, the one with all the old photos of strangers. "Have you been up in the attic since yesterday, Hap?" she asked. "Or Aaron, maybe?"

"Nah." Hap was baffled by the strained look on her face. "Neither of us. I told Aaron to set out mice traps up there yesterday but he ain't gotten around to it. He's the slowest godda—-"

"What about you, kid?" Sandy asked, looking intently at the boy. Lucas shook his head and she pressed him. "Are you sure? Did you maybe have another one of your, uh...I don't know what to call them...one of your *spells*, like yesterday, where you lost track of time?"

"I don't think so," Lucas said, flushing. He stepped toward her. "What's wrong?"

Sandy turned back to Hap and asked if he remembered where they'd left the box she was holding and Hap scowled, not liking the cold feeling he was getting in his gut. "What's causing the itch in your drawers, girl?"

"Please just answer, Hap. It's important."

Hap thought back. "I believe I set it on that dresser on the east wall."

Sandy nodded and took a deep breath. "Good, I'm not completely crazy." She swallowed. "I heard a noise while I was upstairs, and I found the trapdoor to the attic open." She set the box on the tabletop. "Everything was like we left it yesterday except this box was on the floor, all by itself, with this old picture on top."

She lifted the lid on the box and handed a photograph to Hap. Lucas padded over in his stocking feet to look over Hap's shoulder. Hap heard the boy's indrawn breath as goosebumps ran up the back of his own neck. "What the hell?" he breathed.

The black-and-white photograph was of a young man and woman, in their late twenties or early thirties, both thin and tall, standing in front of a well. The well was in the center of a crude barnyard; the surrounding earth was barren and dusty. The woman was pretty, with high cheekbones and long dark hair, yet there was something off-putting about her expression—something cold and haughty—that made Hap take an instant dislike to her. The man had freckles and an attractive smile, but the smile didn't touch his eyes. From their clothes Hap couldn't tell how old the picture was, but he remembered seeing it before, many times; he knew for a fact it had been in the box with the rest of the photos his entire life.

Hap turned to gape at the boy beside him, just as Sandy was doing. Lucas didn't seem aware of their scrutiny; all his attention was on the man in the photo Hap was holding.

"That's me," Lucas whispered. "Just older."

Interlude: Hap and Aaron, 1997

"Christ almighty, son, can you drive any slower?" Hap said.

"What's your hurry, old man? They don't open the doors until seven-thirty."

"Yeah, but the line will stretch to goddamn Utah if you don't quit dilly-dallyin.'"

The Wheatland chapter of the Elks was sponsoring its seventy-sixth annual Memorial Day pancake breakfast at their hunting lodge and campground, nestled between massive boulder formations in the foothills of the Laramie Mountains. It was the only social event of the year Hap always made a point to attend, primarily because he loved where it was held. As a boy he'd clambered around on the boulders near the lodge with his friends while his grandparents looked on; as a young man he'd often hiked with Ellen on an old cattle trail that meandered around the edge of the campground. Hap himself had never joined the Elks—he'd never been comfortable in large groups—but Jacob Cobb had been a member in good standing, and Hap had grown up with many of the boys who were now venerable elders in the organization.

"By the by," Hap said. "If Pat Hinkle's there this year don't go jabberin' and jawin' with him like you did before. He don't need to know our business."

"Oh, good," Aaron said. "For a minute there I thought you'd forgotten to stop busting my balls about that."

Hap grinned. "Nah, you ain't got the point yet."

Thirteen years before, soon after Aaron had begun working for Hap, they'd come to this same pancake breakfast, and Pat Hinkle, a fellow rancher—and a nosey son of a bitch, in Hap's humble opinion—had asked Aaron what Hap was paying him. Aaron had innocently revealed a figure that was more than twice what Hinkle paid his own ranch hands, and Hap, overhearing the conversation, had been incensed, fearing if word got out he was giving Aaron that sort of wage then every man he might hire in the future would expect the same. He'd chewed out Aaron all the way home, and had never since let an Elks' pancake breakfast go by without reminding him to steer clear of Pat Hinkle and anything to do with finances.

"Yeah, you know me and my big mouth," Aaron said, rolling his eyes. "Remember when I told Danny Smith how much money we took in at the cattle auction? Oh, wait, that was *you* talking to Danny, wasn't it?"

"I did no such thing."

"You also bragged to Andy Beston about how much we paid for Junior."

Junior was their prize bull—a magnificent and exceedingly potent Black Angus they'd gotten out of state—and easily the costliest animal on any ranch in the area.

"Stop flappin' your gums and drive," Hap muttered.

As Aaron turned off the highway at the campground entrance, Hap leaned forward to get a better look at the scenery, spectacularly lit by the morning sun. In the square mile or so of land surrounding the Elks' lodge, hundreds of boulders—most bigger than Aaron's pickup and oddly out of place on the otherwise flat and empty prairie—were scattered about, looking to Hap like huge, prehistoric marbles, tossed aside by a giant child who'd grown tired of them and scampered off to play with some other stony toy—perhaps Devil's Tower, or Pikes Peak. Hap shared this with Aaron as they came upon the first outlying boulders, and Aaron laughed.

"Careful, old man. Someone might mistake you for a poet."

"Nah, ain't nobody that dumb." They hit a pothole and Hap grunted, staring up at a boulder the size of a brontosaurus looming over the road. "You shoulda heard my granddaddy go on about this place. He was old enough to remember when the Injuns was still about, and he said this was holy ground to 'em. He said he could see why, too, with the wind whistlin' around the stones and no one out here to talk to but rattlers and coyotes. Him and me came out here once by our lonesome and camped west of the lodge, and at night, when we was sittin' by the fire, I swore I heard Injun ghosts all around, whisperin' in the dark."

Hap's mind was wandering through time. To the left of the road were two Stonehenge-like monoliths, leaning against each other, and he and Ellen—caught outside in a freak storm—had once sheltered beneath them and watched the rain fall for hours. Later that same day they'd gotten naked together high atop a mound not far from the lodge, but well out of sight of anybody, save for a bald eagle circling overhead, and maybe a snake or two sheltering in a nearby crevice. That was early on, of course, back when things between them were still more good than bad: Spontaneous outdoor sex pretty much ended after the first hundred or so knockdown, drag-out fights. They'd never struck each other in their wars, thank God, but he found himself wondering if physical violence might've caused less damage than all the ugly, hurtful things they'd said to each other.

"Woulda left fewer scars, that's for damn sure," he mumbled.

"Beg pardon?" Aaron asked.

"Nothin.' I'm just woolgatherin.'"

By the lodge the boulders were huddled in silent, somber groups, like mourners at a wake. Jacob Cobb might've had no use for religion but he'd been a deeply spiritual man, much moved by the rough, barren grandeur of this place. When Hap was a boy, Jacob had once told him that pagans were in the right of it: if God existed at all, He wouldn't be caught dead in a church; He'd be in the rocks and the woods, the springs and the caves. "*I think maybe you're confusin' God with fairies and suchlike, Granddaddy,*" Hap had said at the time, earning a solid kick in the rump.

Hap told Aaron this story and Aaron chuckled. "I wish I could've met your granddaddy. He sounds like my kind of guy."

"Yeah, I wish you coulda met him, too, son. Anyhow, I always wished he'd had more of a funny bone. Gettin' him to crack a smile was like teachin' a squirrel to waltz. There was this one time me and him was—" Hap broke off as the lodge came into sight. "I'll be goddamned, is that Ezra Simmons up ahead?"

Ezra—an ancient, hairy bear of a man, and the last surviving friend of Jacob Cobb—had moved to Nebraska a few years ago to spend whatever time was left to him with his daughter and her family, but he still had a son and grandson in Wheatland and came back for a visit every summer. Hap waited impatiently while Aaron parked the pickup in the lot by the lodge, then he opened his door and hopped out.

"Ezra! If I knew you was already in town, I'd have brung a bottle of good damn Scotch to celebrate. I can't abide you sober."

Ezra, grinning hugely, had turned around at the sound of Hap's voice and now reached out to grasp Hap's hand in both his own. "Hap, you sorry little pissant. I just got in last night. Howdy, Aaron."

"Welcome home, Ezra," Aaron said. "Howdy, Cyrus."

Cyrus, Ezra's grandson and apparent driver that day, was a forty-something, homely man with crooked teeth and a pug nose. He was nearly as good-natured as Aaron—though nowhere near as smart—and his face lit up when Aaron clapped him on the shoulder. Hap wondered how it must feel to be Aaron and always have folks looking so happy whenever they saw him; Hap couldn't imagine being so universally adored. He himself was greeted far more warily, and though he knew full well it was his own damn fault, he couldn't help but be a little jealous of Aaron's effortless lovability.

"Cyrus," Hap said, "do us all a favor and take your granddaddy home. I don't want my breakfast ruined by him kickin' the bucket while I'm butterin' my toast."

"If I *do* kick the bucket this morning, Hap Cobb," Ezra said, still clasping his hand, "I sure hope your fat round head is inside the damn thing."

Hap laughed but was privately saddened by how old Ezra looked; his once powerful shoulders were now thin and stooped, his gray eyes were watery, and his skin was almost translucent. He was in his nineties, Hap knew, but until recently he'd never appeared to age. There was still some life in the old man, though; his meaty hands gave Hap's fingers a final, painful squeeze before releasing him.

"You look more like your granddaddy every time I see you," Ezra told him. "Your daddy never favored him much, but you sure do."

"Guess I'll take your word for that. I wouldn't know my own daddy from Adam."

As a boy, Hap—whenever his grandfather Jacob wasn't around—had often pestered Ezra about his folks and older brother, hoping to learn more than the next-to-nothing Jacob had told him. Ezra had been willing to share what he knew, but it was very little: only that Hap's father and mother had crossed horns with his grandparents over everything on earth, and that his older brother David was a polite, gentle boy, who seldom spoke and kept to himself. Hap especially pressed Ezra for details about their passing—he knew all three had burned to death in a fire while out of town visiting friends, yet he didn't even know who the friends were, or where they'd lived—but Ezra said Jacob was no more forthcoming with him than he was with Hap.

The four men got in line at the door of the lodge, chatting with each other and everybody else they knew standing close by; the smells of coffee and bacon wafting from the open door made Hap's stomach growl. Aaron told Ezra everything he'd missed since his last visit to Wheatland—deaths, births, accidents, weddings, gossip—while Hap listened on, amazed by how much Aaron knew that he himself didn't.

"How you fit so much crap inside that head of yours is beyond me," he told Aaron during a lull in the conversation.

"Maybe if you left the house every once in a while you'd be better informed."

"Maybe you'd be less of a pain in the damn neck if you'd stop tellin' me what to do."

Ezra snorted. "Aaron's right, Hap. You're the worst shut-in I know. If it wasn't for him, you'd be wandering around that big old ranch of yours, talking to yourself and hiding behind the couch every time someone came knocking at your door."

"He does that whether I'm there or not," Aaron said.

"Know why God gave me two butt cheeks?" Hap demanded as Ezra and Aaron laughed at him. "It's so both of you dipshits can kiss my ass at the same damn time."

The line moved forward as the Elks finally began serving breakfast. Hap glanced back at the faces crowding in behind them and was staggered to see Libby Norton—Ellen's best friend from years ago, and the maid of honor at their wedding—among them.

Oh, Christ have mercy, he thought, sick to his stomach.

He hadn't seen Libby since Ellen's funeral. She'd moved to Torrington shortly after, and all these years later—nigh on thirty—he'd never dreamed he might encounter her at something as mundane as a pancake breakfast. Even when she lived in Wheatland she'd never come to such things.

"I'll be damned," Ezra said. "Ain't that Libby Norton?"

She hadn't changed much at all: Even with her long brown hair streaked with white and a few additional wrinkles around her eyes, Libby was still the prettiest woman in the line, with enormous brown eyes, dark skin, and pronounced cheekbones she'd inherited from her grandfather, a full Apache. Ellen was the only woman Hap had ever met who could hold a candle to Libby for natural beauty, but even Ellen probably wouldn't have aged as well. Ellen's family tended toward an almost cadaverous gauntness as they grew older, while Libby looked as full-figured and vibrant as the last time Hap had seen her. When Ellen first moved to Wheatland, the two women—both strikingly beautiful, both sharp-tongued and full of fire—had been thick as thieves from the moment they'd laid eyes on each other, and it was Libby that Ellen had gone to live with when Hap and she finally called it quits.

"Who's Libby Norton?" Aaron now asked.

"Goddamn Medusa, reincarnated," Hap said curtly. "We're leavin' right now, son."

"What? How come?"

Hap didn't answer, because Libby's eyes had just found his and knocked the breath out of him. He stared in horror as she detached herself from the people she was with and began walking briskly toward them, never once looking away from his face.

"What's wrong, Hap?" Aaron asked.

"It's your fault Ellen's dead, you son of a bitch," Libby had whispered to him in the line at Ellen's funeral, clutching him to her in grief and rage. *"If you hadn't thrown her out she'd still be with us, and so would your baby."*

"That boy wasn't mine," Hap had whispered back fiercely. *"She as much as told me so herself. And I never threw her out! She left of her own free will."*

"Bullshit, Hap. She cried herself to sleep every night for the last two months, did you know that? She stopped eating, stopped caring about everything. She wore herself out crying, and she wasn't nearly strong enough to have that baby. Your baby, Hap, and you know it, no matter what she told you. You broke her heart, and it killed her."

"You don't know what the hell you're talking about!"

"The hell I don't."

"Hi, Hap," Libby now said, standing right in front of him.

For years, every time he'd thought of Libby Norton, he'd been filled with a seething, righteous resentment, but at that moment—seeing her in the flesh again after such a very long time—all he felt was pain. She had loved Ellen nearly as much as he had; she, too, probably still never went a day without grieving for her.

"Hi, Libby." He swallowed past a lump in his throat. "How the hell are you?"

"Well enough." She stepped forward without warning and wrapped her arms around him. Her hair smelled like coconut. "I shouldn't say this, but it's good to see you, Hap Cobb. I didn't think it would be, but it is."

He returned her embrace, blinking hard. "It's good to see you, too, girl."

Holding her, he knew neither of them would bring up the last words they'd exchanged all those years ago; he also knew she'd meant everything she'd said at the time, and probably still thought he was to blame for Ellen's death. He wasn't sure why she was hugging him now with such fierce affection, or why he was hugging her back as tightly, but he couldn't seem to help himself. No matter how badly their friendship had ended, there had once been love between them, and it felt damn good to hold her, to feel her cheek against his neck, to smell the soap on her skin. She was almost the same size as Ellen; she fit in his arms just right, the same way Ellen always had. He released her with a final squeeze, embarrassed to find everybody in the line gawking at them as they stepped apart.

"You okay there, old man?" Aaron asked quietly, leaning in close while Libby greeted Ezra. "You look a little shaky."

"I'm fine," Hap muttered. He'd never told Aaron much about his marriage and he didn't intend to be overly forthcoming in the future, either, but he supposed he'd now have to come up with something to explain why there had been tears in his eyes when Libby let go of him, otherwise Aaron would never give him any peace.

Libby introduced herself to Aaron and held out her hand for him to shake; Aaron told her his name and explained how he knew Hap.

"Oh, Lord," she said, smiling. "You actually live in the same house with him?"

"Afraid so."

"You must be out of your mind."

"Yes, ma'am. I believe I am."

"Just call him pinhead," Hap said. "He don't know to answer to nothin' else."

Ezra asked Libby what brought her to town after all this time and she turned to point at two young girls in the line. Hap hadn't seen them at first because he'd been so focused on Libby. The girls were her granddaughters, she explained, and she'd brought them to visit family friends in Wheatland for a few days; the girls had insisted on coming to the pancake breakfast and dragged Libby along.

Hap stared at the two dark-haired, willowy beauties—they were dead ringers for Libby—and his heart, already hurting, twisted yet again. He hadn't even known Libby had children, let alone *grand*children; it didn't seem possible. It was another reminder of how much time had slipped by, how much had gotten away from him.

"You up and got married after all, then?" he asked. "You always swore you wouldn't."

"I never meant to. It just happened." She grinned her old, wicked grin. "I was more than a little drunk when he proposed, to tell the truth."

"Attagirl. So where's the lucky fella? Don't he like pancakes?"

"This is a 'girl's only' trip. They needed a break from their folks and I needed a break from my husband, so we all ran away from home."

On the spur of the moment Hap invited her to come out to the ranch for a visit that afternoon, but no sooner had the words left his mouth than he knew it was a mistake.

"I best not, Hap," she said, breaking eye contact. "I'd like to, but it's just...it's just we have to get back soon, and the girls and I already made plans." She hesitated. "Thanks for asking, though."

There was a time when Libby had come to the ranch almost daily, to see Ellen. There was a time when the two women and he would sit at the kitchen table, eating the food he'd prepared for them and drinking cheap wine, laughing and talking late into the night, taking turns at the cribbage board. There was a time when it would've been impossible to imagine so many years passing without any contact, impossible to imagine an awkward exchange like this at a pancake breakfast, impossible to imagine they'd one day be reduced to making excuses to avoid a visit that would likely—no, undoubtedly—turn unpleasant, once the shock of seeing each other wore off and their old animosity resurfaced.

"Well, that's a damn shame." Hap tried to hide how much the refusal hurt. "It woulda been just like old times."

They made a little more smalltalk, but then she hugged him again and kissed his cheek, saying she best get back to her girls; he guessed she wanted to beat a hasty retreat before one or the other of them could mention Ellen and mar their brief reunion. She clearly wasn't going to introduce her granddaughters to him, and that told him everything he needed to know about whether or not she had forgiven him.

As did the brief bitterness that had crept into her tone at the mention of the ranch.

She'd witnessed too many of the bad times, heard firsthand all the arguments and recriminations, seen the devastation on Ellen's face whenever Hap said something particularly cutting. The White Creek Ranch had all too often been a battlefield, and Hap couldn't really blame Libby for not wanting to revisit where she believed her best friend had been mortally injured—yet Ellen had done her fair share of the bloodletting, and if Libby were being honest she'd surely have to admit that, wouldn't she? He wanted to cry out and remind her just how many sweet moments she'd also witnessed: she'd seen him twirl Ellen around the kitchen in a spontaneous, sensual dance; she'd listened a million times to them singing songs together and snuggling by the fire; she'd seen the way Ellen came up behind his chair and kissed him on the head whenever she walked past. Surely the good times counted more than the bad; surely Libby could grant him at least that much, after all these years?

"I'd do things way different, Lib, if I could," he murmured in her ear. "I ain't the same dumb son of a bitch I once was."

"Oh, Hap," she murmured back, tilting her head up to smile at him. Her eyes were too bright, and he knew she was on the verge of tears. "Of course you are."

He watched her walk away, his face wooden, trying not to make a spectacle of himself. Ezra and Cyrus didn't seem to notice anything out of the ordinary had just happened, but Aaron was another matter. The younger man's face was full of questions, but for once he had the sense to stay silent, and Hap was grateful.

"Don't stare, son," he said gruffly, turning away from the sight of Libby rejoining her granddaughters in the line. "It ain't polite."

Chapter Ten

"Yes, ma'am," Aaron said into the phone as Lucas nervously toyed with his fork, waiting to hear if there was any information yet about his family. "That was some storm."

Aaron was speaking to the social worker in charge of Lucas's case, a woman from Wheatland named Janet something-or-other. Lucas, Sandy, and Hap were all sitting at the kitchen table—its surface cluttered with the breakfast dishes—and listening to Aaron's side of the conversation. The photo Sandy had discovered in the attic was in front of Lucas and Hap, propped upright against the salt shaker, and Lucas couldn't stop staring at it even as he strained his ears to hear what "Janet" was saying. He didn't really know what to hope for. If his parents had been located and were bad people, would he still have to go back to them? And if they *hadn't* turned up, what would happen then? Would he be put in some kind of foster home? Would it be worse there than his "real" home—wherever and whatever that was?

All the things he had no answers for were beginning to anger him, yet nothing was more maddening than the photo in front of him. The man standing with a woman by an old well had the same wide eyes and long nose as he did, the same freckles on his cheeks, the same thin neck and narrow shoulders. Lucas would've bet anything he also had red hair and green eyes, just like him, but because the picture was black-and-white there was no way to know. The only obvious differences between them were age and height; the man looked to be at least twice as old as Lucas and much taller, towering over the well behind him. The slim, beautiful woman in the photo disturbed him too, but because of his fixation on the man he couldn't spare her much attention.

"We've got everything we need, thank you," Aaron said, bringing him back to the phone conversation. "Our gas generator is going full-out, but it's keeping us nice and warm."

The state patrol had closed the highway between Chugwater and Wheatland. The ice storm had caught the whole southeast corner of the state by surprise, and even Interstate 25 was closed to all but emergency vehicles; Sandy had called her work again to say she was still stranded. Aaron told Janet there was no problem with Lucas staying with him and Hap until the roads opened again; he added that as far as they were concerned Lucas was welcome to stay however long it took to find his family.

He covered the receiver and smiled down at Lucas. "That okay with you?"

Lucas nodded emphatically, then looked away quickly, blinking hard.

"Oh, hell," Hap said, grinning. The old man was seated on Lucas's right and sipping his third cup of coffee that morning. "Now we'll never get rid of the little idjit."

"Hush, Hap," Aaron said. "It was your idea in the first place." He removed his hand from the receiver and listened to something the social worker was saying. His eyebrows rose and he glanced over at Lucas again.

"What?" Lucas asked, unable to control himself any longer. "*What*?"

Aaron held up a hand. "That's—yes, well, that is kind of odd." He listened some more, then said he'd bring Lucas to Wheatland as soon as the roads reopened: Janet was apparently in a rush to meet him. Lucas watched Aaron anxiously as he finally said good-bye and hung up the phone.

"Well?" Hap demanded.

Aaron sat across the table from Lucas and sighed. "No news yet," he said, meeting Lucas's eyes. "Sorry, bud."

Lucas was mostly relieved but he stayed silent, waiting to see what else Aaron had learned. When the man hesitated Lucas felt his stomach knot up.

"Just spit it out, Aaron," Hap said. "What's the part we ain't gonna like?"

Aaron kept his eyes on Lucas. "Nothing's engraved in stone, but Janet said she wasn't sure you'd be able to stay with us after the roads open up." His voice was gentle. "You may have to go someplace else for a while until everything gets sorted."

Lucas bit his lip and Sandy squeezed his hand.

"What the hell for?" Hap protested. "If the boy wants to stay put and we're deficient enough to let him, it ain't nobody else's business!"

"The only other thing Janet told me," Aaron said, "was she'd spoken to the school principal in Wheatland. It turns out there are only five kids named Lucas in the whole district, and all five are accounted for. The principal made the calls himself to make sure no one was missing."

Lucas stared stupidly at him. Just like that, one of the only things he knew for sure about himself had just been proven false. Added to the long list of mystifying things going on—especially the picture of his older "twin" on the table—he suddenly couldn't tolerate his own ignorance anymore. What was next? Would he find out Lucas wasn't even his real name?

"No!" he cried, shoving back from the table. "My name is *Lucas*, and I go to school in Wheatland, *goddammit*!"

He glared at each of them in turn, spoiling for a fight, but no one took him up on it. All he saw were the caring, open faces of the only three people in the world he could recall, and all three were staring back at him with compassion. There was also a tiny glimmer of humor in Aaron's eyes, and Hap's lips were twitching suspiciously at the corners as well. Lucas began to feel ridiculous for his outburst.

"What?" he demanded, flushing.

"Ain't no call for that sort of language, son," Hap said.

*

There were no more pictures in the box of the man who looked like Lucas, but the woman in the old black-and-white photo showed up in two other snapshots. In the first she was standing next to the grill of a mud-spattered Model T, in the second she was seated on a horse, looking imperious. There was no denying her beauty; she reminded Hap of a young Audrey Hepburn, with huge, luminous eyes and an almost regal bearing. But unlike the dark-haired, angelic-looking film star, there was no sweetness in her expression, nor an ounce of playfulness.

"I'd bet my left titty that gal was a world class ball-breaker," Hap said to Lucas as they stared at the photos together in the kitchen. "She gives me the damn shivers, and that's a fact."

It was the third time they'd gone through the box, hoping to see something they'd missed before. Aaron and Sandy were up in the attic looking for anything else that might shed light on Hap's extended—and long dead—family, even though Hap had warned them it was a colossal waste of time. "Ain't nothin' up there but crap," he'd told them. "Granddaddy couldn't abide a single one of our relations—hell, he hated my folks so damn much he near tossed out my birth certificate once just 'cause it had their *names* on it—and these here damn *mystery* pictures is all he held onto by way of what you might call Cobb family history."

Sandy insisted on searching anyway, saying they might as well since they were confined to the house for the day. They were all intrigued by Lucas's resemblance to somebody they assumed was one of Hap's relations—even though Aaron maintained it was nothing but a freakish coincidence—so Hap relented. He and Lucas opted to stay downstairs, however, unable to resist pawing through the photos again even though Hap knew it was pointless.

He glanced at Lucas, seated next to him and currently staring at a blurry photo of a small child playing some kind of game with a stick and wooden ball in the mud of a barnyard. “This box didn’t move itself up in the attic,” he told the boy. “You must’ve had one of your spells again, like Sandy said.”

Lucas looked up from the photo and shrugged helplessly. “I don’t think so.”

“I ain’t sayin’ you did it on purpose, son. It ain’t your fault your brain’s on the fritz.”

Lucas showed Hap the picture he was holding. “What’s this?”

“Don’t know. Just some kid playin’ in the mud.” Hap took a closer look. “That’s our barnyard he’s makin’ a holy mess of, though. See that big rock next to him? It’s still out there.”

“I’m not talking about the kid.” Lucas pointed to the top left corner of the photo, where the image was particularly grainy.

Hap took the picture from him, squinting. “I’ll be damned. That’s a well, but there ain’t been a well in that part of the yard my whole life. The one we got now is by the barn door. Somebody must’ve filled this one in before I was born.”

Lucas took the picture back, comparing it to the photo Sandy found. “It’s the same well.”

Hap shrugged. “Might be.”

“So did this guy who looks like me used to live here?”

Hap studied the boy’s pensive face. “Just ‘cause you look like him don’t mean nothin,’ Lucas. Like Aaron said, it’s just some coincidence.”

Lucas’s green eyes met his. “You don’t really believe that, do you, Hap?”

The boy’s gaze was steady and shrewd, and Hap’s throat went dry as all his drunken misgivings about Lucas from the previous night resurfaced. He was right, of course: Hap really *didn’t* believe it was a coincidence that Lucas looked like the man in the picture. The resemblance was too uncanny; there simply *had* to be a blood tie of some kind, improbable or not. And if the picture had indeed been taken at White Creek Ranch, what did *that* mean? Had the man lived there, or was he simply visiting? If he’d lived there, he was almost certainly a Cobb, same as Hap; to Hap’s knowledge no one but the Cobb family had ever lived at White Creek until Aaron came along. And if the man in the picture *was* Hap's relative, then so was—

"Don't tell me what I think, son," he blustered, trying to ignore the rash of goosebumps on his arms and neck. "You ain't no damn mind reader."

"No," Lucas said, still unblinking. "But I know you're wondering why I'm here." He set the two photos back on the table carefully, side-by-side. "I also know you're a little scared to find out, same as me." He fell silent as he stared down at the old pictures, and suddenly his chin began to tremble.

"Ain't nothin' to be scared of, son," Hap said gently. He ruffled Lucas's tangled head of red hair, praying he was right. "Everything's gonna turn out peachy in the end, just you wait."

"Maybe," Lucas murmured.

*

The dust Aaron and Sandy had stirred up in the past hour was wreaking havoc with Aaron's allergies; his eyes itched and his scalp felt like it was crawling with bugs. "I think Hap's right," he said, tugging a hanky from his pocket and blowing his nose. "We're on a wild goose chase."

"Oh, come on now." Sandy frowned at all the boxes piled in stacks everywhere she turned. The exasperation on her pixie-like features was one Aaron was growing familiar with; she apparently had zero tolerance for things she didn't understand, and her impatience tickled him. "Surely Hap doesn't remember what's in every single one of these silly boxes. Maybe when he was younger he overlooked something."

"Maybe," Aaron said, "but he's been through all this stuff a million times."

"Doesn't it seem strange, though?" Sandy held up a badly frayed afghan before stuffing it back in the box she was rooting through. "Hap told me his family has been in this house since 1866, for heaven's sake, so I'm guessing there must have been *tons* of Cobb family memorabilia laying around the place before

Hap's grandfather went crazy, and started tossing stuff out. Surely he didn't get rid of absolutely *everything* but that one teensy little shoebox of photos?"

Aaron opened a box stuffed with Christmas religious ornaments he'd never come across in all his years with Hap: Hand-painted ceramic candle holders; crocheted white crosses for the tree; a hand-carved, pinewood nativity scene; knitted angels, moth-eaten and falling apart with age. He sealed the box again and set it aside. "Hap always talks about what a cantankerous old codger his granddaddy Jacob was, and how much he disliked everybody with the same last name as him, except for Hap. Maybe he just got a bee in his bonnet one day and decided to hell with it all."

"If that's true it's a real shame."

"Yeah, it sure is. Hap hates that he doesn't know more about his family than he does. He says Jacob once told him a few minor anecdotes about his great-grandparents, but that was the extent of what he was willing to pass on about any of the Cobbs. He never said a single word about Hap's folks, except to say Hap should be thrilled they were dead and gone." Aaron moved a fierce-looking stuffed owl off its perch and started in on another stack of boxes. "I sure wish the old fart hadn't been so thorough, though, when it came to tossing things. I'd pay big money to know why Lucas looks so much like the guy in the picture."

Sandy narrowed her eyes. "You said downstairs that was only a coincidence."

Aaron grinned at her accusatory tone. "I was trying to make Lucas feel better, but between you and me that picture gives me the full-on jitters. It's got to be almost a hundred years old, but I'd swear it's Lucas himself standing in front of that well, all grown up."

"So would I." Sandy opened a metal tin full of knickknacks. "Oh, I'd like to slap Hap's grandfather silly. If he was so dead set on destroying his whole family's history, why hold onto those pictures? It makes no sense to me."

Aaron shrugged, grin fading. "I've got an old picture of *my* folks in my wallet that only brings up bad memories every time

I see it, but I still can't make myself toss it. Maybe Jacob felt the same way about that box." He scrunched up his nose and sneezed, earning a distracted-sounding blessing from Sandy. As he dug out his hanky once more he studied her; she had her hands on her hips and was glaring at the several dozen boxes they still had to go through.

"Okay, fine. I give up." She thrust the tin of knickknacks at Aaron in vexation. "So where *else* can we look?"

Aaron laughed at her as he took the tin and she smiled. Their fingers touched and both of them flushed, though neither said anything. After a brief, awkward pause, their eyes met and lingered, and it was in that moment—as startling and welcome to Aaron as the first time he'd heard ice cracking on the creek on a fine spring morning years ago—that he began to realize Hap may have been onto something after all with something he'd said to him the previous day.

"If I didn't know any better I'd say you got your eyes on that cat-woman," Hap had told him. *"But then again you're too much of an idjit to know a good thing when you see it."*

"You're a real glutton for punishment, aren't you?" Aaron asked quietly. He found himself wanting to touch her again and so he did, reaching out to take her hand.

"Sometimes." Her fingers trembled a little in his, but she didn't pull away. "But I'd prefer chocolate and flowers, if I have any say in the matter."

He laughed again and so did she, then they stood silently for a minute. Aaron loved how he could read every emotion as it crossed her face: delight and surprise, curiosity and shyness, humor and trepidation. He felt all the same things himself, and wondered if his own face was so transparent.

"Hey." Her eyes widened all at once and she squeezed his hand. "Hey, now. Wait just a gosh-darn minute! What about your library?"

Aaron cocked his head. "Come again?"

She sighed. "Sorry. I'm still thinking about Hap's granddad. I'm a pit bull when I get my teeth in something." Her fingers were warm in his. "Do you think Jacob got to the library when he was tossing everything? My mom's always tucking old letters and pictures in her books."

Aaron told her he didn't know, but there was really no point in looking; it would take weeks, for one thing, and Hap and he had read most of the books in it anyway, between the two of them. He added that he could count on one hand the number of times they'd found anything like what she was talking about.

"But you *have* found things?"

"Nothing important. I came across a recipe for rhubarb pie, and I think Hap found a postcard from an old friend of his grandpa's. Just stuff like that."

"How about a family Bible? Lots of people keep things in their Bibles."

He stared at her for a long, long time. "Good Lord, I may be every bit as dumb as Hap says I am. There's a whole bookshelf of old religious stuff down there Hap and I have never even touched. Neither of us has any stomach for that sort of thing."

She smiled with excitement, like a young girl who'd been promised a pony ride. "Well, what are we waiting for then?" she demanded, tugging him towards the ladder.

Interlude: Jacob and Rebecca, 1942

"You're letting that boy run wild," Rebecca said, watching her eleven-year-old grandson gut a fish on a rock by the well. There was a string of a dozen or more trout hanging from the well handle; the boy was cleaning the fish with quick, practiced efficiency. During the summers he spent more time in the creek than on dry land. His back was nut brown and his normally black, tousled hair, bleached by the sun, had turned auburn. "He looks like a little cannibal."

Jacob, her husband, was tending to the chickens and whistling to himself while she hung laundry in back of the house. The door to the chicken coop was wide open and she knew he could hear her even though his only reply was to whistle "Down in the Valley" a little louder. Hap called out across the yard in his high, clear voice, asking if he could cook dinner again that night. The boy was already twice the cook Rebecca was; he could do wonders in the kitchen with just about anything that walked, flew, swam, or grew. She nodded and he grinned happily, telling her he was "gonna fry up these here sons a bitches with a mess of potatoes and peppers!"

"He also *sounds* like a little cannibal," Rebecca said to Jacob.

Jacob stuck his head out the coop door. "Let him be, Becky," he said mildly. "He ain't hurtin' nobody."

Rebecca grimaced, knowing it was futile to argue. The boy's parents had been such fanatics about both profanity and grammar—using a belt on naked skin to punish what they considered unseemly—-that Jacob refused to let her even gently correct Hap for how he talked. Rebecca tried to circumvent this prohibition by always speaking properly in the boy's presence, but as Hap worshipped Jacob and emulated him in every way possible, it was a losing battle. It made no sense to her that two people who read as much as Jacob and Hap had so little regard for proper manners and civilized discourse, but she knew their carelessness stemmed from Jacob's disdain for gentility, loathing anybody who, like Hap's mother, put on airs of any kind.

She'd never bothered to point out that Jacob's behaving like an ignoramus when he knew, nearly by heart, both the *Iliad* and the *Odyssey*—as well as the collected works of Shakespeare, Dickens, and Tolstoy—was every bit as irritating as being pretentious: she knew such an argument would fall on deaf ears.

"What if he ends up going to college someday?" she asked. "What if he ends up being a doctor, or some big fancy lawyer?"

Jacob snorted and turned his head to yell across the yard. "Hey, idjit! You hankerin' to go to college when you're older?"

Hap looked up from his work and gave them a wry look that reminded Rebecca strongly of Reuben, the boy's father. The similarity came as an unpleasant shock; Hap was so different from Reuben that she normally could almost make herself forget the connection.

"Why in hell would I do that?" he yelled back.

"Your grandma thought you might wanna be a doctor or somesuch."

Hap rubbed his nose on the back of his wrist. "You drunk again, old lady?"

Even across the lawn Rebecca saw the twinkle in his eyes; she abhorred alcohol and the boy knew it. "Stop playing the fool, Hap Cobb," she said, forcing a smile, though she was suddenly having trouble breathing. "You're not so big yet I can't take you down a notch or two."

"Sorry, Grandma, but I don't want to go to college. I'm gonna stay put and help you and Granddaddy run this place."

He reached for another fish with bloody fingers and Rebecca lowered her voice for Jacob's ears alone. "That's you talking, Jacob Cobb, not him."

"The hell you say."

"I *do* say. How often do you tell him this old ranch is 'the best damn place on earth?' "

He shrugged. "It's the truth."

"Maybe not for him."

"You got something stuck in your craw, Becky? You look like someone just pissed in your lemonade."

"I'm fine." She lifted a sheet from the laundry basket to hang it on the line. "I just think that boy was made for other things besides tending cows."

"What's wrong with tending cows? It's honest work, and it'll keep food in his belly."

"He's eleven-years-old, Jacob. How is he supposed to know what he wants to do with his life?" She found herself blinking back tears. "Maybe if Reuben had seen more of the world, he wouldn't have gotten so turned around."

"Rebecca!" Jacob snapped.

She blanched, appalled at her own indiscretion. Reuben was a forbidden subject, always, and they turned as one to look at Hap, who was on his way into the barn for something, not paying them any mind. Rebecca apologized.

"Hap ain't gonna get his head turned around, Becky," Jacob said quietly. "He'll be fine."

She hoped he was right, but she remembered Reuben had once been a sweet boy, too, just like Hap. But that was before Elizabeth Colleen Durham wrapped him around her little finger like a blade of grass. Elizabeth may have had the face of an angel, but she was also a shrewish, high-handed, Seventh-Day Adventist who talked as if she'd personally dictated the Ten Commandments to Moses and made no secret about believing the White Creek Ranch and everyone on it belonged in the deepest pit of hell. Even before

Reuben got baptized into Elizabeth's church she'd been unreasonable and erratic, but once Reuben was officially 'saved' it triggered something poisonous in her psyche, and her mind began unraveling. Why Reuben couldn't see her derangement was beyond understanding, but his loyalty to her and her backward, vengeful God was absolute, extending even to the brutal disciplining of their children.

And Rebecca had grown to hate him for it.

"I hope so," she said now, "But what if *he* has a child someday, and he starts to do the sorts of things that—"

"Jesus Christ Almighty, woman! Have you lost your damn mind?"

She shook her head mutely as Hap reemerged into the sunlight from the barn, his skinny torso glistening with sweat and his thin young face intent on whatever it was he was doing now. He'd gone to fetch another bucket for some reason, even though he already had two by the well; the boy was forever making ten times more mess than necessary.

Just like his older brother.

Rebecca lost her grip on the sheet she was holding and put her hands to her mouth. All the things she hadn't allowed herself to dwell on for years were boiling over: Elizabeth and her belt, Reuben's casual brutality, the cloying smell of the salve she'd smeared on the boys' injuries, day after day. Jacob's impotent fury and steadfast refusal to intervene, her own endless, pitched battles with Elizabeth and Reuben, the eventual despair—and if she was being honest with herself, cowardice—that led her, for a time, to abandon her husband and grandchildren, simply to escape the nightmare her home had become.

"What's wrong, Grandma?" Hap called out. She could barely see the boy through her tears; she was only partly aware of Jacob begging her to get a hold of herself.

They'd been right to keep everything from Hap. She knew in her bones no good could come from telling him about what had happened a mere hundred feet from where he was cleaning his fish, over by where the old well had once stood. She also knew she had no right to feel so blindsided by her memories today; she was far from blameless in all that occurred, regardless of not actually being there for the worst of it. She'd played her part just as much as the rest of them played theirs, and the only thing she and Jacob could now do was to keep Hap from learning just how much he'd lost nine years ago.

Elizabeth was right about one thing, she thought, drying her tears with the back of her hand. *The devil is no stranger to this ranch.*

Chapter Eleven

"This is the stupidest thing I've ever done in my whole damn life," Hap said, glancing at Lucas as the boy struggled to help him keep his feet in the snow behind the house. "And between you and me, son, that's saying a mouthful." Lucas grinned at him and Hap grinned back, even though his teeth were clacking from the cold.

"I told you it was a bad idea," Lucas said. "Can we go back inside now?"

"Nah. Now we're here we may as well take a gander 'round the place."

Lucas was small for his age but the arm he'd wrapped around Hap's waist was strong and the heat of his young body felt good against Hap's side. The temperature had risen slightly since breakfast and the gray sky was slowly changing to blue in the west, but the wind was still a murderous butcher, knifing into Hap's ribs with every breath he took. He'd dressed warmly, but even several layers of sweaters and the heaviest coat he could find—Aaron's, of course—weren't enough to keep his frail body safe from a Wyoming winter wind. He clutched Lucas closer, grateful for the boy's solid presence.

"'Aye, aye, Starbuck,'" he said. "'Tis sweet to lean, sometimes, be the leaner who he will; and would old Ahab had leaned oftener than he has.'"

"Huh?" Lucas asked.

"Ain't you never read *Moby Dick*?"

"Nope. At least not that I remember."

"You'd recall if you had, even with your brain scrambled," he gasped, panting as they plunged through knee-deep drifts. "There ain't no other book like it. Anyhow, that big rock is close by. I ain't believing we ain't found it 'cause it's the size of a damn buffalo." His heart was pounding and he felt lightheaded, yet he didn't want to go inside. It had been ages since he'd ventured out in this kind of weather, and it made him feel oddly alive in spite of his discomfort.

"Slow *down,* Hap," Lucas ordered. "You don't sound so good to me."

"Quit your fussin,' boy. You're gettin' as bad as the pinhead."

"I just don't want Aaron mad at *me* when you keel over. With all this snow we'll never find where the well was anyway."

Hap ignored him, knowing Aaron would only blame Hap himself for this bit of idiocy—and rightly so, since he'd been the one who'd browbeaten Lucas into coming along. "Where's that rock?" he wheezed. "It should be right—SON OF A WHORE!"

His knee had just collided with the rock in question; he reeled back in pain. Both he and Lucas nearly fell, but Lucas managed to support him long enough for him to regain his balance. They stood together in the wind as Hap bellowed a blue streak.

"Okay, that's it," Lucas said when Hap finally ran out of steam, "we're going back inside. Can you still walk?"

"Yes, I can still goddamn *walk*!" Hap slowly worked the knee back and forth, not at all sure he was telling the truth. "My damn leg's gonna swell up like a donkey dick, but it ain't nothin' a shot of whiskey won't put right again."

"Aaron's going to kill me. How about we get back inside before anything else happens?"

"How about you stop bein' a whiny old lady?"

Lucas made a face. "Okay, but don't blame me if you fall and break your neck." His mouth twitched in the way that reminded Hap so strongly of his own grandfather. "By the way, how do you know so much about donkey dicks?"

Hap laughed. "You're turnin' into a right mouthy little wise-ass, and that's a fact. You and Aaron ain't allowed to talk no more."

"He said the same thing about talking to *you*."

"I ain't surprised." Hap bent down a little with Lucas's help and brushed snow from the rock that had assaulted him. "Let's sit a spell."

The rock was achingly cold under Hap's haunches but it was good to rest. He peered around the yard as he caught his breath, marveling how alien something so familiar could look when it was all garbed in white. Icicles three or four feet long hung from the roof of the house like ghostly fingers; the wind circled the yard, howling one moment and in the next whispering a sustained, unearthly *hush* in his ears.

"Okay," he said, "this old rock here ain't moved since God created the universe and buggered off someplace else." He glanced over his right shoulder at the barn to get his bearings, then turned to his left and pointed to a spot midway between the tool shed and the house. "So 'bout thirty feet straight that-a-way is where that well in them pictures was."

Lucas looked where he was pointing. "You sure?"

"Yep." Hap dropped his hand but they both kept staring at the spot. "Mind you, there ain't nothin' to see there under the snow but bare ground—and in the spring there won't be nothin,' neither, 'cept for goddamn thistles—but from this rock that's where the well was. I guaran-damn-tee it."

Lucas took a deep breath. "So the guy that looks like me was standing right over there with that lady?"

Hap was startled to see tears in the boy's eyes; he wondered what was ailing him. "Yep," he said. "That's where they was. I just wish it was as easy to figure out *who* they was, too."

"No," Lucas whispered. "Oh, no, Hap, you don't."

*

"I can't believe you and Hap never looked through these before." Sandy fingered the spine of a red, leather-bound book that was one of a dozen or more ancient-looking Bibles scattered throughout a host of Christian literature: *Patriarchs And Prophets*, by Ellen G. White; *A Seal Of The Living God*, by Joseph Bates; *The History Of The Sabbath*, by J.N. Andrew; and on and on—all tucked away on a tall bookshelf in a dark corner of the library. "This one may be older than your house."

The intimacy they'd shared in the attic was still very much on her mind—and she suspected it was on his as well—but she didn't want to scare him off by reaching for his hand again, just in case he was having second thoughts.

Aaron took the red Bible from the shelf with some difficulty; it hadn't been moved for so long it was stuck in place. "I read my mother's Bible cover to cover when I was a kid, but it didn't really speak to me. I was more of a *Lord Of The Rings* kind of guy." He blew a layer of dust off the top of the book and sneezed. "I probably would've enjoyed the Old Testament a whole lot more if all the people in it were hobbits."

Sandy laughed, watching as he thumbed through the book's brittle pages. "Blasphemer," she said. "There are a lot of really beautiful things in the Bible."

"Sure there are. Unfortunately, all I remember is the worst of it—the eye-for-an-eye, going to hell for your sins, stoning-people-to-death kind of stuff. It gave me nightmares."

They both heard a voice yelling outside; Aaron raised his eyebrows and ambled over to the window. "Oh, for crying out loud. Hap's outside with Lucas. It looks like the old jackass hurt his leg."

Sandy was only half-listening. She'd selected a different Bible with notes written in the margins in a thin, spidery hand, but the comments appeared to be mostly about the text rather than anything personal. She put the book back and reached for another. "Okay," she said, "so you prefer the Shire to Sodom and Gomorrah, but what's Hap's excuse? Why hasn't he gone through these books before?"

Aaron shrugged, still staring out the window. "Just not interested, I guess. He always said his granddaddy had zero patience for religion, and it sort of rubbed off on him." He glanced over his shoulder and grinned; his grin did something lovely to her insides. "Can you imagine Hap trying to sit still through a church sermon?"

She shook her head and sighed. "Okay, so help me out, here. Hap's grandfather practically *ransacked* the whole house to get rid of every single thing that annoyed him, but he still held onto all these religious books, even though he had zero use for religion. Does that make a bit of sense to you?"

"Sure. To hear Hap tell it, he and his grandpa were two peas in a pod, and Hap could no more throw out a book than he can say please or thank you. To him, *all* books are holy. Even the Bible."

Sandy loved the low, easy rumble of his laugh; it was impossible to hear it and not want to join in. "I'm not sure it's a good idea to be in the same room with you. Lightning might strike."

"Nah, you're safe with me. Hap's the resident lightning rod."

He looked back out the window at the same moment Sandy tugged yet another Bible off the shelf and opened the front cover. This one was a fragile-looking old relic with gold embossing on its black leather cover. She looked down at the page before her and exclaimed with delight at what she'd found, but her smile froze as she read a little more.

"What on *earth*?" she gasped, fumbling and nearly dropping the Bible.

*

Lucas's memories were flooding back, and he was drowning in them.

"What the hell's wrong, boy?" Hap asked. "You look like you just seen a ghost."

The last vestige of the boy named Lucas almost found that funny.

Almost.

Oh, Hap. I am so sorry.

"Their names were Reuben and Elizabeth," he said quietly. "The people in the picture."

Hap gaped at him for a long minute, his face blank. "Them was the names of my folks, boy," he finally stammered, "but not even Aaron knows that, so just how in *hell* do you? Christ have mercy, the only reason *I* know is 'cause it's on my damn birth certificate!"

Lucas brushed the tears from his cheeks and did his best to respond, but then fell silent again, not having a clue how to begin the story he now knew was his to tell. *Once upon a time,* he thought, as memory upon memory returned to him, each more vivid than the brightly-colored pages of the picture books he had loved so much as a child. *Once upon a time, there was a boy named Lucas, who lived on a ranch in Wyoming.*

*

"What is it, Sandy?" Aaron asked, wondering why she was so unnerved. He looked at the Bible in her hands and saw she'd struck genealogical gold: she'd found at least a portion of Hap's family history. A yellowed vellum page in the front of the book folded out to reveal an elaborate ink drawing of an oak tree. The branches on the tree bore names and dates; linkages between certain branches indicated husbands and wives, others represented parent and child, still others connoted siblings. Sandy pointed to Hap's name: *Hap Edward Cobb, born February 7, 1931.* The branch above, for Hap's parents, had the names and birth dates for Reuben Allen Cobb and Elizabeth Durham Cobb, but it was the spot on the branch directly beside Hap's name—a branch for siblings—that Sandy pointed to next:

David Lucas Cobb, born October 21, 1919.

Aaron felt the hackles on his neck standing on end as he looked at Sandy. "Hap never told me his brother's middle name before. I don't think he even knows it."

*

"So you're sayin' them folks in the picture was *my* folks?" Hap demanded of the boy seated next to him. "And just how in hell would you know *that*?"

"Because they were my folks, too." Lucas's voice was quiet but assured, even as more tears ran down his face.

"You poor little dimwit," Hap said mournfully.

"I'm serious, Hap. We're brothers."

Hap put his hands on the rock for leverage to stand, but his legs wouldn't budge. "The only brother I ever had died in 1933, son, when I was two years old. That's eighty goddamn years ago, and I bet not even your *grandparents* was alive back then, let alone you."

"I know how it sounds, Hap, but it's the truth."

"Look, boy." Hap's eye was drawn to a lock of Lucas's red hair, peeking out from beneath his hunting cap; for a moment he had the strangest impulse to reach out and tug at that patch of red. "I'm older'n Methuselah, and you're such an infant your damn nuts ain't even dropped. You and me *might* be kin—though I ain't got a clue how—but us bein' brothers just ain't possible."

Lucas turned away to study the house. "Pop was bad, but Mama was worse. Both of them liked taking the belt to me, but once Mama got going she just kept on swinging till even Pop said it was too much. Mama always said she was sorry, later, but she had no choice because God told her to. She said the devil was in me, and it was the only thing she could do to get him out."

Rage flared up in Hap, surprising him with its force. Regardless how skewed Lucas's memory was, one thing was perfectly clear: the boy's parents were assholes. "Your mama ain't never comin' near you again," he swore, "or your daddy, neither. I'll put a damn bullet in their heads myself if I have to, but they ain't gonna hurt you no more."

Lucas smiled at him, but the sadness in the smile was heart-rending. "I know the feeling."

Hap spotted Aaron and Sandy in the library window on the second floor, looking down at him and Lucas; his eyes weren't good enough to see Aaron's face at this distance but even so, the younger man's presence was reassuring. Hap would've ripped the tongue from his own head before he'd admit it, of course, but there was no one on the planet whose good sense he valued as much. He almost signaled for Aaron to come join them, but then changed his mind, not wanting the baldheaded fuss-budget to think Hap Cobb wasn't man enough to handle things.

"The pinhead and the catwoman are up there spyin' on us," he told Lucas, trying to lighten the mood. "What say we drop our trousers and moon 'em?"

"She tried to kill you, Hap. I don't know why, but she did."

Hap thought at first the boy was talking about Sandy, then realized who he meant. "Ain't nobody ever wailed on me like you been wailed on, son. Granddaddy would take a switch to my hindquarters if I really had it comin,' but the worst he ever did was make it hard to sit down for a day or so."

"Yeah, Granddaddy was mostly talk," Lucas agreed. "Grandma was nice, too, but she wasn't around anymore because she and Mama hated each other so much she moved to town to stay with Selma. She called Granddaddy a coward for not kicking Pop and Mama out of the house after Pop got saved and started acting crazy, too, and she said she wouldn't move back in as long as they still lived here."

Hap's mind went into free fall. An elderly cousin of his grandmother's called Selma had indeed lived in Wheatland when Hap was a boy, but he'd only met the woman once or twice and had forgotten all about her. How in God's name did Lucas know her name?

"Mama hated Granddaddy, too, of course," Lucas continued, "and him and Pop butted heads over Mama and us and everything else, so Granddaddy took to staying in that little cabin down by the creek, just to get some peace and quiet. I used to stay there, too, when I could, but when you were born I stuck real close to the house. I didn't trust Mama alone with you."

"Hold up there right *now*!" Hap cried. "There ain't no *way* you could know about that old cabin! Granddaddy and me tore it down when I wasn't no older'n you!"

Lucas was as unmindful of his own tears as he was of Hap's outburst. "I went to the cabin that morning to check on Granddaddy because it was so cold out I worried he might've frozen to death. It hadn't started snowing yet, but by the time I got back a few flakes were falling. Mama was out by the well, holding you in a blanket. Just when I saw the pair of you, she started screaming, and she held you over the well, and then she...she just let go." A gust of wind blew across the yard, chilling Hap to the marrow of his bones. "You were only two years old, Hap, and the water in the well was so cold it had ice in it. I started cranking down the bucket rope as fast I could to go after you, but Mama was slapping at me and yelling her fool head off about God's will and the devil being in you, and on and on. She wouldn't get out of my way so I finally hauled off and hit her and she fell down and started bawling for Pop.

"I went down the rope thinking you'd already be dead but you were still somehow afloat, thrashing around like crazy to keep your head above water. I put you on my shoulders and started to climb back up the rope but you were too heavy, and I was too cold, so all I could do was scream for Mama to please, *please* pull us up. She never even answered, but all of a sudden Pop was beside her, and I thought he was going to save us until I heard Mama tell him to give her his knife."

Hap broke eye contact with the boy, stricken dumb. Somewhere in the deepest, darkest recesses of his mind something nightmarish was awakening, conjured by Lucas's words. A flare of memory blossomed briefly into fire, and he saw himself as a small child, wet to the skin and very, *very* cold, surrounded by an appalling, terrifying blackness, with the only light in the world far, oh so far overhead—

Oh, sweet Jesus, he thought as the image clarified.

He remembered clinging to someone's neck.

Someone with red hair.

Someone he loved.

Oh, sweet Jesus.

*

"It's just a bizarre coincidence." Aaron's voice sounded very un-Aaron-like as they both stared out the window at the small, slender young man seated by Hap on the rock. He took the Cobb's family Bible from her and frowned at Hap's brother's name on the page before him.

Sandy felt highly unsettled. "That's what you said about Lucas looking so much like the man in that picture."

Their eyes met. He tried to smile but failed, and they stared out the window once again.

"Who in God's name *is* that boy?" he murmured at last. He handed the book back to her. "Call me crazy, but I think I better go talk to him and Hap right now. Want to tag along?"

Sandy told him she thought she'd stay put and see if she could find anything else. He nodded and told her he'd be back soon, and she listened to his footsteps on the stairs as he went down to the first floor. She almost called out to him to wait, not wanting to be left alone after all in the big, silent house. She shook her head, feeling silly, and returned her attention to the Bible.

Aaron had to be right, she told herself as she lightly ran her fingers over the drawing of the tree. Simply because Lucas *looked* like one of Hap's long dead relatives and shared a name with Hap's brother didn't mean anything. It was just a coincidence—and not even that big of one, given that 'Lucas' was only David Cobb's middle name, not his first.

Her hand stopped moving on the page. Her best friend in college, Lydia Darling, hadn't liked her Christian name, Donna, and had chosen to use her middle one instead; there had been no surer way to rile her than to call her Donna Darling. What if Hap's older brother had disliked being called David, and had gone by Lucas instead?

"It doesn't matter," she declared to the empty room, "it's still just a coincidence."

*

"I begged Pop to pull us up but Mama wouldn't let him," Lucas said. "He argued with her but she got the knife from him and started cutting the rope. Pop tried to take it back but she cut his arm and he let go." His voice roughened. "He gave up, just like that."

The afterimage in Hap's mind of that long-ago day remained maddeningly faint. Had he really been in the well, or was he only sharing some kind of delusion with the damaged boy at his side? How could such a hideous thing have happened—even considering he'd only been two at the time—without him recalling it?

"I thought we were goners, Hap. I thought we were going to die in that freezing water while Mama and Pop just stood there listening to us scream. But all at once Mama stopped cutting the rope and I heard Pop say, "This doesn't concern you, Daddy," so I knew Granddaddy was there, too. Then all of a sudden there was a gunshot, and Mama started yelling, then another gunshot, and before I could figure out what was going on Granddaddy was leaning over the top of the well. He told me to hold on for dear life and he started dragging us up, real slow. You were almost gone by then, I think, but when I told you to grab onto me you got hold of my hair and didn't let go until we made it to the top." The boy shook his head. "I don't know how we ever got out of there. We must've weighed a ton, and Granddaddy wasn't a big man. But he did it. When we got to the top he helped us climb out and we fell on the ground, and that's when I saw them. Pop and Mama, I mean.

"Pop was right next to us, and there was blood all over his coat. He wasn't moving at all, but Mama was squirming around holding her belly and crying. Granddaddy acted like he didn't even see her. He took one look at you and snatched you up, and he told me he had to get you in by the fire right away. He said he'd be back for me in a jiffy, but I needed to make my own way if I could. I asked him what about Mama and he said to leave her, but when he took you inside Mama called my name and told me to come to her. Her coat was all bloody, too, and she cursed me something fierce, saying God would make you and me and Granddaddy all burn in hell for eternity for what we'd done."

Hap closed his eyes.

"I didn't mean to do it, Hap," Lucas whispered. "I swear to God I didn't. I just remember wishing she'd shut up. I didn't even know I'd picked up Granddaddy's gun where he'd left it by the well." He paused for a moment and listened to the wind. "The only thing I remember is how loud it was, and then the whole world got real, real quiet again. Just like now."

The boy was no longer crying, but Hap was. Crying like he hadn't cried in years. He cried in silence, not blubbering, just wiping his nose on his mitten and letting the tears spill down his face. His foolish old heart believed the boy's story—believed it utterly—no matter what his brain was telling him. He remembered something his grandfather had once told him: *"Just 'cause a thing ain't possible,"* he'd said, *"don't mean it ain't true."*

"Granddaddy piled blankets on us by the fireplace and told me to keep you warm while he heated water. He put us to bed after we'd soaked in the tub and he stayed with us until we fell asleep, but when I woke up later he wasn't there. I found him outside knocking down the well with a sledge hammer, and Pop and Mama were gone. I went out and asked him what he was doing but he told me to get back inside." An incongruous smile crossed Lucas's face. "He pitched a fit and called me an idjit, and said if I took one more step he'd cane me so bad *the crack of your little butt'll start spinnin' like a goddamn pinwheel.*"

Lucas's voice had deepened into a spot-on imitation of Jacob Cobb. Hearing Jacob's gruff, profane, and much loved voice again after so many years made Hap grin, even through his tears. "The old man sure had a fine goddamn way with words, didn't he?" he said.

Lucas's smile faded when Hap asked what happened next. He told him Jacob worked like a dog all day and didn't come inside until dark, after he'd knocked down the well and half-dug a new one closer to the barn. "I wasn't sure at first why he knocked down the old one," he said, looking where the well had stood. "It didn't make any sense to me at the time, but I finally figured it out. He didn't want me to see what he'd done, and that's why he wouldn't let me come close."

"Oh, Jesus Christ," Hap whispered when he saw where the boy was staring. "That's where he put 'em?" He wiped his face, trying to calm himself as the boy nodded. He was in considerable discomfort from the cold and when he shifted on the rock his legs and feet were so numb he felt as if he were part-man, part-statue. "Why didn't he just dig a grave for 'em?" he asked thickly. "It woulda been a hell of a lot easier."

"Maybe he thought they didn't deserve a Christian burial."

Hap had no answer for this. He wept more and tried to rub feeling back into his limbs.

"I couldn't sleep that night," Lucas said. "I did my chores in the morning same as always, but every time I passed where the well used to be all I could think about was what was down there, under all that busted up rock and dirt. I came inside and saw Granddaddy feeding you at the table like nothing was wrong and I ran back out on the porch and sicked-up everything in my stomach.

"Granddaddy put you down to nap midday and the two of us came out here to talk." He patted the rock beneath them. "Right on this old rock, as a matter of fact. He said he was going to fetch Grandma in Wheatland, but he wanted to make sure I knew what to say if anybody came looking for Mama and Pop. He told me we could never tell anybody except Grandma the truth. Not even you. You were too little to remember anything, so he said it was best to say our folks died in a fire while they were out of town, and got buried elsewhere. He said nobody really cared for our folks anyway, not even the people in Mama's church, and they'd believe anything we told them.

"After he left for town I sat by your crib for a while watching you sleep, but it was so quiet in the house I started getting real antsy. The longer I sat there the quieter things got, like we were still down in that well together, sinking deeper every second. I could hear you breathing in your crib, and I could hear *me* breathing, but every other sound in the world kept getting farther and farther away, swallowed up whole by the quiet. I couldn't sit still anymore, so I built up the fire in the wood stove to make sure you'd stay warm, and I grabbed my coat and went outside.

"There wasn't a highway back then, remember? There was just an old county road with potholes big as moon craters. I headed toward Chugwater, but I didn't get very far before it started snowing. I knew I should head home straight away but before I got turned around there was more snow falling from the sky than I'd ever seen in my whole life. I slipped and fell, and in about two seconds flat I couldn't see a dang thing but snow.

"I knew better than to close my eyes but I couldn't help it. All I wanted to do was just fall asleep, and forget about everything. I stretched out on my back and tried to come up with one good reason to get up again, but then I'd think about all that had happened and I couldn't seem to make myself care enough to even try.

"Then I thought of you.

"I started fretting about what would happen if Granddaddy and Grandma couldn't get back home, and how scared you'd be if you woke up with everybody gone, and how whatever happened to you would be my fault. I could picture you screaming bloody murder with no one to hear you or pick you up and hold you, and I hated myself for leaving you. I was your big brother, and it was my job to take care of you when you needed me, instead of just lying around in the snow feeling sorry for myself.

"I can't tell you how long it took me to open my eyes again, but I didn't think it was all that long since there was only a little bit of snow piled on top of me by the time I got back on my feet. I didn't really know which way to go, but I swore right then and there to make it back to you, no matter what—even if it meant walking in circles in that stupid blizzard; even if it meant crawling on my hands and knees until I finally found my way home.

"And that was when I saw Sandy's car heading for me on the highway."

*

Hap started when Lucas's rush of words came to an end. He'd lost himself in the boy's tale, and the final syllables took a few seconds to penetrate.

"Come again?" he asked. "What do you mean, *that's when you saw Sandy's car*? The two of you just met up on the highway two days ago."

Lucas shifted on the rock and looked Hap squarely in the face, and Hap's breath caught in his throat. The boy seemed to have aged ten years in as many minutes; his eyes were sunken in their sockets and his skin was ashen gray.

"I'd forgotten who I was, and what I was doing out in a blizzard. I don't know why it took me so long to remember everything, but that's what happened. Honest to God."

Hap gaped, waiting for more, but Lucas simply gazed back at him in silence.

"Christ have mercy." Hap felt as if the boy were playing him for a fool. "You're telling me you took a little *snooze* like Rip Van Goddamn Winkle and woke up *eighty years* later? That's...Jesus Christ Almighty, that's *bullshit*, son!" He began sputtering with indignation but Lucas reached up and rested a hand on his cheek, silencing him. The gentleness in his touch brought tears to Hap's eyes.

"I wish I knew more, Hap, but I don't. I think maybe I fell asleep on the ground the day I ran out of the house, and I didn't wake up again until..." Lucas hesitated, "...well, until you needed me, I guess. I could be wrong, but I don't think so." Hap blinked, speechless, and Lucas dropped his hand. "I don't know where I've been all this time, or if it was good or bad. I figure maybe I'm not supposed to know. Eighty years sure seems like an awful long time to lose track of, but something tells me it's just a drop in the bucket when it comes to stuff like this."

"What in *hell* are you talkin' about, boy?"

Lucas shrugged. "Family, I guess. Friends, too, sometimes, like you and Aaron. The folks we love, and can't stand to lose. The things we do to each other, for better or worse. Everything, and everybody, that time doesn't have much to do with." He looked around at the ranch speculatively. "Do you think Granddaddy ever found me out there all those years ago? Or if anybody did? I wonder if I ever got buried."

"Christ, boy, don't—"

"I guess it doesn't matter. I guess all that matters is I'm here now, and I got to see you again." Lucas's chin quivered and his eyes spilled over once again as he took Hap's hand in his own, cradling it. "Better late than never, right?"

Hap's heart faltered in his chest as he struggled to grasp what the boy was telling him. He raised his head and saw that Aaron had come outside and was walking toward them; the concern he saw on the younger man's face filled him with a keen, tender grief all his own. Hap saw Aaron mouth his name and begin to walk faster.

"It's time to go, Hap," Lucas said.

*

Aaron knew he was being irrational—spooked into thinking like a superstitious old peasant by nothing more than a name in a Bible and an odd feeling in his gut—yet he couldn't help himself. He looked on the back porch for his boots and his winter coat but they were missing; Hap must've snagged them before going outside, too lazy to retrieve his own coat and boots from the front closet. He went to the entryway to get another set of boots and thrust his arms into the sleeves of one of Hap's old coats, then passed through the dining room on the way back to the porch. Sandy's cat was curled up by the wood stove, near Hap's rocking chair. The cat had somehow acquired Hap's lap blanket from the chair seat and was using it as a bed, and Aaron grinned.

"Good kitty," he said. "Don't move a muscle till Hap gets a gander at you, okay?"

He stepped out the back door and saw Hap and Lucas still sitting quietly on the rock across the yard, so immersed in their conversation that neither seemed to notice him. He began walking toward them, mocking himself for feeling anxious, but when he was only twenty yards away or so, he saw Lucas lift one of Hap's hands in his own in an oddly grownup gesture, like a father comforting a son. A few moments later Hap finally saw Aaron, and the look that came into the old man's craggy, ornery, and oh-so-familiar face—a look Aaron had never once seen there in all their years together—startled him so much that tears sprang to his eyes.

"Oh, Hap," he breathed.

*

"We ain't never gonna tell Hap nothin' about his folks, or Davy, that we ain't tellin' everybody," Jacob Cobb said. "All he needs to know is the three of 'em died in a fire when they was away, visitin' friends."

Rebecca was kneeling by a small, crude grave in a copse of pine trees by the creek. The day was bitterly cold, but the wind wasn't as bad in the trees, nor the snow so deep as elsewhere. "No." She had no problem not talking with Hap about Reuben and Elizabeth—nor lying to him and the rest of the world about how they'd died—but Davy was another matter. "Hap needs to know the truth about his big brother. He deserves at least that much, and so does Davy."

She was hollow inside from weeping, as hollow as the grave they'd just dug for their grandson. The day before, Jacob had found David's body a mile or so away, out by the road. Coyotes and God only knew what else had been at him during the nineteen hours he'd been missing; they'd left little more than bones and a few fragments of his red coat—and blood, too, of course, an icy red slick in a valley of white. When the boy hadn't come home last night she and Jacob had feared the worst, but she'd prayed they were wrong and he'd still come back to them.

But he wouldn't.

If God were interested in justice, Davy was surely better off wherever he was—someplace far kinder than this hellhole of a ranch—but she couldn't help fearing otherwise. She hated herself for considering such a notion, hated herself for thinking so poorly of God as to question whether Davy had been condemned to hell for finishing what Jacob had started. If ever a human being had deserved to die it was Elizabeth Cobb; surely God knew just how much that woman had been begging for a bullet in the head. It terrified her to think Davy's soul might be in torment for all eternity for an act she wished she'd done herself; she was sure she'd spend the rest of her days in unrelieved misery for not being the one who'd pulled the trigger.

She would've gladly paid whatever price was necessary for the privilege.

"We can't tell Hap about Davy," Jacob said, squatting beside her and taking her mittened hand in his own. The sorrow on his face was

nearly more than she could bear. "We just can't, darlin.' It would open up a goddamn kettle of worms, and before you know it we'd be tellin' one damn lie after another to keep him from findin' out about his folks."

"I agree there are things he should never know," she said, squeezing his fingers, "but how can it hurt to tell him who his brother was, and how much he loved him?" She brushed newly fallen snowflakes off the plain white stone they'd laid flat on the grave as a tombstone, and her voice broke. "He needs to know where Davy's buried, too."

The entire conversation was an abomination: here they were, debating what lies to tell Hap, and meanwhile the murdered bodies of her son and daughter-in-law were moldering in the earth under a ton of debris from their old well, and her older grandson David was dead, too, asleep in a remote grave where no one was ever likely to find his remains. She and Jacob—after they agreed on the most believable story they could come up with—would soon be beset by friends and neighbors, all wishing to console them. Their kitchen would fill with flowers and casseroles, there'd be offers of help and heartfelt tears from all quarters.

And only she and Jacob would be aware of how undeserved any such consolation was.

"I know it ain't fair, Becky," Jacob said. "But the second we start tellin' Hap about Davy, he's gonna keep at us till one of us slips up someday and says too damn much, and I swear to you he won't thank us for it. We can say Davy was a good boy, but anything else is just beggin' for trouble."

Rebecca looked down at the tombstone again, her resolve waning. Would Hap indeed be happier knowing nothing about David? There was so little she and Jacob could share with him that wouldn't give him nightmares, so little they could say that wouldn't mire him in filth and sin, along with the rest of them. Davy's kindness and loyalty, his courage and gentleness, were forever bound to Elizabeth's madness and Reuben's cowardice; nearly every sweet memory she could share with Hap was soiled by turmoil, grief, and downright cruelty, and she couldn't fathom how to separate the good from the bad in the telling. Yet how could she stay silent about Davy when to do so was such a betrayal of the love she had for him? How could she ever live with herself?

Oh, Davy, she thought. Please forgive me, my love. Please forgive us both.

They shouldn't be able to get away with any of this. In a civilized place, three people couldn't just vanish off the face of the earth and have their absence explained away by saying they'd died in a fire elsewhere, leaving no remains—the idea of getting away with such a tale would be absurd. But the White Creek Ranch was not a civilized place. It was a prehistoric wilderness, the 'Wild West,' with the nearest homestead miles away and no one to question their story. They could commit atrocity after atrocity on this land of theirs and no one would ever be the wiser. No one but themselves.

And God, of course. God would always know.

She brushed the snow from the stone once more—a stone soon to be covered by weeds and pine needles, and never seen by anyone who didn't know exactly where to look for it—and she gazed at the initials Jacob had chiseled into it: DLC. "We should've left off the 'D,'" she said absently, too tired to think any longer. "He wouldn't have liked it."

Davy had always preferred his middle name. All his friends and teachers had called him Lucas, but David was the name his parents had chosen for him, and they'd steadfastly refused to call him anything else. It was one of the few things Jacob and Rebecca had agreed with Reuben and Elizabeth about; they'd never cared for the name Lucas in the first place.

"What he don't know won't hurt him none," Jacob said.

*

Aaron plowed through the deep snow as if it weren't there, but he still wasn't in time to prevent Hap from sliding off the rock to the ground, landing hard on his bony ass.

"Hap!" Aaron cried, dropping to his knees beside the old man. "Hap!"

Hap was shaking violently and his skin was blue from the cold, but he was still very much himself. "Pipe down, peabrain," he gasped. "I ain't deaf."

"Where's *Lucas*?" Aaron helped Hap lean back against the rock. "He was just here two seconds ago!"

Hap gestured weakly at the ground and Aaron made a small, wordless sound of denial deep in his throat as he saw what had caught Hap's attention: From the house to the rock, there were three distinct sets of footprints in the otherwise pristine snow—his own, Hap's, and Lucas's—but the smallest set, Lucas's, now led to the west, toward the horizon. The boy himself was nowhere to be seen but the trail he'd left continued on farther than Aaron's eyes could follow, farther than anybody could walk in half an hour, let alone a few heartbeats.

"God*damn*," Hap breathed. Aaron heard the grief in Hap's voice; his own throat closed as he turned back to stare into the old man's teary eyes. "Aaron," Hap rasped. "Lucas. He was...he..."

"Save your strength, old man," Aaron murmured, seeing how hard it was for Hap to speak. His gaze kept returning to the boy's footprints; he felt as if he were hallucinating. "Sandy just found a Cobb family Bible, and it says your brother's middle name was Lucas. Did you know that?"

"No shit?" Hap's eyes widened. "I'll be...I'll be a son of a bitch." He tried to smile, but failed, utterly. "Guess maybe... maybe we shoulda paid more attention to those...those goddamn books, you think?"

Aaron swallowed. *This is a dream*, he thought. *This whole thing is nothing but a dream.* "What happened here, Hap?" he asked at last. "Where did Lucas *go*?"

"I don't rightly know, son." A faraway look came into Hap's eyes as he gazed at Lucas's footsteps in the snow. "I guess I ain't sure of nothin' no more."

Aaron swallowed, forcing his mind back to necessities. "We have to get you inside, Hap. You're freezing."

Hap nodded, too, but made no move to rise. He reached up a hand and patted Aaron's cheek, something he'd never done, and the pain on his face nearly broke Aaron's heart. "Aaron. I ain't said some things I shoulda said a long time ago. Lucas comin' back like he did...it makes me think I oughta say 'em now, while I got the chance. You're the best...and I mean the *very* best goddamn... goddamn *pinhead*...I ever knew in my whole sorry life." His restless hand stilled on Aaron's cheek, and his face shook. "Tell me…tell me you know what I'm tryin' to say to you, son. I can't bear for you not to know."

Aaron couldn't speak but he nodded, and it was enough: Hap closed his eyes in relief for a moment before opening them again.

"I'm so cold." His voice was a whisper. "Best we go inside now."

Chapter Twelve

Sandy watched Aaron lift the receiver of the kitchen phone for the third time in the past twenty minutes, dial the sheriff's office in Wheatland, then hang up yet again before allowing it to ring.

"What in God's name do I say?" he asked, just as he had twice before. He sank back in his chair at the table, across from her. "Glenn will think we've been dropping acid out here."

Sandy gave him the same answer she had earlier; it seemed all they could do was repeat themselves. "I don't know what to say, either. I wish I did."

The two of them were alone, watching through the windows of the kitchen as the sun sank from sight, pulling the night sky over the earth like a down comforter. Aaron had put Hap to bed two hours before; the old man was exhausted but before he fell asleep Aaron checked his temperature, pulse, and blood pressure; all were more or less normal, save for his temperature being slightly high and his blood pressure slightly low. Hap had been so weary he'd barely even objected as Aaron fussed over him.

"I'm fine, son," was all he'd said, closing his eyes, "leave me be." He'd drifted off to sleep and begun snoring the instant Aaron finished tucking him in.

Sandy worried Hap was very far from fine, but she also guessed there was little Aaron or anybody else could do for him. She was no doctor, but she knew what was ailing Hap wasn't physical. True enough, he looked awful: when he'd first come inside, his skin was ashen and he'd been trembling all over, as if with palsy. But what else could be expected? Lucas's inexplicable disappearance was bad enough, but Sandy suspected it was only part of the old man's distress. She was not yet privy, nor was Aaron, to what Lucas might've told Hap when they'd been sitting on the rock together, but—if the shellshocked look in Hap's eyes was any indication—it had been devastating.

After Aaron had put Hap to bed and told her what he'd witnessed, she'd gone outside with him again, needing to see the boy's footprints in the snow with her own eyes. For forty minutes—as Hap slept in the house and Aaron followed Lucas's tracks to the west—she'd stood in the cold, staring after Aaron until he returned and took her back inside.

"The footprints end in a little patch of pine trees down by the creek," he'd told her, "but Lucas isn't there." He'd hesitated, then, swallowing hard. "The snow was cleared away from the ground by where he took his last step, and some earth was pushed away, too, and there was a stone with the letters 'DLC' carved into it, just sitting there for me to find, a couple of inches deep in the soil. God only knows how long it's been there, but I think…I think it's a gravestone."

It has to be a trick, she'd thought. Fourteen-year-old boys didn't just didn't wander off into nowhere, in broad daylight, leaving nothing of themselves behind but footprints in the snow. *Especially* not the boy she'd found in a blizzard and sat next to during meals for the past two days; not the boy who'd laughed with her, and talked to her, and teased her; not the boy with red hair and green eyes, and bruises on his back; not the boy who—

Not the boy she'd begun to love.

It isn't real, she'd told herself, again and again. She was still telling herself the same thing. *It's impossible*.

"God," she murmured now to Aaron at the table. "If this is just some kind of bizarre dream I'm having, I sure wish you'd make me wake up."

Aaron took her hand. They'd been holding hands off and on ever since he'd brought her back inside; she suspected the warmth of his fingers in hers was the only reason she hadn't turned into a gibbering lunatic.

"If I tell Glenn the truth," Aaron said, apparently still fixated on a conversation with the sheriff, "he'll have a lot of questions for Hap. I'd really rather not put him through that ordeal, if we can help it."

Sandy felt the muscles of her face twitch in spite of herself. "You mean Glenn, or Hap?"

He grinned at her. "Glenn, of course. Talking to Hap is against the rules of the Geneva Convention."

She managed a shaky laugh, but sobered again almost at once, too frazzled for any real levity. She ran her thumb along the side of his index finger, calming herself; of all the remarkable developments of that day, the physical warmth that had sprung up between them was the only thing that made any sense to her at all.

"I'll do, or say, whatever you think is best for Hap," she said, "but I don't know how we can spare him talking to Glenn. Glenn won't just look at…at those footprints out there, and at that stone you found, and let things go at that."

"I know." He sighed and gazed out the window again, though there was now little to see because it was nearly full dark. "So that's why I don't think we should show him anything. I don't like lying to Glenn, but he wouldn't believe us if we told him the truth. Hell, *I* don't believe it, and I was right there." He met her eyes. "We could just say Lucas took off on his own, and we don't know where he went. God knows *that's* no lie."

Sandy supposed he was right, but a small part of her still wanted to disagree, wanted him to tell the sheriff everything: Glenn was a professional skeptic, trained to see hoaxes where others saw mysteries or miracles, and there was nothing she'd rather hear at the moment than somebody in authority saying there was a rational, scientific explanation for those footprints in the snow. But the larger part of her knew there was no explanation that would ever suffice. Wherever Lucas had gone, there would be no finding him. Not now, not tomorrow, not ever.

He was gone, and that was that.

"Hey," Aaron said, squeezing her hand. "Hey, now."

"I'm okay." She wiped her nose on her sleeve and took an unsteady breath. "I'm just really sad."

He nodded, and she loved him for not trying to hide his own grief, nor jolly her out of hers. "Me too."

He leaned down to kiss the back of her wrist, and she smiled at him through her tears.

*

Hap Cobb woke at midnight. For a minute, he didn't remember anything of the day that had just ended, but then it all came back at once.

Lucas.

His big brother: David Lucas Cobb. Their mother and father, Reuben and Elizabeth; their grandparents, Jacob and Rebecca. The whopper of a lie he had been told—and swallowed whole, all his life—about a fire that never happened. The pictures in the attic, the gentleness of his brother's hand on his face, the sound of his brother's voice as they sat together on the rock that afternoon, talking.

The well behind the house.

He felt an ache in his chest and he curled up beneath his blankets, knowing he was done sleeping for the night. Maybe forever.

He listened to the silence of the house until he couldn't bear it, then he sat up in bed, reaching for his reading lamp. Soft white light mingled with the yellow and red flames of the propane fireplace, banishing the worst of the shadows to the corners of the room. Ordinarily he would just grab a book if he couldn't sleep, but no book—not even *Moby Dick*—could help him tonight. He flung off his blankets and rose to his feet, obeying an odd, restless impulse to be up and moving.

He was only dressed in long johns, but Aaron had left a robe for him on the chair by the bed, in case Hap needed to get up in the middle of the night to use the bathroom, as he nearly always did. He slid into the robe and and a pair of slippers and tottered across the room, then opened his bedroom door and stepped in the hallway. There was a nightlight at the end of the hall that allowed him to make his way to the stairwell without bumping into things; he put a foot on the first step and began to climb, not really knowing why he was going upstairs but doing it anyway. At the top of the steps he shuffled past the bathroom and the library—now using the bathroom's faint nightlight to guide him—and didn't stop until he reached the door of Lucas's bedroom.

Lucas's bedroom, and his own as well, when he was a child.

He opened the door and stepped into the room. It was empty, of course; even before he flipped on the light he could feel the absence of life. The bed was made but Hap assumed the sheets and blankets were still the ones Lucas had been using; Aaron probably hadn't gotten around yet to changing them. He wandered over and sat on the foot of the mattress. He stared around the room, not knowing what he was looking for but believing there was a reason he had come.

The room had originally been his brother's before it was his; he knew that much. He had no memory of those days, of course, but he imagined everything still looked pretty much the same, save for perhaps the bed. He had a vague recollection of his grandfather moving him from the nursery to this room when he was four or five, and watching Jacob assemble the bed he was now sitting on—the bed that used to belong to Hap's parents—and saying, "*A big boy like you needs a big bed.*" Hap had never considered what bed Lucas had slept on as a child, but now knowing what he did about their mother and father, he very much doubted it had been half as nice as this one.

"Sons'a'bitches probably strapped him to a goddamn torture wheel before kissin' him goodnight," he muttered.

Hearing his own voice unsettled him. The room had been silent before, but now it filled with echoes. He almost felt—if he listened hard enough—he'd be able to hear every word ever spoken there; he could almost hear himself as a small child talking to his grandfather, and his grandfather answering, and further back yet—before his own birth—Lucas being made to pray aloud while kneeling on the floor, watched over by their controlling, ever-vigilant mother. No doubt the prayers he was made to utter in Elizabeth Durham Cobb's presence were of the forgive-me-Lord-for-being-such-a-miserable-sinner variety, but when she left him alone at last, did he pray for something more? Did he know enough to pray for the parents he deserved, instead of the parents he'd been given? Did he maybe stare up at the ceiling and ask for love and understanding—or at the very least, a little *sanity*—from the people who were supposed to be taking care of him? Hap wanted so badly to step back through all the years and sit beside the boy's bed as he slept, wanted so badly to be there when his dreams were bad, to hold his hand and comfort him, to tell him all would be well.

We talked just today, he thought. *But now he's a million goddamn miles away from me.*

A sob rose in his throat. He lurched to his feet and hurried into the hallway, flipping off the light and closing the door behind him with trembling hands; he fought to control his breathing, so as not to wake Sandy, whose room was directly across the hall.

Directly across the hall, with its door standing wide open.

"Oh, Christ," he sighed, barely able to see in the faint illumination cast by the nightlight down the hall. He couldn't believe he hadn't noticed the open door sooner; he'd been so intent on getting to Lucas's room he'd somehow missed it. After all the ruckus he'd been making, he was certain Sandy was indeed awake, and had witnessed his breakdown—she was probably watching him with pity at that very moment, even as he squinted through her doorway, trying to force his eyes to adjust to the darkness. He waited with dread for her to break the stillness but she said nothing; he was still waiting when he was able to see at last, with great relief, that she wasn't there after all. Her bed was empty.

Relief gave way to curiosity.

"Well, now," he murmured, "looks like the catwoman's out past curfew." His lips twitched, in spite of everything, and the ache in his heart, though still burdensome, lessened the slightest degree. "I'll be damned. Guess the pinhead fancies girls more'n cows, after all."

His lips twitched again and he shook his head; when he stepped down the hallway it was with a lighter tread. On a whim, he opened the door to his beloved library, just to make sure everything was in order, and seeing that it was lifted his spirits, too. At least this one small corner of his world was still intact, all his earthly treasures still safe and sound. Piles of books stood here and there like sentinels in the night, watching over the rest of the collection, and he nodded at the pile closest to him.

"You're doin' a bang up job, there," he grunted. "At ease, soldier."

Back downstairs, he wandered into the kitchen. Moonlight was streaming through the windows, and in the brightest patch of it, by the table, he saw Wilbur. The cat was seated on his haunches like a gargoyle, his eyes fairly glowed as Hap carefully edged around him on the way to the back door.

"Goddamn cat," Hap said reflexively.

Looking out the window of the porch door, he could see remarkably well; the moon was still nearly full. He could see the rock he and Lucas had sat on, and their bootprints in the snow, and where Lucas had gone off by himself, headed west. The ache in his heart returned, but this time it wasn't quite so fierce; this time it brought more to the table than just pain. This time it came with a generous side of gratitude, as well as a sudden revelation to sink his teeth into:

I ain't scared, he realized, astonished.

Always in the past, his grief at the passing of those he loved—most notably Ellen and Jacob, but many others, too—had been heavily tainted with fear: fear of his own mortality, fear of losing not just himself but everyone and everything he'd ever known, fear of reaching the end of his life and, with his last fitful gasp, knowing absolutely, and with no hope for reprieve, that it truly *was* THE END—no coda and no epilogue; no heaven, no, purgatory, no hell—only silence, only an empty page, only a mute, wasted corpse on a slab at the morgue. Only this, and nothing else.

But Lucas had changed everything.

"I'll be damned," he murmured. He found himself unable to look away from the footsteps in the snow. "I *will* be goddamned."

*

Aaron rose from his bed in the morning, slowly and carefully, so as not to wake Sandy. She was deeply asleep, curled on her side with one arm under her head and the other stretched across the mattress where a moment before Aaron had lain. Their lovemaking the night before had been sweet and gentle—they were both too tired for anything more energetic—and they'd fallen asleep early, Aaron on his back and Sandy pressed against his side, her arm across his chest. He didn't think either of them had moved more than once or twice in the night, and he was surprised by how well he'd slept—especially given how many years it had been since he'd shared his bed.

Guess the long famine is finally over, he mused, smiling as he dressed.

The sun was well up; he'd overslept. He was astonished by this as much as anything. Granted, he'd had other things on his mind the night before than remembering to set his alarm clock, but he usually woke well before his alarm went off, anyway. What was perhaps even stranger, though, was that Hap hadn't immediately come to see what was wrong. The last time he'd overslept, the old man had barged in at dawn, threatening to turn the hose on him.

He dressed quickly, beginning to worry. Even if Hap had somehow guessed that Sandy was in the room with him, he still doubted the old fart would've let them sleep so long; with Hap Cobb tact and consideration always took a backseat to scheduled meal times.

He slipped into the hall and closed the door quietly behind him, then padded down to Hap's room in his stocking feet. Hap wasn't there and his bed was unmade—another disquieting anomaly, because Hap always made his bed after rising. He closed the door again to keep the room hot like Hap liked it, then hurried to the kitchen, chewing on his lip.

Wilbur was the only living soul in the kitchen. The cat was sleeping in a patch of sunlight; he opened a disinterested eye and closed it again when Aaron said good morning and bent down to rub his belly. Aaron straightened again, and it was then he noticed a piece of paper on the kitchen table, with a pen beside it. From where he was standing he couldn't see what was written on the paper, but the messy scrawl was plainly Hap's; Hap had worse handwriting than the average second grader.

For no good reason, Aaron's heart started hammering in his chest.

Instead of walking over to look more closely at the paper he went to the back door, noting that Hap's boots were right beside it, on the mat, and his coat was hanging from the coat rack in the corner. He stared at the boots for a long time, telling himself all was well—*Hap wouldn't be caught dead outside without his boots*—yet his heart, ever the heretic, refused to simply take on faith the reasonable thing his brain was telling him. A chill ran down his spine, and with a muffled cry he charged on the porch and tore open the outside door. Barely feeling the cold, he leaned outside, anxiously searching the vast, white-shrouded prairie behind the house.

"HAP!" he howled, feeling ridiculous but unable to help himself. The old man would of course appear any moment in the kitchen behind him, demanding to know why he was standing there holding the door open and yelling his damn-fool head off; he'd put on a pot of coffee and the two of them would start their day, the same as always, bickering about everything under the sun, world without end, amen.

"HAP! WHERE ARE YOU?"

The wind ripped the scream from his lips, tossing it high in the air and tearing it to pieces, then resumed—with what sounded to Aaron's ears very much like a weary, patient sigh—the thankless job of filling in yet another lonely set of footprints in the snow, headed west as far as eternity.

*

Dear Pinhead,

I ain't scared no more so don't you be neither. Guess Lucas coming back like he did means this ain't all there is like I thought. Don't know for sure why he in particular got picked to come back, but I ain't complaining. I also don't know why he was made to wait so damn long. Maybe he got put in storage, or some damn thing like that, or could be God's just a halfwit like you, and can't tell time for shit. Who the hell knows?

Anyway, don't worry none. It's just time for me to be seeing what's down the road, since I've seen all of this here stretch I care to. I'll be fine, so don't fret yourself none on my account, or on your own, neither. You and the catwoman are going to be fine, too—maybe a damn sight more than fine. I might be jumping the gun a tad but I get a feeling this old house may soon be crawling with a whole damn litter of baldheaded, peabrained little fartsniffers. I sure as hell hope they take after their mother instead of you in the smarts department, though, or folks will think there's been a whole lot of inbreeding going on around here.

Anyhow, don't go making a fuss. We'll see each other again. I swear to Christ we will. I was thinking about good old Ahab this morning, and how he says "Stand close to me, Starbuck; let me look into a human eye; it is better than to gaze into sea or sky; better than to gaze upon God." He was right about that, and that's a fact. Looking you in the eye all these years like I done taught me at least that much, if nothing else.

Bye for now.

P.S. Keep that goddamn cat out of my library.

Acknowledgments

Heartfelt thanks to Gordon Mennenga, Marian Clark, and my editor at Culicidae Press, Mikesch Muecke, for thoughtful, inventive, and multilayered feedback on this decidedly oddball story. It was a long journey from first draft to final copy, but I'm so grateful I got to work with all three of you along the way.

Love and gratitude as well to all my family, friends, and students, but with a special shout-out to Shaorong Yan, Lisa and Edward Leff, Pena Lubrica, Dave Dugan, and Tonja Robins. While I was writing this book, y'all kept my stomach happy, my soul at peace, and my liver overworked, and I don't know what I would've done without you.

www.ingramcontent.com/pod-product-compliance
Lightning Source LLC
Chambersburg PA
CBHW030815310726
48980CB00006B/500/J

* 9 7 8 1 6 8 3 1 5 0 0 7 7 *